DIAMOND
IN THE
RUFF

DIAMOND
IN THE
RUFF

A WIGGLE BUTT MANOR MYSTERY

CINDY GOYETTE

LEVEL
BEST BOOKS

Author Photo Credit: Jon D'Emilio

First edition

ISBN: 978-1-68512-952-1

Cover art by Michael Verdun

This book was professionally typeset on Reedsy.
Find out more at reedsy.com

For Noah, my little "duman"
RIP
2009-2022

"I'm suspicious of people who don't like dogs,
but I trust a dog when it doesn't like a person."

— Bill Murray

Chapter One

The massive bridge from mainland Washington to the village of Orca Cove lay before me like the highway to hell. Not that Orca Cove's a bad place. Quite the contrary. It's just that heights scared the bejesus out of me—and it was going to take every bit of courage I could muster to cross it.

The sky was hazy as the sun threatened to burn off oppressive dark gray clouds. Spikes at the top of the bridge disappeared into the fast-moving fog. The looming structure reminded me of green metal toothpicks, supporting a wobbly death trap in the sky. It took my breath away and not in a good way.

Come on, Charlie. Put on your big girl pants and suck it up.

I tried to concentrate on the quaint town on the other side and the refuge it would provide. But all I could think of as I navigated my rental car across the bridge was that the Pacific Northwest was long overdue for an earthquake. Wouldn't it be my luck to be on this bridge when it happened? I imagined I would feel suspended in the air forever during the plunge, but death would come quickly as the ice-cold water below swallowed us whole.

"I know," I said, glancing down at my buff Cocker Spaniel, Noah, fast asleep on the seat beside me. "Stop being so dramatic." But as I white-knuckled our way across the bridge, Noah was oblivious. He continued to sleep off the meds I'd given him to make the flight from New Jersey more tolerable. His snore reminded me of what an overweight lumberjack might sound like after a few too many beers. Hard to believe such a rattling noise came out of a twenty-two-pound fur ball, so adorable people often mistook him for Lady from *Lady and the Tramp*. A thorn in my side, but I was prone to overreacting when it came to my boy.

Four miles seemed a long time to contemplate one's death. Cars behind me honked as I drove just under the speed limit, my eyes intent on the few feet of road in front of me. I tried to stifle the hysteria that rose in my chest and choked me.

Deep breaths, Charlie.

I did my best to ignore the impatient drivers behind us. Fate threw in a pack of serious bicyclists, making the bridge even more narrow. I focused on the toned calves pumping the pedals on the bike of the woman in front of me, while wishing there was another way onto the island. But my unemployed status and dwindling bank account didn't allow for luxuries like a private boat or seaplane.

Exiting the bridge, I let out a long breath. "That was stressful," I said to Noah.

More snoring. Well, it was terrifying for *me*.

The sleepy town always made me feel like I'd entered a time warp and had surfaced in the 1950s. Quaint buildings, with brightly painted mismatched architecture for each mom-and-pop shop, boutique, and restaurant, lined the streets. Because orcas frequented the area and drew many tourists, everything had a nautical theme, and murals of killer whales and other sea life decorated the buildings. Despite its appeal, the town remained a best-kept secret, and even during the height of the season, crowds were few and far between.

Couples walked hand-in-hand down sidewalks, others pushed strollers, and many had a canine friend on a leash. I knew from previous visits that many of the residents were retired, and there was a high population of artists on the island.

Back on solid ground and with this storybook town before me, calm released like water from a dam, washing my trepidation out to sea.

Not wanting to visit my aunt empty-handed, I stopped at the town bakery and bought two giant molasses cookies, my aunt's favorite.

As I started up the hill to Aunt Jo-Jo's house, I felt excited at the prospect of seeing her again. She was not only my favorite relative, but she'd also been my savior growing up when my mom went off the deep end—which was more often than I'd like to admit. I spent snippets of my childhood on this island, and some of my best memories were of my time here. But I'd been remiss, having not visited her since my uncle passed away about five years ago. Life had gotten in the way. First, there was college, and then the life-changing decision I'd made to leave my tedious corporate job for the police academy. Like most people my age, I was perpetually broke, and travel wasn't in the cards.

But my aunt seemed to understand, and we kept in touch through email and weekly phone calls. She was still my sounding board when dealing with my mom's antics. Those calls kept us close, but there was nothing like face-to-face time.

Aunt Jo-Jo's Craftsman house perched on the hillside like a proud bird overlooking its kingdom. From it, she had a fantastic view of the water and the, *gulp*, bridge. The house was painted royal blue with white shutters. Colorful gardens surrounded the property, and a small dog park flanked the west side of the house. A banner reading *Future Home of Orca Cove's First Agility Course* stretched across the fence. A handful of dogs frolicked on lush grass while owners sat on benches in animated conversation.

A more modern structure sat behind the home, painted the same shade of blue. A hotel for dogs–Wiggle Butt Manor.

Ten individual rooms were decorated with children's furniture, on which the four-legged guests slept. Each room had a theme. There was a *One Hundred and One Dalmatians* suite, a Lassie room, and one had French Bulldogs and a Paris theme.

I parked in the gravel driveway behind a mud-splattered Jeep Cherokee with an *I love Golden Retrievers* bumper sticker peeking out from beneath the dirt.

Rousing Noah with a quick belly rub, I got out of the car and stretched. The chill of the late September air reminded me that fall was around the corner. "Come on, Boo." I slapped my thigh.

Noah's flowing ears swayed as he jumped to the ground. He followed me like a shadow as I walked up to the pet hotel and rapped on the door. When no one answered, I opened it and stuck my head inside. "Hello?"

Barking erupted from the back room when we entered. The lobby held a desk and two overstuffed chairs, along with a giant bucketful of dog toys. A collage of photos taken of guests over the years hung on the wall. Noah gave me a look that said: *what the heck, I thought I was the only one.*

"You've led a sheltered life," I said. "You're not one of a kind."

Noah was not a "dog person," and he couldn't care less about the canines eager to greet him. He glanced toward the barking dogs, yawned, and then leaped onto a chair and curled into a compact ball. I opened the door that led to the pet rooms and made my way down the hall. A wall of guest suites was to my left. Dogs of all sizes and colors stuck their noses out of low, barred windows to greet me. I bent down and said hello to each of them. I didn't want to be rude.

The door at the end of the hall opened as Martha stepped inside. "Oh, dear!" She patted her chest as if she needed to restart her heart. "Charlie! You scared me half to death."

Martha had worked with Aunt Jo-Jo for as long as I could remember. They argued constantly, but they'd take a bullet for each other. Martha's curly gray hair looked like a startled ferret on her head, and her glasses were askew. She wore faded overalls and lime green Crocs.

"Sorry to scare you," I said. "We just got here. Is everything all right?"

"One of the dogs is AWOL," Martha said. "That teenager we hired must have failed to latch the kennel, and when I opened the hotel door, the slippery rascal bolted."

I grabbed a leash off the hook. "What's the breed?"

Martha scratched her head. "Basic brown dog. Size of a lab, soul of a scoundrel. Answers to Maya, if she'd ever bother."

"I'm on it," I said.

Heading back to my car, I called for Noah to join me. Not buying into the urgency, he lumbered off the chair and followed. Back in the rental car, we set off down the street, driving up and down the hilly roads that made

4

up the neighborhood. Charming houses had well-manicured lawns, and vibrant flowers were abundant.

I watched the road while quickly scanning the bushes for a hiding dog. I wished I would have asked how long Maya had been missing. A dog like that could make it to the main road in minutes. I prayed a car wouldn't hit the runaway.

I soon spotted a tan blur leap over a six-foot fence three streets down, disappearing into a backyard. Slamming on the brakes, my arm automatically jerked out to stop Noah from flying off the seat. I told him to stay, grabbed the leash, and jumped out of the car. I was five-foot-ten, and for once, I didn't curse my height.

Standing on my toes, I could easily see over the fence and into the yard. The dog chased a flock of chickens while a middle-aged woman dressed in a low-cut top and shorts that might have fit her twenty years ago yelled at Maya to stop. Yielding a broom, she chased the dog in circles with little effect.

"I'm here to help," I yelled over the fence. "Maya, come here!"

If the dog could flip me off, she would have. The look she gave me had the same result. Maya was on a tear.

"Do something," the woman said, near tears.

I put my foot onto a nearby wheelbarrow, pulled myself up on my forearms, and swung my leg over the fence like they'd taught me in the police academy. Dropping into a crouch on the other side, I straightened and stepped between Maya and a chicken seconds before what would become the last moment of the feathered creature's life.

"Come here." I leaned down to the dog's level and motioned her forward.

But Maya had other ideas. She charged at me, knocking me on my backside before pushing off me like a diving board, ready for round two.

I struggled for breath as I reached up, and almost caught her mid-flight, but she dodged me, leaving me lying on the ground flat on my back.

I got to my knees, then staggered to my feet. "Okay," I said, out of breath. "You win, you slippery devil."

I swear she laughed at me.

Out of ideas, I looked at the woman still wielding the broom like a baseball bat, and the chicken, who ruffled her feathers as if she was trying to pull herself together. They didn't look impressed by my ungraceful moves.

Apparently satisfied that she'd proven her point, Maya walked slowly over to me and ducked her head, allowing me access to her collar. Getting a firm hold of it, I gave Maya a nod. She'd earned my respect. Pushing my hair out of my face, I turned to the woman. "Sorry about that. We'll get out of your way."

Neither the woman nor the chicken looked particularly grateful.

Dragging the dog, who continued to lunge at the flock behind us, we made our way back to the car, where Noah still snored undisturbed. *Yin and Yang*, I thought as I shoved Maya into the backseat.

"Wait," the woman called, running toward me.

Keys in hand, I paused by the door.

"You dropped this." She handed me my phone, covered in mud and what I guessed was chicken poop.

I carefully took it, holding it by the corners, trying not to gag. "Aw, thanks."

"And thanks to you, too, Maya," I said under my breath.

I got into the car and looked in the rear-view mirror, about to back out of the space, when I spied Maya biting down on one of the cookies I'd planned to bring to my aunt. A twinkle sparkled in her eyes, and she held my gaze as she swallowed.

So, this was how it was going to be?

Back at the hotel, I pulled into the driveway and sat for a minute, rubbing a shooting pain in my knuckles. Martha paced the yard. "Thank goodness you found her," she said, coming to stand at my rolled-down window. "No one gets hurt on my watch."

I got out and pulled Maya out of the backseat by her collar. "This dog can fly," I relinquished control to Martha. "How old is she?"

"Fifteen. Can you believe it? Age hasn't slowed her down one bit. I was about to get her out because her owner was supposed to pick her up. So glad you found her before Lucy got here, or she would have had a fit. She loves that dog like a child."

I knew the feeling. I glanced back at my fur baby and clicked my tongue to call him. Noah leaped off the front seat and stretched by my feet.

"Maya almost knocked me on my patootie when she bolted for freedom," Martha said. "For a moment, I thought I'd be joining your aunt in the hospital."

"Thank God that didn't happen. One woman down is enough. This dog is amazing for her age. Glad we got her back in one piece."

"Funny," Martha said as I followed her inside. "Lucy's an hour late. That's not like her."

"Well, good thing," I said.

"I hope she gets here soon. Despite Maya's antics, I don't mind having her here, but we're fully booked, and I need the room."

Inside the hotel, Martha placed Maya in a kennel, so she'd be safe. Noah resumed his spot on the chair.

"How was your trip?" Martha asked.

I tucked a wayward hair behind my ear. *Don't show your ears,* my mom always said. *They stick out just like mine.* As if she were standing there giving me the stink eye, I freed my hair and let it frame my face. "Trip was long but uneventful. Just glad to be here so I can help. When did you last see Jo-Jo?"

"Yesterday. She's ornery as ever. I feel sorry for the staff at the rehab. She's bossing them around like they work for her, and I know how that feels."

I laughed.

When Martha called last Wednesday, I immediately knew something was wrong. My aunt had been in a car accident that left her with a fractured hip and leg. She'd been in the hospital for a few days before they moved her to a rehabilitation facility where she underwent physical and occupational therapy, which would prepare her to come home in a week or so. She wouldn't be able to manage the pet hotel for several weeks, maybe months. I'd recently lost my dream job and had yet to figure out what I wanted to do next. Plus, I loved dogs. Helping would be the perfect distraction for me and would benefit my aunt at the same time. A win-win.

"I guess I should head over to the rehab," I said. "Mind if I leave Noah with you? He's still sleeping off the drugs."

"No problem," Martha said. "Compared to Maya, he's a piece of cake."

Chapter Two

After signing in at the front desk at the rehab center, I followed the sound of Aunt Jo-Jo's infectious laughter to the end of the hall and into a big therapy room. There were padded tables, pulleys hanging from the ceiling, a mock kitchen, and even the front half of a car where patients practiced transitioning from their wheelchairs to the passenger seat.

With one arm in a sling, Aunt Jo-Jo operated her chair with the other, failing to navigate the cones set out for her, knocking them down instead. She laughed like a kid driving a wayward bumper car. Her ramrod-straight therapist wasn't amused.

Aunt Jo-Jo looked good—a bit thin, but not much different from the last time I'd seen her. The resemblance to my mother slapped me in the face, although the differences between them were significant. While my aunt welcomed her advancing age and kept her silver hair twisted in a bun behind her head, my mom dyed hers pink and wore it in a pixie cut.

I hadn't heard from my mom for a few months. That's what she did—disappear on some grand adventure that I would only hear about once it ended, usually badly.

Memories started to surface, but I threw a blanket over them as the self-help book I'd recently read warned me *not* to do. Not going there today, that was for sure.

When my aunt spotted me standing in the doorway, she broke into an even bigger grin. "Charlie," she said. "What are you doing here?"

I raised my arms. "Woot, woot, surprise! I'm here! Looks like you're a danger to the community in that wheelchair."

Martha thought it would be best if I arrived unexpected. Give my aunt a lift. But Aunt Jo-Jo didn't seem depressed. She wasn't one to let life's punches get her down. Still, I was glad I'd come.

Aunt Jo-Jo gave a belly laugh. "What are you gonna do? Write me a ticket?" She wheeled herself my way, and I bent down to hug her. "I can't believe you came all this way, Charlie."

"Of course, I'd come. Looks like you could use a hand."

"You try navigating this darn thing with one arm. And this chair they gave me is a dud."

"The chair is fine," her therapist said, extending her hand to me. "I'm Claire, and we're done for the day. You can take Crash back to her room if you'd like."

Once Claire was out of earshot, my aunt cupped her hand around her mouth and whispered, "Claire clearly needs a suppository, or a stiff drink, or maybe both. She's too darn serious."

I bit back a smile as I stepped over a crushed cone and took control of the wheelchair. "Which way?"

"My room is depressing," Aunt Jo-Jo said. "Let's go out on the porch and get some fresh air."

Maybe Martha was right. My aunt did need a distraction.

I followed Aunt Jo-Jo's directions to a wrap-around porch that gave a breathtaking view of the Salish Sea. And that damn bridge. Positioning the wheelchair to enjoy the scenery, I covered my aunt with a blanket from a basket nearby and sat on a rocking chair beside her. "This place looks nice."

"Window dressing," Aunt Jo-Jo said. "It's a prison. And the food stinks."

I laughed. Her no-nonsense personality always left me smiling. "I'll sneak you in some good stuff now that I'm here."

We watched an enormous tanker ship languidly pass by.

"How long can you stay?"

"A few weeks, maybe a month." I rubbed a sore spot on my knuckles and then stuffed my hands under my thighs so Aunt Jo-Jo wouldn't notice the swelling. The visit was about her, not me.

"I don't want to keep you away from the academy," she said.

"No worries. Martha and I can handle the hotel. You just concentrate on getting better. I knew you broke your hip and leg, but what happened to your arm?"

"Dislocated my shoulder. It's worse than my leg and leaves me with one wing."

"I'm sorry. Tell me about the accident."

She shrugged a slight shoulder. "Don't remember it. When I came to, I was in the hospital. I'm just glad no one else got hurt."

Martha was short on details when she'd called me. I made a mental note to ask her if she'd learned anything more about what happened when I saw her next.

"What about your job?" Aunt Jo-Jo said. "You haven't even graduated from the academy. How are you able to take a break?"

I wasn't ready to go into the long story about why I'd left the police academy. I didn't mind my aunt knowing. I just couldn't muster the energy to go there yet. "Don't worry about it," I said. "It's all good."

She didn't look convinced, but thankfully didn't push the issue. "Did you bring Noah?"

"I did. He's back at the hotel with Martha."

"I can't wait to meet him. Make yourself at home. Probably want to change the bedding on the sleeping porch daybed. Nobody's slept there for so long."

"I will."

My cellphone vibrated in my pocket. I pulled it out and checked the message.

Martha: *Worried that Maya's owner hasn't come for her yet, and no answer when I call. Can you swing by her house on the way home and see if she's there? Lucy Masanova. I'll forward you the address.*

I banged out a response. *I'll stop by after I finish with my aunt, who sends her love.*

Okay, I improvised a bit, but I was sure my aunt would express her best wishes if she knew I was talking to her friend.

I didn't want to bother Aunt Jo-Jo with the problem of Lucy being late for Maya—she'd try to manage things from her hospital bed—and I wanted her to concentrate on getting better. I spent the next hour with my aunt, watching the ships meander by while she filled me in on the lives of the staff at the rehab. She'd not only learned their names, but knew their family situations as well.

"They take better care of you if they like you," she said, her voice low.

I checked my watch. Maya's mom was now several hours late.

"I've got to go." I stood. "Want me to wheel you to your room?"

"No. Leave me here. I want to sit in the fresh air for a while. Got to squeeze out the last bit of summer while we can."

"Okay. Tomorrow I'll bring you some good coffee and a breakfast sandwich."

"Bless your heart," Aunt Jo-Jo said.

I kissed her forehead. "Behave," I said, starting down the steps.

My aunt's raucous laughter told me that was the last thing she intended to do.

Chapter Three

I powered my rental car up the hill until it crested on flat ground. A wall of Pacific Madrone trees, curving smooth red trunks leaning back from countless winters of beating wind, guarded the property to my right. The afternoon sun glistened on the water to my left.

At a break in the trees, I spotted a mailbox. The address was wearing off, but I could still make out the numbers. Lucy Masanova's house. I pulled over onto the shoulder of the road and parked.

I remembered Lucy from one of my stays with my aunt and uncle in my younger years. She was the town librarian, and she seemed as old as the hills when I was a kid. She must be pushing at least ninety by now. And while I didn't remember her being mean, I recalled she was a sourpuss. Long before they were fashionable, purple-framed glasses hung from a chain around her neck, and she wore long skirts, cardigans, and sensible shoes.

The rusted gate was locked. "Hello?" I called. The sound of chirping birds responded. Once again, my long legs came in handy as I scaled the gate and landed on the other side.

A brick pathway led to the house. Overgrown grass had forced its way through the decaying mortar. Multi-colored wildflowers swayed in the gentle breeze and brushed against my calves as I made my way toward the house. The structure itself was weather-beaten. Peeling violet paint, and windows gray from grime or age.

The screen door banged open and shut at the will of the wind. A water bowl that had attracted bugs sat on the porch next to an old, well-chewed boot—the work of Maya, no doubt. As manic a dog as she was, I wondered if a foot had been in the shoe when Maya claimed it as hers.

The window next to the yellow front door was ancient. Its wavy glass, pock-marked with imperfections, distorted the room behind it. I could hear some noise from inside, but I couldn't make out what it was. I knocked on the door and waited. No answer.

Cupping my hands against the window, I strained to see inside. Tattered light blue love seats faced each other in front of a brick fireplace, dark with soot. Ratty red, green, and yellow Afghans lay draped over the sofa backs.

My mother went through a phase where she made similar blankets, crocheting whenever she was still, using remnants she'd found on sale at the local yarn outlet. The colors were at odds, but I could count the gifts she'd given me on one hand, and each one was special to me. I still had one of those mismatched screamers in my apartment back home. I often pulled it out on the dreariest of days, cuddling with Noah on the big chair by the window and reading a novel. No matter how captivating the story, thoughts of my mom were ever-present. There were good times, too, after all, and I cherished those memories.

Knocking on the wooden door, I called out, "Hello, Ms. Masanova? You home?"

Still no answer.

I walked around to the backyard. Neglected shrubbery, grass, and more wildflowers were all overgrown. Rusty garden tools leaned against the back of the house. At the rear door, I knocked again. Waited. When no answer came, I turned the doorknob—locked.

I made my way back to the front of the house, stopping momentarily to scratch the bug bites rapidly multiplying on my ankles.

After knocking on the front door one more time, I tried the knob. It opened.

Why would Lucy leave the house unlocked? Orca Cove was small. People felt safe and didn't see the need to lock their doors, but folks were usually more vigilant when going out of town. Did that mean Lucy had returned from her trip? Perhaps she'd come home and was at the hotel to pick up Maya.

I took out my phone and called Martha.

"Has Lucy come for Maya yet?" I asked once we exchanged pleasantries.

"Nope, still no word from her. Did you get to her place?"

"I'm here, and the door is unlocked. I hear something inside, but no one is answering. There's no car."

"Lucy doesn't drive," Martha said. "She'd walk here. Always walking, that one. The hills don't seem to bother her even though she, like Maya, is older than dirt."

"Do you think I should peek inside?"

Martha didn't hesitate. "I'm sure she wouldn't mind. I'm getting worried."

"Okay," I said. "I'll call you back if I find anything."

I disconnected the call and pocketed my phone. I'd only made it through four weeks of the police academy before I had to give up my dream of being a cop. We hadn't gotten to the section on breaking and entering yet, but I didn't think checking on a missing woman would constitute a felony. At least, I hoped not.

As I stepped inside the house, the screen door banged shut behind me. I nearly jumped out of my skin. "Jeez." I patted my thumping heart.

Books and knitting material cluttered the house. Dusty knick-knacks crowded shelves. In the dining room, newspapers and mail covered a table. One chair was overturned, and a stack of letters had cascaded onto the floor. I checked the date of the newspaper on top of the pile. It was from five days ago.

A musty smell mingled with fragrant ocean air.

The sound was clear now, and I recognized it right away. Songs from *The Sound of Music*. Julie Andrews crooned about raindrops and kittens over and over as the needle stuck on the record playing on the turntable.

I let it play on.

I took in the collection of LPs next to the record player. Lucy was quite the collector of show tunes.

My radar went up a notch. One wouldn't leave a record playing when going out of town. Something wasn't right. Goosebumps pimpled my arms.

I moved on. Upstairs, I found two bedrooms. One appeared to be a nostalgic snapshot of a young person's bedroom. Posters of pop stars from years ago plastered the walls. One bed was plain and neatly made. The other had dust-covered stuffed animals two feet deep. The closet door was open, and two full moving boxes were on the floor. A peek in the closet revealed T-shirts and jeans in a woman's size on one side and a small child's clothes on the other.

There was a double bed and a dresser in the second bedroom. A suitcase, half-packed, sat on the neatly made bed. Was it half-packed or half-unpacked? I couldn't be sure.

An overwhelming desire to leave washed over me. I turned and took the stairs two at a time. By the front door, I glimpsed a purse lying on the floor. I stopped short and nudged it upright with my foot. A wallet and keys were inside.

Outside, I placed another call to Martha and told her what I'd found.

"That doesn't sound good," she said, worry creeping into her voice. "She's about five hours late to pick up Maya. Now, if she were my dog, I'd never come back, but Lucy adores that little devil."

"I think I should call the police," I said.

"I agree," Martha said. "Something's amiss."

Chapter Four

I waited at the front gate for the police to arrive, occupying myself with playing on my phone.

When it dinged in my hand, I almost jumped out of my skin. I had a good case of the creeps, and I kept glancing over my shoulder and staring at the house like someone was inside watching me. The structure seemed to groan, crying out for much-needed repair. It reminded me of a drawing in a book Aunt Jo-Jo used to read to me, where an older woman lived with her many children in a house shaped like a shoe. I was half fearful and half envious of the family, as I'd always wanted siblings. But the house always seemed scary to me.

I opened the text message that came through. It was from my mother, who insisted on going by the name Gabriella, even though her name was Kim.

Hi, baby. Can you do me a favor?

I didn't even know where she called home these days. She had no idea what was going on in my life, either. The last time I saw her, about six months ago, I was miserable in my desk job, and she wanted money. I'd bet my last dollar that the favor, once again, was to bail out her latest mistake.

A police cruiser pulled up and parked behind my rental. I shoved my phone back in my pocket without responding to my mom.

The officer stepped out of his car and adjusted his gun belt before he walked toward me. He was slightly taller than me, which was nice for a change. I was tired of towering over everyone. He tucked his chestnut brown hair, a bit long for a police officer, behind his ear. He had a pleasant face with a square jaw and a bright smile. His nose looked like it was slightly swollen from a fight, upsetting an otherwise perfect picture. "Everything okay, Ma'am?" he asked.

I hated being called ma'am. It made me feel like I should roll up my support hose and take an antacid. "I called because Lucy Masanova, a client of ours at Wiggle Butt Manor, hasn't picked up her dog like she was supposed to. I came by to check on her, and things don't look quite right."

A voice crackled over the radio clamped to his belt. He listened for a moment, then reached down and lowered the volume. "How so?"

"Her purse, with wallet and keys, were on the floor. Music played, and someone had tipped over a chair. Oh, and her suitcase was on the bed. Since she was supposed to go out of town, I don't know if that was there for a few days or if she just got back."

He raised an eyebrow. "You went inside?"

The whole felony thing pushed its way forward from the back of my mind. I aimed for nonchalance. "Oh, yeah, I also found it odd that the back door was unlocked."

"If you know Lucy," he said, "everything about her is odd."

"I remember that about her. But I thought I should report it, nonetheless."

He looked me over carefully, like he was seeing me for the first time. "I didn't know Jo-Jo had hired anyone new. Where did you say you were from?" He took off his sunglasses, giving me a look at soulful brown eyes that almost sucked me in. *Down, girl. He's probably in love with himself.*

"Jo-Jo McMullen is my aunt. Since she's in the hospital, I came to help."

The knowing look on his face made me feel suddenly exposed. "So, you're the legendary Charlie?"

I swallowed hard. "Legendary?"

He flashed a sly smile. I felt left out of a joke and wondered just what my aunt had told him about me. Having never heard about him, I was at a considerable disadvantage.

But he moved on. "I heard about the accident. She doing okay?"

"She has a long road to recovery, but she's in good spirits."

"Good to hear. You got ID?"

I sighed. I'd been in town a few hours, and my name would already be in a police report. I felt a pang of longing for the job I'd almost had. Walking over to my car, I took my wallet from my purse on the front seat, retrieved my license, and handed it to him.

"Jersey," he said, like it was another planet. "Charlie Calderbank from New Jersey."

If he came out with a Jersey joke, I'd scream. "I'm aware."

He chuckled and took out a stack of notecards held together with a clip. "I thought I detected an accent." He scribbled down my information and handed my license back.

I glanced at his name tag. "Officer Sabato, does Lucy have family? Someone we can call who might know where she is?"

"Not that I know of," he said. "My nana calls her a spinster."

"Nana?" What was he, five?

He shrugged and shook his head with a little laugh. "Always called her that."

"Doesn't someone else live here?" I thought about the spare bedroom and clothes that belonged to an adult and a child, but I didn't want to admit I'd snooped that much. Even to me, it seemed I'd crossed a line.

"Not that I know of," he said.

"Well, I don't really know Lucy, but of course, I'm concerned. Martha at the hotel said it's not like her to be late. And we've got her dog. The hotel is booked. Can anyone care for her until we find Lucy?"

"Maya? Don't think anyone's gonna volunteer to watch that demon disguised as a dog."

"She has a reputation?"

"I'd say a quarter of my calls are complaints about Maya. She has a talent for jumping fences and terrorizing the neighborhood."

I knew a chicken who would attest to that. "Is she vicious?"

"Never knew her to hurt anyone, but she acts like she wants to tear your throat out sometimes. She especially likes to intimidate other dogs. Yet, she has a sweet side. It's hard to stay mad at her."

I felt lucky Maya hadn't gone after Noah when I'd had them in the car together. Maybe Noah's indifference kept him alive. Or maybe it was the cookies.

I felt confident that Martha would keep a close eye on Noah, but I didn't want him alone with Maya with what I now knew. I wanted to get back to the hotel. "Do you need anything else?"

"Not at the moment. You staying at your aunt's?"

I nodded.

Officer Sabato clicked his pen open. "You got a number I can put on file?"

I rattled off the numbers, and he added them to the notecard with my other information. On my way back to my car, I said, "Please let me know when you locate Lucy."

"Of course."

I could feel him watch me drive away. I kept sight of him in the rearview mirror until I started down the hill and Lucy's house disappeared from sight. Half intrigued, half irritated, I didn't know what to think of him. I just hoped he found Lucy soon, so Maya would become somebody else's problem.

Chapter Five

Back at the hotel, I told Martha about my contact with Officer Sabato. "He's a hottie, that one," she said, as she stapled a flyer titled **Help Build the Agility Course** on the corkboard.

I squatted down and gave Noah some attention. "I don't trust someone that handsome."

Martha slid her glasses down her nose and looked at me. "Why's that?"

"Women always throw themselves at men like him. Who needs the competition?"

Martha shook her head. "You're beautiful, smart, and kind. You could get any man you want."

I laughed. "Yeah, right." I'd spent my teenage years hating my height, my almost flat chest, and lips that looked like I'd overdone a Botox injection. Add my new rheumatoid arthritis diagnosis and the fact that I was unemployed, and yes, I was quite the catch. Also, I wouldn't be in Orca Cove for long. It wasn't wise to get too attached to anyone. I scratched Noah behind his ears.

"Does Lucy live with someone?"

"Nope," Martha said. "She's on her own."

I told her about the spare bedroom. "It looked like a young woman and a little girl lived there."

Martha shook her head. "Are you kidding me? Those people moved out years ago. She hasn't gotten rid of their stuff?"

"Well, there were boxes that indicate that she might have started packing. But there were clothes in the closet and toys still on the bed."

Martha made a clicking sound with her tongue. "Guess she never got over losing those girls. Anyway, are you in for the night?"

I was sure there was a story there, and I'd like to hear it someday, but Martha was checking her watch, and I knew she was eager to end her day. "Yes," I said. "No plans. What needs to be done with the dogs?"

"Just fed them, but if you could walk them before going to bed, that would be great. I'm tired of coming over here every night and doing what Jo-Jo usually does."

"Got it covered," I said. "Just one more question before you go. Do you know where Lucy was headed? Why she boarded Maya?"

"You know, she didn't say. I do know it was a last-minute reservation. She usually lets us know her plans months in advance. But she's a strange one, keeps mostly to herself, so I'm not surprised she didn't tell me where she was going. She's closer to Jo-Jo. Maybe she knows."

I bid Martha goodbye and took Noah into the house. The screen door led to the sleeping porch, my room for the time being. A French glass door separated my quarters from the main living area, which meant any guests who came had to traipse through my room to get to the rest of the house or use the side door into the kitchen. It wasn't the most secure or private place I'd stayed, but in Orca Cove, one didn't worry about such things.

After stripping the daybed, I went down to the basement with Noah following and started the washing machine. In the kitchen, I fought the can opener to open a can of tuna. Turning the crank made the joints in my hand scream, but eventually, I managed the task. After making a sandwich, I ate standing at the counter and washed my food down with a glass of tap water. Since Aunt Jo-Jo had been laid up for the past week, I figured most of the perishable food had spoiled. I cleaned out the refrigerator and planned to stock up on groceries in the morning.

Lucy invaded my thoughts. I checked my phone, but there were no updates from Officer Perfect, so I assumed her disappearance was still a mystery.

Once I transferred the sheets to the dryer, I unpacked as many items as would fit in the only empty dresser drawer I could find. Leaving the rest of my stuff in my suitcase, I kicked it into the corner of the room. Lining up my medication—one prescription, and five supplements on top of the dresser—I realized I'd forgotten to take my pills that day. I'd only been on them for a few weeks, and it wasn't a habit yet.

I hated the reality that I had to swallow any meds. Until recently, I hadn't taken as much as an aspirin since I was a kid. Most of the men who had streamed in and out of my mother's life had addiction issues, and I never wanted to go down that path. But my rheumatologist had convinced me how important my new regimen was if I didn't want permanent joint damage. At thirty, I was too young to be handicapped by such an unforgiving disease.

Other than the stiffness and swelling in my hands that made it difficult to open a can or button a blouse, most people didn't notice anything was wrong with me. But I knew. I'd lost my place in the police academy and subsequent career in law enforcement because of it. And I feared it would progress, as it usually did, leaving me old before my time. No way around it, it sucked.

All my settling in left me exhausted. My watch read eight o'clock, but it was eleven Jersey time. No rest for the weary. I had dogs to walk. Ten, to be exact. I figured it would take me a while to walk them all. I started with a border collie with mismatched eyes and an abundance of energy. Noah tagged along on each walk.

Saving Maya for last, I cautiously reintroduced her to Noah. Her tail swooshed, and she didn't seem like she wanted to eat him, so I clipped a leash on her and set off down the street with both dogs. Maya was hyper-alert. The energy buzzing off her was almost visible. We walked two blocks. It was now close to nine, and the sun had long since gone down. The only light came from a lone streetlamp at the four-way stop. At the end of the street, a pathway disappeared into dense woods. It looked eerie in the dark. The fur on the back of Maya's neck stood up as she pulled us toward the gravel path. I yanked her back. "Not tonight, girl. That's a discovery for daylight hours."

As I turned to head back to the house, Maya continued to lunge toward the trail, getting more and more worked up by the minute. Caught up in the excitement, Noah barked, something he rarely did. "You guys are creeping me out," I said.

23

Upping my muscle, I dragged both dogs behind me. When I got to my aunt's property, I heard the door of the pet hotel slam, and a shadow darted across the lawn. "Hello?" I called.

Whoever it was disappeared into the darkness. A moment later, I heard an engine come to life down the street, and then an unremarkable pickup truck drove by, lights off. I couldn't make out the occupants or much detail about the vehicle.

The hair on the back of my neck rose, much like Maya's had at the beginning of the path. "Come on," I urged the dogs, pulling them toward the hotel.

The door remained unlocked, as I'd left it. I eased it open and flipped the light switch on. The guests barked in greeting. I checked each room, finding all the residents accounted for. But the door to the storeroom in the back stood open. I thought I'd pulled it shut behind me when I'd grabbed a leash. I was too tired to be sure. Nothing seemed out of place.

Still, someone had been there.

Maybe it was the teenager who worked part-time at the hotel. I'd yet to meet her. Perhaps she'd run in to grab something she'd forgotten from her shift that day.

The salty scent of the ocean was strong in the room. Odd. Though the water was close by, I'd never noticed it before. The Pacific Northwest smelled more like pine than the salty Jersey shore scent that now permeated the air.

Feeling uneasy, I took both dogs back to the house. Maya would stand watch tonight. Sometimes, a devil dog was the best company.

The daybed was comfortable, and a good cleansing cross-breeze came through the screens from three sides of the room. I'd loved sleeping in the country air whenever I'd visited and would fall into the deepest sleeps of my life. A lot of special childhood memories occurred in this room. I remembered going to the library whenever I came to town and choosing a book with great care, my aunt would read to me before I drifted off to sleep in this very bed.

But tonight, tension tightened my muscles after what had transpired that day. The flimsy door between me and the outside world provided little security. Noah curled up alongside me as he always did. His body curved against my chest so I could feel his little heart beating. It was a shock when Maya jumped onto the bed uninvited and settled against my back, making me the filling in a dog sandwich. I looked over my shoulder at Maya, who stared back at me with knowing eyes. White hair on her snout was the only thing that gave away her age.

When Maya relaxed, I stared at the ceiling and relived the events that had brought me to the other side of the country and this charming town. In a way, Aunt Jo-Jo's accident was a welcome distraction from my life that was falling apart, piece by piece.

I'd always wanted to be a cop. Athletic and tall, I wasted my attributes at my monotonous desk job. I went through my days on autopilot and knew I had to do something to get myself out of my funk. If my mom had taught me anything, it was that an emergency was always around the corner. I'd saved enough money to tide me over while I quit my day job and became a police recruit. I knew the job was a gamble since I had to pass the academy and a probationary period before I'd be able to consider myself secure in my employment. But the opportunity excited me and filled me with a sensation of hope I hadn't felt in a long time.

Turned out, I excelled at the classes in criminal law, and the physical training that seemed difficult for many of my classmates came easily to me. But then, about a month in, I woke up with a swollen, painful hand. My mother's curse had curled up and lunged at me like a cobra strike.

At first, I thought a spider had bitten me. What else could explain the sudden swelling?

A trip to the doctor led to a referral to a rheumatologist. Bloodwork showed I had Rheumatoid Arthritis, a disease I knew nothing about. I thought only older people received the diagnosis. I soon learned others suffered from an ailment that was more than stiff joints. Turns out, they use low doses of cancer drugs to treat RA, and at first, they made me nauseous.

Although I tried, I couldn't hide it for long. It quickly became apparent I wouldn't be able to fulfill the duties of a police officer. I was in tears when

I told my class sergeant and gathered my stuff, leaving my budding career and dreams behind.

Tonight, those tears came again, as they often did when I was alone with my thoughts. I let them come as drowsiness engulfed me.

The happenings that had occurred since my arrival in Orca Cove, coupled with my pending life choices, threatened to keep me awake. But I felt somewhat secure between two dogs, even if one would sleep through a plane crashing into the house.

As if sensing my unease, Maya inched closer. The heft of her body against my side had the same effect as a weighted blanket.

I'd be able to sleep. Maya had claimed us as members of her pack, and she would protect us, I was sure.

Chapter Six

I woke, uneasy that someone was watching me. I startled, remembering where I was and that the night before, somebody had been in the hotel while I walked the dogs. My eyes popped open, and I met Maya's expectant stare. Not only was the dog encroaching my space, but she had a paw on either side of my shoulders, and her breath was not the most pleasant thing to wake up to in the morning.

"Jeez." I gently shoved Maya to the side. "Who'd expect you to be an early riser, old girl?"

Noah, on the other hand, snored peacefully, undisturbed by the sunlight warming the room.

Sitting up, I rubbed my eyes, then massaged the stiffness in my hands. The view from the screened-in window of the water was like something from a brochure. My gaze left the tranquil scene and found chaos on the floor. The contents of my suitcase had erupted all over the room. "What the heck?"

Maya wagged her tail, thumping it against the covers, and Noah groggily stretched.

I gave Maya the stink eye, and she yawned. "Did you do this?" Pulling back the blanket, I got to my feet. "Bad dog."

Rapping on the door caused me to jump and Maya to let out a string of aggressive barks.

"Hello?" a male voice called through the door. The door was one of those metal ones that allowed air to pass through, but it was difficult to see inside. Thankfully.

I froze, then looked down at my tank top and sleeping shorts. Realizing that whoever was there could easily see through the screened windows if they tried, which would allow them to see more of me than I was used to offering up. I dropped to the floor and pulled the comforter off the bed, rolling myself inside like the stuffing in a cannoli. "Just a minute," I called.

Scrambling to my feet, I unlocked the door and pushed it open. Maya rushed past me and leaped through the doorway and into the yard. My eye roll was instantaneous.

Officer Perfect stood in front of me, shielding his eyes from the bright morning sun. I followed his gaze to the mess on the floor, mainly the two bras on top of the pile. I cringed and kicked the clothes under the bed while pulling the blanket tighter around me. Maya looked at us from over her shoulder while she boldly did her business on the lawn. I thought about my unruly hair, but I couldn't spare a hand to do anything about it without dropping the comforter. I figured my breath was almost as bad as Maya's and stuffed the folds of my covering against my mouth as a barrier. While keeping an eye on Maya in the yard, I tried to act like I hadn't been caught off guard. As though I walked around wrapped in a blanket all the time. "What's up?"

"Morning, Jersey. Just wanted to see if Lucy surfaced and picked up Maya. Since she just darted past me, I'll take that as a no."

I returned my attention to Maya—a tan blur that disappeared into the trees surrounding the property.

Officer Sabato sighed. "I'll get her. Be right back."

The leash was on the floor. I kicked it his way. "Good luck," I mumbled through the quilt.

Once he was gone, I dropped the blanket, picked a pair of jeans off the floor, and yanked them on. I managed to brush my teeth in the bathroom and rake a comb through my hair while Noah watched me patiently from the doorway. I slid a hoodie over my tank top as Officer Sabato came up the driveway, pulling Maya behind him.

"Someday, I'm just gonna let her run," he said. "But I'm afraid that if anything happens to her, she'll haunt me for all eternity."

I forced a smile as I took the leash from him.

Officer Sabato crouched down and reached out to pet Noah. "Hey, pretty girl."

There it was. "He's a boy. Note the blue collar." I realized I sounded grumpy as soon as the words were out of my mouth, but it was a pet peeve of mine.

"Sorry." He held up his hands in surrender. "Didn't mean to offend."

"Sorry," I echoed. "Haven't had my coffee yet. No word on Lucy then?"

"Afraid not." He scratched his head. He looked unsure of his next move, and I almost felt sorry for him. I wasn't making this easy. "You have breakfast yet?" he asked.

"What? No… I mean, what?"

He laughed. "Not a big deal. I just thought…I have some questions about Lucy and her leaving Maya behind. I'm hungry and…."

I bent down and scooped up Noah for no other reason than I didn't know what to say. I had no comeback.

"Never mind," he said. "I'm sure you have things to do. Just let me know if you have any more information."

Boy, I was a jerk. But the damage was done. "Of course."

"Well, have a nice day." He handed me his business card and turned to leave.

No wonder I was single. I wished there was a way to take my foot out of my mouth, but the moment was gone. I pulled the door shut behind him and lowered a squirming Noah to the floor.

Chapter Seven

I walked the last three of the ten guests, a poodle, a Great Dane, and a mixed breed whose crinkled skin and alien eyes reminded me of Yoda. After giving them treats, I locked the dogs back in their rooms before Martha arrived to take over.

It was cool enough out that I could leave Noah in the car, but I hoped the rehab center would allow him to visit my aunt. Making a quick stop at the coffee shop, I ordered two regular coffees and two breakfast sandwiches to give Aunt Jo-Jo a break from cafeteria food.

I noticed the same sign that Martha had tacked on the bulletin board at the hotel about the upcoming century ride taped to the wall. The fine print told me about the plan to build an agility course in the dog park. The race was a fundraiser to help my aunt cover the cost. It touched me that the town would come through for her, as I knew how proud she was to have a place where people could gather with their dogs.

At the rehab, I clipped on Noah's leash, gathered up our food, and stopped a nurse as she left the building. "Are dogs allowed to visit patients?"

The nurse squatted down and patted Noah's head. "This lovely girl can go in for sure. The patients will love her."

I took a swig of coffee so I wouldn't lash out at her as I did at Officer Sabato. But I wanted to scream. *Can't you see he's a boy?* Why did no one notice the blue collar? Maybe I needed to buy him a motorcycle jacket or a bow tie.

Inside, I stopped to sign in, then paused for several residents to say hi to Noah.

My aunt sat in a wheelchair in her room. The news played on the television mounted on the wall. An uneaten tray of food sat on the table in front of her. A sour look stained her face. She was so intent on the politician speaking at a news conference that she didn't notice me in the doorway. "Give me a break!" she yelled at the TV.

"Good morning." I walked Noah into the room.

Aunt Jo-Jo's expression immediately brightened. "Noah, baby! You're even more adorable than the photos your mama sent me." She patted her side and clicked her tongue.

Noah obliged and trotted over to her, letting her rub him down.

"My, isn't he the sweetest?"

When Noah had had enough, which took a while, he lay down at her feet.

I arranged my aunt's breakfast on the table within her reach, then settled into the vinyl chair across from her.

"Bless you." She took a sip of coffee. "I can't stand the swill they serve here. And powdered eggs should be outlawed."

I took a bite of my sandwich. "Agree."

"How are things back at the hotel?"

I lowered my food onto the paper on my lap. "For starters, Lucy Masanova never showed to pick up Maya. And that dog's a handful. I can understand why everyone refers to her as the devil, yet she's a cuddler."

Aunt Jo-Jo laughed. "She has a sweet side. She's just a bit bold."

Bold like a cocky rock star. I rolled my eyes. Even Noah sighed.

"I hope nothing's wrong with Lucy," my aunt said. "It's not like her to be five minutes late, let alone a day late."

"It does seem like something might be wrong. I called the police so they can look for Lucy. It's not my place. I'm not a cop."

Aunt Jo-Jo smiled at me like I was coy. "You mean it's not your jurisdiction. It's about to be your job. You're almost a cop."

I bit my tongue. I wasn't ready to go there and tell my aunt about the change in plans because of a stupid health problem. Besides, I couldn't stand the look of pity on people's faces when they learned the truth. Most folks didn't understand how life-changing RA was. That it was more than just

31

arthritis, like that wasn't enough.

It was too much to go into, especially since my aunt had her own problems.

"Anyway," I said. "Any idea where Lucy could be?"

"She was going to Atlanta to see her nephew. Maybe she decided to stay longer."

"Wouldn't she have called?"

Aunt Jo-Jo put her sandwich down and shrugged. "Maybe she did. I haven't seen my cell since the accident."

"Good point. Hopefully, Lucy decided to stay longer, but I doubt she'd leave her house with the record player on and her purse lying on the floor."

"Oh, dear," my aunt said, dropping her sandwich into its wrapper. "That is troublesome."

"Anyway," I said. "Officer Sabato will figure it out."

"Officer Sabato, he's such a sweetie."

"Really?"

Aunt Jo-Jo raised an eyebrow, and her eyes twinkled.

What was it with Officer Perfect and women drooling over him? I moved on. "I'm guessing Lucy never even left town."

My aunt's mood darkened. "I'm glad you called the police."

Chapter Eight

After spending a few hours with my aunt, watching the physical therapist help her perfect transferring herself from the wheelchair to the bed, I could tell Aunt Jo-Jo was exhausted. I kissed her goodbye and promised I'd be back in the morning with more good coffee and the muffin she yearned for.

Since it was a cool sixty-five degrees, I felt safe leaving Noah in the car. I parked in the shade with the windows lowered a few inches and ran into the grocery store—a no-frills building, dark and overflowing with over-priced goods. I'd be broke in no time if I continued shopping there. But it beat crossing the bridge to hit the chain stores on the mainland. I bought a few things: fruit, vegetables, and salmon, all foods that were supposed to fight inflammation. RA was ruling my life, and I hated giving it so much power. I was in line to check out when I gave in to the urge to have something sweet. I hurried back to the baking aisle and bought a box of brownie mix, telling myself that I would make them for Martha and Aunt Jo-Jo, but I knew I'd sample some. What was life without the occasional treat?

Back at the house, I unpacked the groceries, mixed up the brownies, and put them in the oven. After doing a few chores, I found Martha in the office, working on the books. Constant howling made it hard to be heard.

"How's Jo-Jo?" Martha yelled over the racket as I settled on the chair across from the desk with Noah on my lap.

"Therapy takes a lot out of her," I said.

Martha nodded. "I predict she comes home in the next few days. She's a trooper."

"She is. Who's making all that noise?"

Martha looked over her glasses at me. "Who do you think?"

I laughed. "Maya, of course. Why don't you educate me on what needs to be done besides feeding and walking the dogs?"

"I've got the books," she said. "It's what I've always done. The books, cleaning, and some dog walking. If you could help with the feeding and walking, it would be a lifesaver. We also have Kyleigh to help with walks, but she's not very dependable. Comes from a troubled home. Jo-Jo believes she can save the girl by giving her a purpose."

"That's Aunt Jo-Jo, gruff on the outside, tender on the inside. I haven't met Kyleigh yet. Does she drive?"

"She's sixteen, but I don't think she has her license yet. Someone always drops her off and picks her up. Why?"

I told Martha about the person I saw leaving the hotel and then the truck driving off the night before.

"Hmm," Martha said. "Sounds suspicious. I don't see anything disturbed or missing. At least nothing jumps out at me."

"Do you think it could have been Kyleigh?"

Martha thought for a moment. "Could have been. She has a key. And her uncle drives a truck." There could have been two people, for all I knew. I hadn't been able to see inside the truck.

I shrugged. "I'll lock up between walks at night from now on, just in case."

"Can't be too careful, I guess."

The alarm on my watch sounded. The brownies were done. I lowered Noah to the floor and got to my feet.

Martha turned back to the books and said over her shoulder, "Can you take Maya? I can't stand the noise anymore, and she's driving the other dogs nuts."

I sighed. Would I ever be done with the mischief-maker? Taking the grateful pup from her room, we headed back to the house.

The enticing aroma of brownies greeted me when I walked through the door. Pulling the Pyrex pan out of the oven, I laid it on the back burner of the stove to cool while I took an overdue shower.

When I emerged from the bathroom, Maya was lying under the table, paws crossed and watching me. Noah rushed forward to greet me with a wagging tail as fast as a hummingbird's wings. He was the happiest dog I knew.

Maya, on the other hand, looked quite proud of herself. "What did you do?" I took a quick tour of the house, expecting to come upon some sort of destruction. But everything was in its place as far as I could tell. Maybe I was imagining things. Nothing a brownie couldn't fix.

I went to the stove, thinking I'd take a corner piece, imagining gooey chocolate melting in my mouth. But the whole thing was gone. Not just the brownies, but the glass pan I'd baked them in.

I spun around, searching the counters. I even looked in the oven, wondering if my memory of taking them out was false. Was I losing my mind?

Feeling safe with Martha across the way, I'd left the kitchen door unlocked. Was the same person who'd been at the hotel last night a brownie thief? A shiver rippled down my spine as I thought about someone being inside the house while I was in the shower.

I glanced back at Maya, still watching my every move. No one could have come through the door with her on guard, I was sure. And she seemed to know something. Whatever had happened to the brownies, Maya had the answer. I crossed the room toward her. She gave me an intense stare, ready to play the game of who would look away first. What was I going to do, interrogate her?

As I crouched before her, something bit into my foot. I let out a cry and lifted my heel. A shard of glass protruded from my flesh. I pulled the piece out, recoiling when I saw it was covered in blood. Oh, wait…not blood. I gave it a sniff. Chocolate!

"God damn!" I jumped on my good foot to the counter, where I grabbed a few paper towels and held them against my wound.

"Really, Maya? You ate the dish?"

Maya licked her lips.

My heart pounded. Chocolate was toxic to dogs. And glass couldn't be good for them either. Reaching under the table, I grabbed her collar and pulled her toward me. About fifty pounds of dead weight. She would not make this easy. Face-to-face, she exhaled sweet brownie breath, like she was rubbing it in.

I sighed. "Noah, come here."

He trotted over, cheerfully giving me a kiss on the chin. More brownie breath. No way could Noah have reached the cake as it cooled on the stovetop. I'd shoved it all the way back to be safe. But Maya would have no trouble reaching it. And once it tumbled to the floor, Noah wouldn't be able to resist the gift from above.

Before my mind could wander too far down the path toward huge vet bills and possible canine death, there was a knock at the door. I hopped over and pulled it open. Officer Sabato stood on the other side. He took his sunglasses off and gave a lopsided smile. I was not in the mood.

"What?" I snapped.

He looked down at the foot I held three inches off the floor. "You're bleeding, Jersey."

Blood, not chocolate, had made its way out of my foot. "How perceptive of you," I said through clenched teeth.

My sarcasm seemed to bounce off him. He walked past me and into the kitchen, where he pulled out a chair. "Sit. I'll get something to fix that."

I wobbled. I had no choice but to take a seat.

Plopping down on the chair, I picked up my foot to inspect it while Officer Perfect went into the bathroom.

"I don't know how," he called from the other room, "but I'm guessing Maya had something to do with this."

I met the dog's intense stare. I swear she was enjoying the chaos she'd created.

Officer Perfect came back into the room carrying a box of oversized Band-Aids and a towel. Kneeling before me, he took my foot in his hand.

I immediately pulled back. "I can do it."

"I have no doubt," he said calmly. "But let me help. I have a merit badge in first aid from the fourth grade." He placed my foot on his knee.

Good thing I'd shaved my legs.

Wrapping the towel around my heel, he put pressure on the wound. I winced. "I've got to get the dogs to the vet. They ate chocolate. It's dangerous for them. And where the heck is the glass pan?"

He looked over his shoulder at Maya, who had lain down and settled her head onto her paws. I half-expected her to request a lawyer.

Officer Perfect carefully put two bandages on my foot and handed me my sneakers that sat by the door. I wouldn't have been surprised if he offered to tie my laces.

Once my shoes were on, I stood, unable to put much weight on my tender foot.

"Where the heck is the pan?" I repeated.

Officer Perfect pointed to a pile of glass stacked haphazardly in the room's corner. It was licked clean.

"I'm not even gonna guess how she managed that," he said. "I'll drive."

"You don't have to take us. I'm perfectly capable of..." But I knew driving was going to hurt.

"I know," he said. "But I'll take you just the same."

He clipped leashes on both dogs and offered me his arm. I pretended not to see the gesture and walked on my tiptoes toward the cruiser. He put Maya in the back seat and then climbed in front. Reluctantly, I slid into the seat next to him, hugging Noah to my chest.

I had a momentary flashback of going on a ride-along in Red Bank while I was in the academy and felt a pang of longing for the life I'd almost had.

"What's your first name?" I asked as we headed to town.

"Why, you got a complaint to file?"

I broke into a slow smile as a rush of warmth enveloped me. "You just bandaged my foot. I feel like we should be on a first-name basis."

"Nick." He offered his hand, and I shook it. "Nice to meet you, Jersey."

"They ate the pan?" The vet tech wore scrubs adorned with colorful cats. She looked familiar, but I couldn't place her. "You mean a Pyrex glass pan?"

I sighed. I wouldn't have believed it if I hadn't seen it myself. "We found a pile of glass, licked clean. Hopefully, they didn't ingest any of that. At the very least, they ate a whole batch of brownies."

Nick leaned down and patted Maya's side. "You've really outdone yourself, old girl."

I turned to the nurse, who looked like she was fresh out of high school. Yet I was going to trust her with my sweet boy's life. I had no choice. "I've looked in both dogs' mouths, and there aren't any cuts as far as I could tell. If they ate glass, surely they would have cut themselves."

"We'll get X-rays to be sure."

Cha Ching. I didn't even care about the cost; I just wanted them to be okay.

The vet tech took Maya's leash. She stopped and looked at me more closely. "Charlie? Is that you?"

I nodded and gave her a closer look. Although I knew some people from my time on the island, I hadn't been here in years, and this girl was young enough that she would have been in her late teens the last time I saw her. Then it came to me. "Riley?"

"Yes," she said. "We used to play together in the woods. I grew up down the road from your aunt."

"Good to see you," I said. But I couldn't focus on anything but Noah and Maya at the moment.

Riley reached for Noah's lead, but I picked him up and squeezed him, unwilling to let him out of my sight. "I love you, little guy," I whispered, my lips against the top of his head. "Please be okay."

Riley met my eyes, which were brimming with tears. "He'll be okay," she promised. "Chocolate is toxic for dogs, but we can induce vomiting. Unless the glass… Well, we need to get X-rays."

I relented, placing Noah on the floor. Snuggling him one last time, I relinquished control to Riley. She gave me a hopeful half-smile before guiding both dogs away.

"I'm sorry," I said to Nick, wiping sloppy tears from my face. "I just love that little guy so much."

"Understandable." He gave me a reassuring pat on the arm. "He's a heartbreaker."

I nodded and tried my best to control myself. I didn't know what I'd do if something happened to Noah. I swore that sometimes he was the reason I still functioned. He'd gotten me through my darkest days. First, issues with my mom, and then being forced out of the academy. I'd go into debt to save him, but I imagined horrific medical bills on the other side of this. And I felt responsible for Maya as well.

"Let's sit," Nick said. He offered his arm to help me make my way to the bench across the room.

I held back a saucy remark about him treating me like an old lady. I felt like an old lady. I gave in and accepted his help.

We settled on the bench. "I bet Maya has an iron stomach," he said. "I wouldn't worry about her."

"I am worried. I shouldn't have left the brownies within reach. I'm used to a short dog."

Nick patted my arm. "How long have you had Noah?"

I wiped my eyes and sighed. "Since he was a puppy. He's four now."

"I can see he's well-loved."

If he kept being so nice, I was surely going to lose it. I felt as anxious as a criminal waiting for the jury to return. I wished I could pace, but my aching foot told me that was out of the question. "What brought you over?" I asked, hoping to refocus the conversation.

Nick kicked his boots out and crossed his ankles. "Still trying to figure out this whole missing Lucy Masanova thing. She told people she was going to visit her nephew in Atlanta. I contacted him and he said she'd called him out of the blue, saying she wanted to see him. But she never showed. Before that, he hadn't heard from her in years."

"Weird. Did he tell you anything else?"

"He seemed disinterested," Nick said. "I get the feeling oddness runs in the family."

Chapter Nine

Forty minutes had passed, and the vet had yet to update us on Noah and Maya's conditions. I sat massaging my aching hands while Nick took a few phone calls, standing just outside the door.

I watched him pace. His khaki work pants showed a slim waist. The bullet-proof vest he wore made his top half look bulky. I tried not to let my mind wander to what he might look like in regular clothes.

He's being nice because he's bored. I imagined there wasn't a lot of criminal activity in such a small town, and his biggest problem was under sedation in the back room. Still, as my thoughts drifted to what if, I reminded myself that I didn't live here, and the last thing I needed was a long-distance relationship. As if he'd even be interested.

Nick caught me staring in his direction and gave a sly grin.

I looked away before he could see the heat burning my cheeks, and became fascinated with a mark on the linoleum floor.

A few minutes later, the vet came out. He was a compact little guy with a bald head and bright green eyes that made everything else about him irrelevant. He offered me his hand. I stood and shook it. "I'm Dr. Powers," he said.

"Charlie Calderbank," I told him as Nick came back through the door.

"Nice to meet you." He nodded at Nick. "Officer."

"Doc," Nick said in return.

"How are they?" I couldn't handle small talk. I'd explode if I had to wait a minute longer for the news.

"They'll be fine," he said. "X-rays showed no glass in their stomachs, so we induced vomiting and then gave them charcoal to absorb anything that was left." He shook his head. "It appears both dogs had a bit of a party, but they'll be fine. They should be able to go home in about thirty minutes."

I let out a long breath. "Thank you so much." Tears of relief stung my eyes. Nick must have thought I was a mess, but I didn't care. Noah was going to be okay. And Maya, too. I surprised myself with how worried I was about the rabble-rouser.

"I've been Maya's vet for more years than I can count," Dr. Powers said. "She's always getting into something, but she has a cast-iron stomach. Is Lucy out of town?"

"Yes," I said. "Maya's a guest at our pet hotel."

Dr. Powers looked confused.

"Charlie is Jo-Jo's niece," Nick said. "She's helping out while her aunt recovers from her accident."

"I heard about that. How is she?"

"Better every day," I said.

He nodded. "That's good. Everybody loves Jo-Jo."

"She is lovable," I said. "Anyway, I can't thank you enough."

"It's why we're here," Dr. Powers said. "Give your aunt my regards."

"I will."

When Dr. Powers returned to the back room, I let out another giant sigh of relief. Nick scratched his head. "I'm afraid duty calls. I can try to swing back for you and the kids when I'm done."

"Don't worry about me. I can get a ride."

"Well, if you can't, let me know." He jotted down his number on an interview card and handed it to me. I already had his work number, but this one was different. Was he giving me his personal cell number? "Call anytime."

When I took the card from his hand, he held onto it for a minute, a suspicious look on his face. "You punch someone?"

I followed his gaze to my hand, so close to his. My swollen knuckles were obvious. I held tighter to the card and pulled it out of his grip. "You should see the other guy," I said.

He laughed. "I can imagine. Talk to you later."

I watched him leave and then placed a call to Martha. She agreed to come and get me as soon as she finished checking out one of our guests.

Riley brought out the dogs, and I scooped Noah up into my arms, nuzzling the top of his head with my chin.

"What a sweet little guy," she said. "Of course, Maya's a regular."

"Thank you for taking such good care of them," I said.

"My pleasure." She handed me a small piece of paper. "That's my number. We should get together, catch up."

"I'd like that."

Riley was about a year younger than me. She'd been a nice kid and had made my stay on the island a little easier years ago. It was nice to connect with a familiar face.

Maya jumped onto the backseat of Martha's Cherokee, as if nothing had happened. Noah sat on my lap in the front seat. Although my bank account had taken a hit, neither dog seemed any worse for wear. I turned to look at Maya. "I hope it was worth it." She licked her lips, telling me it was well worth it, and she would do it again if given the opportunity.

I kissed the top of Noah's downy head and turned my attention to Martha. "No word from Lucy?"

"Not a peep." She navigated the SUV onto the main road. "I wonder if Officer Sabato knows anything."

"He didn't. At least not when he left about thirty minutes ago."

Martha raised an eyebrow.

I explained he took us to the vet and waited with me until he got a call.

"Seems like he's crushing on you," she said with a wink.

"It's not that!"

Martha laughed. "I know Lucy. You don't see him hanging around me asking questions, do you?"

I buried my face in the fur on Noah's head, grateful he was doing okay. "Anyway," I said, "even if he were interested, it doesn't mean I am. And since

I'm only here for a few weeks, I'm not. End of story." It was best not to even think about a future with a man like Nick. Even if there wasn't the distance problem, that kind of life wasn't in my deck of cards.

Martha shook her head. "If you say so."

"I do."

"Mind if I stop at the feed store?"

"Not at all."

We pulled into the parking lot. While Martha ran inside, I took the dogs for a short walk on the patch of grass between the store and a gas station, while favoring my sore foot. The dogs sniffed every inch in front of them, and my attention drifted to the gas pumps where people stood fueling their cars. A cherry red Mustang caught my attention. The driver leaned against the car, checking his watch while he waited for the gas tank to fill. Neatly trimmed blond hair and a goatee framed his handsome face.

For a minute, I wondered if a side effect of my medication made me check out every man I encountered. It wasn't usually my way. Typically, I was so oblivious to male attention, my friends had to elbow me when someone hit on me.

The man looked my way and smiled.

I focused on the dogs. He was probably taken with them. And people in the Pacific Northwest were friendly. I was sure there was nothing more to it.

When Martha came out with a shopping cart full of dog food, I put the dogs in the car's backseat and helped her load her purchases in the back. Then we started toward the hotel. From the side mirror, I could see the blond guy with the sports car watch us leave.

Chapter Ten

When we pulled into the driveway of the hotel, Martha waved at a teenager who was being pulled along the driveway behind a pack of four dogs. Although the pups appeared to be in the driver's seat, I appreciated her ingenuity. Why hadn't it occurred to me to walk several at a time? "Is that Kyleigh?" I asked.

"The one and only," Martha said.

The tone of her voice told me she wasn't as crazy about the girl as my aunt was.

Kyleigh had black hair that hung to her waist. She wore baggy cargo pants that looked like she borrowed them from her father. A shapeless sweatshirt and army boots completed the look. Her wild mane hid what looked to be a pretty face. Something about her was familiar, but I couldn't place why.

I got out of the car with Noah while Martha took Maya from the back seat. "Hi," I said, approaching the girl. "I'm Charlie. I'll be helping out for a bit."

I towered over her. Kyleigh was lucky if she cleared five feet. She looked up at me through long lashes. A flicker of interest flashed across her face before she returned her attention to the dogs. "Hi," she mumbled and started to walk away.

"Just let me help Martha unload the supplies, and I'll take two of those dogs off your hands," I called after her.

She stopped and waited.

I hobbled back to the house with Noah. I was getting the hang of not putting pressure on my sore heel and walking without pain. I put Noah inside, scooped up the broken glass, and threw it in the trash. After lugging two thirty-pound bags of food into the hotel storage room, I caught up to Kyleigh and the pack of dogs outside.

She offered me two leashes, and I was in control of a standard poodle and a pit-mix. We started down the road. "So, I guess you like dogs," I said.

She looked at her feet. "They're okay."

"A job's a job," I said, opting for a different tactic.

She shrugged again. This was going to be harder than I thought. I wasn't exactly good with kids or a sparkling conversationalist myself. I tried to get comfortable with the silence.

Kyleigh took the path Maya had wanted to go down the night before. I imagined she usually took the dogs there, which was why Maya had found it so enticing. Gravel crunched beneath our feet, the rocks biting into my aching foot. I adjusted my stride to minimize the pain. Tall trees stood on both sides of the narrow path. We didn't fit side-by-side, so I followed behind her.

At the end, the path opened to a small beach where the ocean lapped gently onto the pebbly sand. "You can let Louie off leash," she said. "He likes to go for a swim."

"Which one is Louie?"

She reached over and unhooked the poodle's leash, and Louie pranced along the water's edge for a minute before plunging into the ocean after a stone Kyleigh threw. She sat on a beached log, and I settled beside her, thankful to take pressure off my foot. In silence, we watched Louie, who had submerged his head underwater in search of the rock. He was under for so long, I thought about wading out to force him up for air, but before I could commit to standing, he came up himself, a flat rock grasped in his jaws.

He trotted back to us and dropped the stone at Kyleigh's feet before he went for round two.

"You're a cop, right?" She kept her attention on the water.

My aunt must have told her. "No," I said, eyes on the horizon. "I decided not to do that." I wasn't sure what made me share my situation with this girl

I hadn't said two words to when I hadn't told my aunt.

"Good call," she said. "I hate cops."

"Why?"

"Macho jerks who want to throw everyone in jail."

"I'm sorry that's been your experience," I said.

She shrugged. "No big deal."

I bet there was a story behind her mistrust of police officers, and I weighed if it would be smart to go there. She reminded me of an abused animal. When you thought you'd gained their trust, they would flee, thinking you were going to cause them harm. I wanted to ask her if she had been at the hotel the other night, but before I could form my question, Louie dropped a woman's black pump with a sturdy block heel at our feet. "Strange for someone to lose that at the beach," I said.

Kyleigh stood up and made her way to the water's edge, the dogs by her side. Shielding her eyes from the sun by flattening her hand like a visor, she scanned the area. I walked forward and did the same. About twenty feet away, I spotted a stockinged foot bobbing in the water next to a floating log.

"Oh, no!" I ran along the shore, ignoring the pain in my foot and dragging the pit bull behind me. From my vantage point, I could see a body submerged in the surf. Kyleigh came to stand beside me.

"Holy Moly," she said. "That's Lucy Masanova. I recognize the scarf."

I thought about dragging her out of the water, of trying to revive her. But one thing was clear: it was too late for Ms. Masanova. She'd obviously been there for quite some time. I pulled my phone out of one pocket and Nick's card out of the other. My hand shook as I punched in his number.

"What's up, Jersey?"

"Lucy Masanova is no longer missing," I said. "You better come over right away."

Chapter Eleven

Kyleigh and I stood guard over Lucy's body. I had no idea what the tide schedule was, but I feared if I left her unattended, she would float out to sea, never to be found. Kyleigh quietly put Louie's lead back on and kept the dogs a few feet back from our discovery.

I didn't know what to do with my emotions. I'd seen a dead body before, but that was after the mortician had worked their magic to make the deceased look at peace. But this was a drowning victim, so bloated and distorted, she didn't look real. I didn't want to break down in front of Kyleigh, who seemed strangely composed, so I kept it together.

The scrunch of heavy boots on the trail announced Nick's arrival.

Just before he got to me, a wave broke, lifting the body, causing Lucy's hand to rise above a log. In her open palm lay a gold chain with a butterfly pendant. Colorful and not symmetrical. Crude. My stomach knotted as I realized it belonged to my aunt. I'd made it for her when I was in the third grade. It was one of a kind. She wore it beneath her clothes, so others rarely saw it, but she said it was a way of keeping me close to her heart. I swallowed hard as I tried to process what it might mean and how it came to be in Lucy's possession.

Before I could make sense of it, Nick came to a stop in front of me. He took off his sunglasses and looked me square in the eyes. "You okay?"

I nodded and tried to keep my breathing even. He followed my gaze to the silk scarf that floated on the surface of another breaking wave.

Nick took a few steps closer to the water's edge and squatted down for a better look. He keyed his radio and asked the dispatcher to summon the medical examiner to the location.

Nick shook his head. "Damn shame."

Kyleigh, who had been standing back by the tree line, took a step forward and cleared her throat. "I have to go."

"I'll need a statement," Nick called out, but Kyleigh was already dragging the dogs back up the trail.

"Not like you don't know where to find her," I said. But I wondered why Kyleigh couldn't wait to get away from him. For some reason, I felt protective of her. Although it was difficult to imagine, I wondered if Nick was one of those arrogant cops she was wary of.

"So, you two just stumbled upon Lucy?" he said.

I blew out a long breath. "Yes. We were walking the dogs. I feel bad because Maya tried to lead me here last night, and I wouldn't let her."

He ran a hand through unruly hair. "I'd dismiss that as a coincidence, but it's Maya we're talking about. I swear that dog can read our thoughts."

"She's freaky that way," I agreed. I risked another look at the body. But the hand and the necklace were under water, and I could no longer see them. It was almost as if I'd imagined it. Almost.

He stood and dusted his hands off on his pants. "Well, I think your time with Maya is about to end. Lucy's nephew is in town. He flew up after I called him yesterday about the missing person's investigation I'd started. I mentioned you were itching for someone to pick up Maya. He said he'd come and get her."

Funny, but I felt a pang of regret. I was getting attached to the scamp.

Before I could sort through my feelings, an attractive woman dressed in jeans and a flannel shirt came walking down the trail. She had swept her blonde hair up into one of those messy updos that were more complicated than they seemed. At least that's what happened when I tried to match the look. I noticed a simple silver cross hanging around her neck. "Hey, Nicky," she said with a familiarity that, for some reason, stung. "What've we got?"

A look of happiness flickered across his face at the sight of her. But then he seemed to remember the somber occasion, and he became serious. He gestured toward the water's edge. "Looks like Lucy Masanova's been found."

"Oh, no," she said, hands on hips as she looked at the body. "I'd heard she was missing. I hoped it was just a misunderstanding."

"Hard to tell what happened at this point," Nick said. "She loved to walk even if she wasn't that steady on her feet. Could have fallen or had a medical issue."

"Or?" Her perfectly tweezed eyebrows shot up.

"Foul play." Nick shrugged. "Something's not right at her house. But those things rarely happen in Orca Cove."

The woman looked at me then, like she just registered my existence. She extended her well-manicured hand. "I'm Alex."

I shook her hand, trying not to react to the pain that shot up to my elbow from her firm grip. "Charlie," I said.

She smiled, but it didn't touch her eyes. "Our parents must have wanted sons."

I got that a lot. People often thought I was a guy before they saw me in person.

"Alex is the medical examiner," Nick said. "Why don't you let us do our thing? Processing the scene is going to take a while. I'll stop by for your statement on my way out."

I nodded and started up the path toward the hotel. I wanted to stay. Crime scenes fascinated me. I'd gone to the police academy for this moment. But I had no reason to stay other than morbid curiosity, and I wasn't about to admit to that. And in my short time in the law enforcement inner circle, I'd learned that cops hated wannabe cops.

Even though I understood, I felt like a little kid not invited to play with the big kids.

And I wanted another look at that pendant. I guess I could have mentioned it to them, but that would involve Aunt Jo-Jo, and I wasn't about to offer her up to them on a silver platter.

Chapter Twelve

Deep in thought, I walked back to the hotel. I hadn't known Lucy well, but finding a dead body still made my stomach roll. I couldn't imagine what people who knew her better might feel. She didn't seem popular, but a life lost was almost always hard to handle. I felt even worse, considering how difficult I'd heard she was, and wondering if anyone would miss her.

Lucy had probably been there, dead, the whole time. Maya tried to tell me, and I pulled her the other way. Boy was I a schmuck.

When I emerged from the woods, I stepped back onto the road as a red convertible sailed up the hill and pulled up in front of the hotel. The blond guy from the gas station got out of the car. He ran his hands through windblown hair, patting it back into place before he noticed me approaching the property.

His smile was welcoming. "Good day," he said in a liquid drawl that reminded me of sticky sultry nights, key lime pie, and fireflies. "I'm here about a dog."

"Maya?" I came to stand before him, figuring he must be Lucy's nephew. He couldn't yet know his aunt's body was just found. Nick would deliver that piece of information in person, I was sure. I would not break the bad news.

"That's the one." He extended his hand. "I'm Austin."

"Charlie," I said.

"Nice to meet you, Charlie." He pronounced my name without the R.

I wasn't sure if the tingly feeling that rushed through my body came from my RA or if Austin's southern ways were affecting me. "Maya's in her room. Come with me and I'll get her for you."

He walked beside me. "Are you the one who was worried about my aunt and called the police? The officer who notified me she was missing said it was someone from the pet hotel who reported it."

"That would be me, yeah." I didn't have the heart to tell him that the story was about to get a lot worse.

"Well, thanks," he said. "Hopefully, she just went off somewhere. She's a bit of a loon."

Boy, he was making this hard. I felt guilty knowing more than he did. We stepped through the door to the hotel, bumping shoulders. Maya immediately started howling, setting off a chain reaction. The noise was deafening and made further conversation impossible. I grabbed a leash off the hook on the wall and opened the door to Maya's room. She stopped yapping and danced in a circle, making it hard to snap the lead in place. "Calm down, Missy. Someone's here to see you."

But she only got more excited at the sound of my voice. After several unsuccessful tries, I managed to attach the leash and bring her into the lobby where Austin waited. "Here you go." I handed him control.

Maya's ears pinned back against her head, and the hair at the nape of her neck rose like parties before a judge. A low growl through snarling teeth caused Austin to take a step back. He held his hands up. "Easy, girl." He looked at me, wide-eyed. "Is she vicious?"

I bit my lip so I wouldn't laugh. "She's a bit of a miscreant, but I don't think she'd hurt anyone. Then again, I don't know her well."

Austin seemed to second-guess his offer to care for the neighborhood nightmare. I almost volunteered to keep her, but before I could make my decision, he started dragging Maya to the door. "Sorry if she's been any trouble," he said over his shoulder. "Figure out what I owe you for the extra days of care, and I'll write you a check."

I waved as he passed through the door. Maya dug in, but he was three times her size, and he pulled her to the car. After wrapping her leash around the center console so she couldn't escape, he got into the driver's seat. I had a bad feeling and had to stop myself from intervening. Apparently, Austin was Lucy's next of kin and I had no right to butt in, but as I watched him drive away with Maya looking longingly back at me, her expression so sad, I wanted to cry.

Chapter Thirteen

Once Austin drove off with Maya, I went back to the house to check on Noah. He greeted me at the door, dancing on his hind legs and insisting on a kiss as he always did, before letting me pass into the room.

"Back to just us," I said. "Hope Maya's wild ways didn't rub off on you too much. Lord knows we don't need that kind of nuts. I just hope crazy pants is okay." Noah trotted after me to the kitchen, where I offered him a piece of jerky, which he gratefully accepted. All was good in his world.

He followed me out the door and to the pet hotel, where I hoped to find Martha so I could share the bad news about Lucy. But Kyleigh stood alone in the lobby, looking lost. As I got closer, I noticed her eyes brimmed with tears.

"Hey," I said as gently as I could.

She jumped and turned to look at me, then wiped her eyes with the back of her sleeve.

"How well did you know Lucy?" I asked.

She shrugged. "My aunt said to stay away from her. Said she was unstable."

"Still," I prodded. "It's not every day you find a dead body. I'm a bit freaked, I gotta admit."

She looked at me through a veil of hair. "But you were a cop."

"I was almost a cop. And cops don't see dead bodies all that often." At least I hoped not. And I would guess in a tranquil place like Orca Cove, it would be even less likely.

Kyleigh shrugged again.

"Well, if you want to talk, I'm here." We now shared something that would bind us together for life. I'd never recall this day without thinking of her tortured soul. I wanted to comfort her, but I didn't know how.

The front door opened, and a Golden Retriever bounded into the room with Martha behind him. The dog ran straight to Kyleigh. They'd obviously met before. For a moment, a beautiful smile replaced the girl's miserable expression. Kyleigh rubbed the dog down as his tail thumped against the wall. When they were done with their mutual admiration fest, the dog trotted over and said hello to me as well. "Who do we have here?" I asked, massaging his jowls.

"Meet Bruce," Martha said. "He's my sidekick. We just came from visiting Jo-Jo. She's itching to come home. I tried to tell her to relax and enjoy people fussing over her because that won't happen here."

I bet Martha would take good care of my aunt, even if she did so with complaint. Like Maya, her bark was worse than her bite.

I hated to ruin a good time, but I couldn't keep the news of Lucy's death from Martha a moment longer. "I'm afraid we have some bad news," I said.

Kyleigh wanted no part of it. "I'm gonna water the plants." She hurried out the door.

Once we were alone, I filled Martha in on what we'd found on the beach.

The color drained from Martha's face. She backed slowly to the chair Noah slept in, waved him away, and then sat down heavily. Noah ran to me, acutely aware that something was wrong.

Bruce picked up on it, too, and settled himself between Martha's legs. "I was afraid something bad had happened. It wasn't like her not to come for Maya. Guess we get to keep the little devil."

"Actually, her nephew Austin picked her up."

"Nephew?" Martha took off her glasses and wiped her eyes with her thumb. "I'm surprised he'd come. Lucy was close to him when he was a kid, but I got the feeling he stopped keeping in touch. Last time we spoke, she went on and on about how alone she was and that if he couldn't even send a birthday card, she should take him out of her will and leave her money to the library."

"Well, he got here pretty quickly once Nick told him his aunt was missing," I said.

Martha raised an eyebrow. "Is that so?"

I turned to the window, watching Kyleigh as she sprayed water from the hose on some over-ripe tomato plants. "Tell me about Kyleigh. She's intense."

"She's pretty moody," Martha agreed. "She's had a hard life, with her mom leaving and all."

"When did that happen?"

Martha scrunched up her face as if she were trying to recall. "Years ago. She lives with her aunt and uncle now. I'd be moody too if I had to live with those deadbeats."

I had questions, but the conversation halted when Kyleigh came back into the room. "I'm going home," she announced.

"Need a ride?" I asked. "I'm going to see Aunt Jo-Jo and tell her what happened before the gossip chain reaches her."

"No, I'm good," the girl said.

"Oh, for heaven's sake," Martha said. "Take the ride. You don't live that close."

Kyleigh looked like she wanted to be anywhere but cooped up in a car with me. But few people had the guts to say no to Martha.

We drove in silence, Noah on Kyleigh's lap. She absently stroked his head, her gaze out the window. My thoughts drifted to the things I had to do. I needed someone to follow me to the mainland so I could return the car. The town was walkable, and I didn't have the funds to keep paying for a rental. Especially after the vet bill I just paid.

"Turn here." Kyleigh pointed to a narrow road, framed by tall pine trees. Without her to guide me, I wouldn't have even noticed it was there.

I maneuvered the car down the rutted single lane road for about half-a-mile before we came to a clearing where a beat-up rusty trailer sat sliding off its foundation. Someone wedged thick pieces of wood against the leaning structure to keep it from falling onto its side. But a strong wind would probably cause it to give up the fight. It looked uninhabitable, and I felt negligent leaving her in such a place.

Kyleigh made no move to get out of the car. She hugged Noah to her chest and sighed. "Was Ms. Masanova murdered?"

I wondered why her mind would go there. She didn't have the additional information I had about finding her house unlocked and her things left behind. Even with what I knew, I didn't conclude that Lucy had been killed. She could have gone for a walk before her trip and had a medical emergency. Martha said Lucy walked a lot. Murder seemed like a leap, even to me. "I don't know," I said. "It could be as simple as an accidental drowning. But only the medical examiner can tell us that."

"Alex." She sighed. "She always looks at me weird. Gives me the creeps."

Kids were like dogs in that way. I trusted their instincts. I filed that little piece of information in the back of my mind. Something about her didn't sit right with me either, but if I was being honest, it was probably because of her close connection to Nick.

"It would be freaky to have a killer on the island," she said.

"We don't know that we do," I reminded her.

Her hand went to the door handle. Before I could ask another question, she gave Noah a squeeze, and she was out of the car and heading into the trailer. I noted crushed beer cans and trash littering the property. Poor girl. This was no way to live. I had a feeling there was a lot more to Kyleigh's life than a crooked trailer that would explain her morose affect. I was glad Aunt Jo-Jo had taken the girl under her wing. I knew I shouldn't get too involved as the last thing the kid needed was to have someone barge into her life and then pull out, which I would do when I returned home. I made a U-turn and started to leave the property and head back to the main road when a half-primed red pickup truck rocked up the driveway. A bad feeling enveloped me. The truck came to a stop, parking nose-to-nose with my vehicle.

A wiry man wearing a grungy gray shirt, jeans, and cowboy boots got out and stomped toward me. "What are you doing on my property?" he barked through my rolled-down window, adjusting a cap that sported a marijuana leaf.

"Hi." I tried to muster up some charm, but I could tell by the look on his face that I was coming up short. "I'm Charlie."

"Okay," he said. "What are you doing on my property, Charlie?"

Somebody was in a mood. I pointed over my shoulder at the trailer. "Just dropped Kyleigh off."

"You shouldn't be here." He spat on the ground.

"Kyleigh's had a rough afternoon," I said.

"That ain't your business."

Something told me I would not reach this guy. My "oh-crap" meter was in the red zone. "Okay, I'm leaving."

The man, a few inches shorter than me, crossed his arms and stared me down. "See that you don't come back. This is a private drive. Go."

Message received.

I put my car in drive. He stood his ground, and I had to back up and drive around him to make my exit. I didn't relax until I'd made it to the main road.

Chapter Fourteen

Noah was as popular at the rehab this time around.

"What a pretty girl," a nurse said as we passed by.

I swallowed a comeback. I didn't want to be that difficult woman who overreacted to what people said about her dog. Okay, I was that person, but the world didn't need to know.

I was still shaky after my run-in with the man at Kyleigh's trailer.

Aunt Jo-Jo sat in her wheelchair in front of the TV, yelling at a politician who answered questions from reporters. When she saw me, she clicked the off button, and the screen went dark. "I can't take the boldfaced lies these people tell," she said. "They said my blood pressure is up, and they wonder why."

"Maybe you shouldn't watch the news," I suggested.

She ignored me and called to Noah. "Come here, Handsome."

Noah obliged and stood on his hind legs to give her a kiss and accept some serious petting before he curled up at her feet.

I sat in the chair across from her. "How you feeling?"

"I'm doing well. Doctor said I'll be home in a week."

"Awesome," I said. "That's great. But I have some bad news."

I filled her in on finding Lucy, then waited while she took a minute to process the information. Her eyes became moist, and she dabbed them with a tissue. "That breaks my heart. I wouldn't call Lucy a friend, but she was part of Orca Cove for a long time. The crazy old lady who lived on the hill. She added a dash of color to the town."

"I've surmised as much."

"Maya's going to take it hard. Dogs experience grief like we do, only we can't explain what happened to them. I wonder what goes through their little heads. She'll be confused."

I told her about Austin taking Maya. "I'm not sure he knows about Lucy yet. I didn't think it was my place to tell him, but I imagine Nick has by now."

She gave an impish smile. "Nick? You're on a first-name basis now?"

I busied myself picking imaginary lint off my pants. "Well, he seems to be around a lot because of the investigation."

"Maybe he fancies you," she said with a wink.

I rolled my eyes. She sounded like Martha. "He doesn't. He's just doing his job. And I was wondering if your cell phone would help him. Give him a clue as to if Lucy called you about leaving Maya longer. Might help him with a timeline as to what happened."

"I haven't seen my phone since the accident. I assume it's in my car."

"And where is your car?"

"Guessing it's at the impound lot. If you go, can you get my other stuff? I'd gone shopping just before the accident and had some bags in the back. Oh, and there's a green metal box. About the size of a shoe box, but flatter. I'd appreciate it if you get that, too. It belonged to Lucy. She asked me to hold on to it for her."

"Do you know what's in it?"

"Not a clue. But I should probably find out, given what's happened. Please get it and bring it to me."

"Sure thing." I slapped my thigh to get Noah's attention. He looked up at me and wagged his tail. "You ready to go, Boo?"

He shook himself and stretched. I bent down to attach the leash to his collar. "By the way," I said. "Do you know where your pendant is? You know, the one I made for you?"

Aunt Jo-Jo jerked her good hand to her neck, feeling for the necklace I'd never seen her take off. "Oh, dear," she said. "They must have taken it off me when I got to the hospital. I'll ask the nurse to track it down."

I wished that was the case. But I knew where it was. It was at the coroner's office with Lucy Masanova's body, and it was only a matter of time before the police traced it back to my aunt. Did she really not know Lucy had it? Was how she lost track of it forgotten like the accident, or was she keeping something from me? I couldn't see that being the case.

And I didn't want to give her anything to fret about just yet, so I kept my worries to myself. I kissed her cheek and took Noah from the room.

We'd made it to the car when my cell phone chirped. I illuminated the screen and read the incoming text message. Nick. *I need to get your statement. I'll be by the hotel in about an hour.*

That would give me just enough time to get my aunt's things from the impound lot.

Chapter Fifteen

The car impound lot was on the outskirts of town. The sun had started to set, and a strong breeze whirled falling leaves. A whoosh of crisp autumn air blew my hair back.

I walked up to the office as a woman placed a *closed* sign in the window. "I'm sorry," I said. "I know you're heading out, but can I get some things out of my aunt's car? I'll be quick about it. It's kind of an emergency."

The woman tapped long, thin fingers on crossed arms. "Who's your aunt?"

"Jo-Jo McMullen."

"I figured as much," she said. "We only get a few totaled cars a year, as the island is so small. Hers is the only one we have right now. How's she doing?"

"Well," I said. "Thanks for asking. Hoping she'll be home in a week."

"I keep thinking about her. I saw her the day before, and she seemed so out of sorts."

"Really? About what?"

"It was Lucy." The woman lowered her voice as if there was anyone around to hear. "I don't like to gossip, but that Lucy, she's a strange one. Whatever she said, your aunt didn't take it well. Jo-Jo was red in the face."

"Did you hear anything?"

"Just Lucy saying she wished she'd never trusted Jo-Jo, and that she wanted her box back, whatever that meant. Then she stormed off in a huff."

I wondered why my aunt hadn't mentioned this. She'd made it sound like they were just acquaintances. You rarely trusted acquaintances with something valuable. "Where did this happen?" I asked.

"At the coffee shop," she said.

So, chances were, more people witnessed this exchange. It wouldn't take long for the police to find that out. I was no investigator, but if Lucy was murdered, my aunt was looking like a person of interest. Lucy had my aunt's necklace, and they'd argued before her death. I felt sick to my stomach. But, in my heart of hearts, I knew my aunt had nothing to do with Lucy's death. I felt guilty for even letting my mind go there.

"The car's out back," the woman said. She held the door open for me to step inside. "I've got to be someplace, so I'd appreciate it if you could be quick."

"I will be."

I followed her to the back of the building, where she let me out the rear door and pointed to a crushed Honda Civic across the lot. The thought of my aunt surviving the crash with such severe damage made my heart catch in my throat. The impact folded the front of the car like an accordion, crushing the silver metal and shortening the car by several inches. I hurried over to it, trying not to think of my aunt sitting in the carnage, helpless while waiting to be rescued.

Since the woman had been nice enough to let me in after closing, I decided I'd look for the cell phone and the box and come back for the other things another day.

The driver's side of the car was so badly damaged, it was impossible to open the door. The airbag had deployed, making it difficult to see inside from my vantage point. I went to the passenger door and wrenched it ajar. It let out a tremendous groan. The contents of Aunt Jo-Jo's purse were on the seat and all over the floor. I tossed each item aside as I searched the car, finding her planner, which I placed on the dashboard, but no phone. Dropping to my knees, I blindly felt under the front passenger seat, coming up with a package of travel-sized tissues and some lipstick.

It was a stretch to get my hand under the driver's seat, but I could feel a flat object. Pulling it toward me with my fingertips caused pain to shoot up my arm, but inch by inch, it came closer. I realized I wasn't breathing and forced a deep breath when it was within reach.

I sat back on my heels and looked down at the phone. I saw the shattered screen, but I was sure we could work around that. I got to my feet and shoved the phone into the back pocket of my jeans.

Walking back to the rear of the car, I saw that the bumper was dented. It had to have been a two-car collision. If she'd been rear-ended, at least the accident wasn't her fault. Unless the damage was old.

The car was undoubtedly totaled. It was an old car, and I doubted the insurance company would pay much for it.

I didn't have the keys to open the trunk, and I couldn't get to the release by the driver's door. I bet her recent purchases and the green box were in there.

The woman waited by the back door at the office, anxiously checking her watch. "Did you find what you were looking for?" she called.

I'd need more time to get access to the trunk. I didn't feel good about leaving without the green box, but I didn't have a choice.

Walking back to the building, I said. "I'll come back for the rest."

She let me in the building and followed me down the hall. "Please tell your aunt that Clara sends her best."

"I will. And I'll be back tomorrow."

I made a mental note to find a set of keys so I'd be able to get into the trunk. If that green box belonged to Lucy and she wanted it back, it just might hold a clue to her death.

Chapter Sixteen

Back at the house, I plugged my aunt's phone into the charger. It was totally dead. I figured it would take a while to reboot. Since I didn't have her password, I wouldn't be able to look at her messages, anyway. I took a bottle of Fat Tire out of the refrigerator, popped the cap, and took a satisfying swig just before there was a knock on the door. Taking the beer with me, I found Nick standing on the lawn staring at the water, his back to me.

I went outside and stood beside him. "How'd it go?"

He sighed, then gave me a sideways glance. He rubbed his hand across the stubble on his face, clearly tired. His gaze settled on the beer I held. Checking his watch, he said, "I'm off duty in exactly three minutes. Think I could have one of those?"

I smiled. "Of course, I'll be right back."

I found Noah in the house, staring forlornly at the cabinet where his food was kept. I filled his bowl with kibble—he was also used to receiving his evening meal in exactly three minutes. No idea how he knew how to tell time. While he inhaled his food, I grabbed another beer and went back outside. Nick had taken a seat on the front porch step. I lowered the bottle, so it rested against his shoulder. He reached up and took it. I settled on the stoop next to him and for a few minutes, we sat in silence, staring at the darkening sky. He clanked his bottle against mine and said, "To Lucy, may she rest in peace," before taking a drink and letting out a long breath.

I took a sip as well. The bitter brew was cold as it assaulted the back of my throat, but it went down smoothly. "Any idea what happened?"

"Alex will do an autopsy, but I gotta say, I'm worried."

"So, it looks like foul play?"

He looked over at me, and I could tell he was weighing his words. "I really shouldn't say."

"I understand." But I figured that if it wasn't something sinister, he would have said so.

"I grew up here," he said. "I left for college at Portland State when I was eighteen. After a few years of working for Portland PD, I came back home. I've been Orca Cove's eighth cop for five years now. I can't remember a homicide in this town in my lifetime."

"I'm sorry," I said. "Do you get support from a bigger agency?"

"Don't think there's a rule book. But I can probably reach out to my buddies in Portland if I have any questions. Working there, I saw too many heartbreaking things. Made me wonder if I was cut out for the job. But when a position came open here, I thought it would be the perfect fit. We get some family squabbles, have a few local drunks, tourists who get out of hand, that kind of stuff. Oh, and let's not forget about Maya. But so far, nothing that keeps me up at night."

I laughed. "Don't think I'll ever forget about Maya. Lucy's nephew, Austin, came to collect her, by the way."

He nodded. "That's good."

"Did you give Austin the news about his aunt? I figured it was your job, so I didn't say anything when I saw him."

Nick took another tug of beer. "I went by the hotel, but he'd checked out. Stopped by Lucy's house and he wasn't there either, but he seems to stay there. Tried to call, but his phone is off. Went straight to voicemail."

I rolled my beer bottle between my palms. "I'm sure he'll turn up."

"I was going to take your statement, but I'm beat. Can you swing by the station tomorrow?"

"Sure."

He rubbed at the stubble on his chin. "I have to get Kyleigh's statement, too."

"That should be fun. I gave Kyleigh a ride home. A man kicked me off the property."

Nick shook his head. "So, you met Ray Boyce?"

I laughed. "He's charming."

Nick cracked a smile. "Charming like a pissed off rattlesnake."

"Yeah, that about sums it up."

"Be careful going over there," he said. "Not only is Ray a jerk, but he has a mean streak."

"I feel bad for Kyleigh."

"I hear you," Nick said. He finished his beer and yawned. "I'm gonna head home and take a shower. I must reek of death."

"You don't."

"Oh, so you're smelling me now?"

I laughed. "Don't flatter yourself. Reek seems like something one couldn't miss."

He gave a slow grin. "Well, Jersey, thanks for the beer and the conversation." He stood and placed the empty bottle on the porch. "I'll see you later."

"Okay," I said. I thought about offering an ear if he needed to talk later. A lot of people believed stuff like seeing a dead body rolled off cops' backs, but I knew they suffered trauma like the rest of us. And Nick told me he didn't fancy the ugly part of the job. I bet most cops didn't. None of my classmates in the academy had superhuman qualities, and I sure didn't. Vicarious trauma was real and only recently recognized in the law enforcement field. But I stopped myself from saying anything. Nick probably had a support system, a girlfriend or wife, for all I knew. Maybe Alex. That thought bothered me more than it should have.

I watched him get into his car and drive away, and then absently petted Noah while I finished my beer in the quiet. Once done, I walked all the dogs, three at a time before locking the hotel up for the night.

After eating a quick salad and a sandwich, I shut the windows. The temperature had dropped, and the wind had picked up again. With the doors locked, I felt pretty safe. I got into bed with my aunt's day planner and opened it to this month.

And there it was. The day before her accident, my aunt had lunch plans with Lucy, as she had the week before. Maybe it didn't mean anything. Just like their argument that was witnessed by Clara and God knew who else. I was sure my aunt could offer an explanation. But the pendant was another story. Try as I might, I couldn't come up with a good reason for Lucy to have it in her clutches as she died.

It was hard to fall asleep with the questions that knocked around in my head. One thing I knew for sure—my aunt was not a killer. But with what I knew so far, the police might see things differently. I had to find them a credible suspect before the investigation focused on her.

Chapter Seventeen

A thunderous boom yanked me from a deep sleep. I bolted upright, sitting up straight, my heart palpitating. I held my breath and waited, listening. It was dark outside, and I could only see a foot or so in front of my face. My hand automatically reached for Noah, who was alert beside me. For a moment, I couldn't distinguish between a dream and reality. Just when I'd convinced myself the noise was a figment of my imagination, it sounded again. Something slammed against the sunroom door.

Noah let out an unimpressive woof. "Shush," I said. I didn't breathe as I silently got out of bed and tiptoed to the door, blindly feeling for the baseball bat I'd left out before I'd gone to bed. I turned back to Noah, who'd followed me. "You stay," I said, dropping my voice to a whisper.

I was unsure of my next move. Should I confront the source of the noise or grab my phone and dial 911 while Noah and I hid in the closet?

Before I could decide, it happened again. The door shook, as if someone was ramming it with their shoulder. I flipped the porch light on, hoping it would scare whoever or whatever it was away. I heard a scraping noise against the wooden floorboards of the porch and then a howl.

Noah and I exchanged a puzzled look. I moved to the window and peered outside. A face appeared on the other side of the screen. I jumped back and instinctively swung the bat, punching a hole in the mesh and cracking the glass. Unflinching brown eyes stared back at me. They were at the level of my thighs. Was my tormentor on their knees? My brain attempted to make sense of the events unfolding, but my hyper-alert state gave me tunnel vision. I was in fight-or-flight mode. I tried to grapple with the fact that whoever was out there was about three feet tall. At this hour, that didn't make a lick of sense. I chanced a second look and saw a dog pacing on the porch. Maya.

I went limp with relief and leaned against the wall for a moment while my heart restarted. "Jeez," I said, glancing back at Noah, who stood on the bed beside me.

He looked at the door, willing me to open it.

Bat still in hand, I gingerly unlocked the door and eased it ajar, stumbling back when Maya burst into the room. She had a major case of the zoomies— darting across the floor, bounding from the daybed to the chair, dragging a clanking chain behind her. She finally stopped to sniff Noah, then jumped back on the bed and barked at me in greeting.

I let out a second breath. "Where the heck did you come from?"

A gust of wind reminded me that the door was wide open. I walked back to it and looked out into the darkness. All was quiet except for the sudden hoot of an owl. I pulled the door shut and clicked the lock into place.

Turning my attention back to Maya, I shook my head. Her tongue lolled out of the side of her mouth. She looked quite proud of herself. "Good God, girl, what brought you here in the middle of the night?"

I leaned the bat against the wall by the door and crossed over to Maya, whose tail thumped in gleeful anticipation. I rubbed her head and then inspected the heavy chain that was fastened to her collar. It was hooked to a piece of wood that was splintered. I undid the cable and looped the restraint in circles, then laid it on the end table.

Maya nudged my arm with her head, which I took as a thank you, and gave her a few pats. "Did you break free?" Anger bubbled inside of me, thinking of her chained to something, left outside in the cold. Dogs were family and belonged in the house, where it was warm. I realized not everyone thought that way, but then I wondered if they should have a dog in the first place.

Where had Austin left her? Had he tied her up and left town? Or was he still here and just didn't want Maya inside with him? Either way, Maya didn't deserve to be treated like this.

Still spooked, I rechecked the door, confirming the lock was in place. After making sure both dogs had water and giving Maya a midnight snack, I took the baseball bat back to bed with me. Clicking on the bedside lamp, I got under a blanket and opened my book. But I couldn't concentrate. Noah and Maya snuggled beside me. Noah fell asleep quickly, but Maya stayed alert, snapping her head up at each sound. Every time she looked around, I did the same, fear bubbling in my chest. The knowledge that Maya would defend us wasn't enough. She hadn't been able to protect Lucy, after all, and I couldn't help but think that there might be a killer at large.

Orca Cove no longer felt like the safe place I'd thought it to be.

Chapter Eighteen

Somehow, I fell asleep. Still tired, I woke to the sound of a car door slamming. Turning my head toward the window, I could see Martha walk to the hotel from her Cherokee. Maya leapt off the bed and stood on her hind legs, resting her paws on the windowsill, watching Martha disappear inside the hotel. Noah stretched and yawned.

Relieved that it was just Martha arriving at work, I relaxed and looked back at the ceiling. It had been a busy few days, and I hadn't given my ever-changing life situation much thought. But a dream I'd been having before sleep was ripped away from me, dangled in my mind, and I tried to recall what my imagination had conjured up in the few hours I'd slept.

I'd been at the police academy at the range. The firearms instructor stood behind me, yelling for me to reload my gun faster. But I couldn't get my fingers to release the clip I'd emptied into the target. Everyone else had finished the drill and holstered their weapons. All eyes were on me while I fumbled with my gun. Tears splashed down my cheeks as I realized something was wrong with my hands.

Only it hadn't been a dream. The instructor made me holster my weapon, and I left the range in shame, with my classmates whispering behind my back.

The next day, I'd called in sick and had gone to the doctor. When she saw my swollen hand, she referred me to a rheumatologist who ordered a bunch of tests.

My class sergeant had been kind. He took me into his office and promised to work with me while I waited for the test results, but kindly warned that if

71

I couldn't take part fully soon, I wouldn't be able to remain at the academy. I remembered him saying, "Law enforcement is your calling. You react quickly and appropriately under stress. I've been impressed by your performance so far, and I hope you can fix whatever is wrong."

For the next week, I continued attending academic classes, but they excused me from firearms training and defensive tactics, including handcuffing and anything involving fine motor skills.

As the days went by, the swelling in my right hand got worse, and then started in the left. I researched RA online and had pretty much diagnosed myself before the doctor did. I cried when I shared my fate with my sergeant. I no longer met the requirements to be a police officer, and the department had no choice but to let me go. With a heavy heart, I emptied my locker and turned in my equipment. I would never become a cop.

That was a month ago now, and here I was, 3,000 miles away with no idea what I would do with my life.

I didn't want to return to the boring corporate job I'd had before I'd gone through the grueling process of getting accepted into the police academy: the written test, the interviews, the psychological and physical exams, and the lie detector test. Hundreds applied, but only a few were selected. When I got the job, I was proud for the first time I could remember.

And it was all over in the blink of an eye.

I had no desire to return to sitting behind a desk all day. There had to be another option. Before I could figure that out, I'd gotten the call from Martha.

This morning, I held out my hands and studied them, despising them for betraying me. My knuckles were twice the size they used to be, and the constant stiffness and pain I felt was hard to ignore. There was no cure for RA. I only hoped that the meds would stop my joints from further damage. My research showed that most people with one autoimmune disease often developed others. I had no idea what my future held, and I was only thirty years old. It all seemed unfair.

Maya scratched at the door, and I knew my pity party would have to be placed on hold. I got out of bed and pulled on my jeans. I used Noah's leash on Maya, as I trusted him not to run off. I walked both dogs over to the dog park, my mind still on my way-too-realistic dream.

Nobody else was at the park, so I let Maya off leash and watched her run around in the fenced-in area, marking her territory as she went. Noah didn't wander more than five feet from me. Not well-trained, just insecure, but I liked not having to worry about him.

I sat on top of a picnic table and Noah jumped onto the bench and sat next to me, leaning against my leg. The wind had died down, and the sky held the promise of a nice day. We watched Maya expend her energy—as if that could happen. When I saw a woman walking briskly toward the park with a German Shepard, my radar kicked in. I called to Maya, "Come here, girl."

She ignored me. I got off the table and took quick strides to reach her before the Shepard entered the park. Leash at the ready, we played the game where she was almost within reach, and then she darted away before I could take control of her. "So, this is how it's gonna be?"

The regal German Shepard was focused on us as he passed through the first of two gates, and I knew I didn't have long to get the upper hand. I tried to sound as stern as I could. Command presence, my class sergeant had called it. But Maya remained unimpressed.

I turned to the lady with the other dog, about to plead my case for her to give me a moment before she entered the park, but she'd already opened the second gate.

What happened next seemed to unfold in slow motion. The Shepard charged, ears pinned back, eyes fixed on us. "No!" I called, bracing for a fight between Maya and this proud canine. But he didn't go for Maya. He whizzed past us and grabbed Noah by the neck.

Noah let out a yelp, and so did I.

Mama Bear came out, and I lunged for the dog. But before I could take hold, Maya charged past me and smacked into the Shepard like a bowling ball, sending him stumbling. He dropped Noah as Maya pinned him to the ground. Respect was instant as the Shepard looked up at the snarling Maya, standing bravely over him, daring him to make a move.

I bent down and scooped Noah into my arms. I saw that Noah was shaken, but he wasn't bleeding. He dug his paws into my shoulders and hugged me like a frightened child. He didn't look any worse for wear.

The woman didn't even pick up her pace.

I turned to Maya, who continued to stand guard over the newly submissive dog. Our eyes met, and I hoped mine expressed my gratitude to her.

The woman lumbered over, a look of annoyance on her face.

Really? Her dog had attacked my dog, and she was miffed?

"Can you control your rotten dog?" she snipped.

My mouth dropped open. Anger rushed through me. "My dog? Your dog attacked mine. Maya was only protecting Noah. If your dog is vicious, he should be on a leash."

Her laugh was curt. "Maybe you should get a real dog instead of that pretty stuffed animal you're holding."

I swallowed a nasty comeback and fought the urge to settle this the Jersey way and knock her silly. I thought about ordering her off my aunt's property, but I knew she took pride in having a space for the locals to bring their pets.

Still carrying Noah, I snapped the lead on Maya and pulled her behind me as we left the park.

Inside the house, I let Maya go free and dropped to the floor. Sitting cross-legged, I conducted a closer inspection of Noah, who appeared to have forgotten the incident. He licked my chin. He seemed fine, but the encounter still shook me. Maya watched us from across the room. I called to her with a click of my tongue. She trotted over. "Now you listen," I said, reaching up and rubbing her back. "Thank you."

She lowered her head and pushed it against mine. You save me, I save what's dear to you. Like it or not, we were in this together.

I found Martha in the hotel and told her about our ordeal that morning. "That Shepard belongs to Mary Boyce. We've told her countless times to control her dog. She shouldn't bring him to the park if he can't behave."

"Seems like she ignored you. If it weren't for Maya, I'm not sure how bad things would have gotten." And then it dawned on me. "Boyce? Any relation to Ray and Kyleigh?"

Martha stuck her finger in her mouth and pretended to gag. "Ray's wife. They're both just awful people." She set her glasses on the desk. "I thought Lucy's nephew took Maya."

"Seems she prefers it here with us." Since I wasn't staying long, I hoped Martha or Aunt Jo-Jo would feel the same loyalty toward the nefarious pooch. But in the end, it wouldn't be my call. My New Jersey apartment allowed only one pet.

Martha shrugged. "Well, we can watch her a little while longer, I guess. At least until we find out what Lucy's nephew has planned for her."

"I don't trust him," I said. "Anyone who would tie up a dog in the cold—"

Martha held up her hand. "Say no more. We'll figure something out."

"Do you need help walking the dogs?" I asked.

"Kyleigh should be here any minute. It's her job this morning."

"That works. I want to bring my aunt her phone."

"Tell her to hurry up and get better. Enough lounging around. There's work to be done."

I laughed. "You're too much. I'll be back to take the pups for a stroll this afternoon."

"Sounds good," Martha said.

The town coffee shop buzzed with locals and tourists who spilled out of the boutique hotel next door. Most of the village was dog-friendly, and they had an outside patio where pets were welcome. Noah and I got in line behind a few customers.

I recognized Alex, the M.E., two people ahead of me. She didn't see me, though. She was deep in conversation with a middle-aged woman.

"How can you be so ungrateful?" the older woman said. "After all the sacrifices I made so you could have a bright future."

Alex whipped her head around and checked out the crowd, but if she recognized me, she didn't let on. "Shush," she said in a barely audible whisper. "Why do you always have to rub that in?"

"Because you seem to forget where you came from. You with your fancy fingernails and highlighted hair. When I was raising you, I could barely afford to feed us. And here you are, a successful coroner, and you can't even help your mother out when she needs it."

Alex gritted her teeth. "I'm a medical examiner, not a coroner. I'm a physician."

"For dead people," her mother snorted. "And may I remind you that you couldn't have gotten that fancy degree if you had a child to raise like I did."

"I'm well aware of that, Mother," Alex hissed. "This is not the place for this discussion. I'm leaving." Alex turned and headed for the door, colliding her shoulder against mine. She made eye contact with me and visibly recoiled. "Sorry," she said and continued on her way.

"We didn't order our coffee yet," her mother called after her.

But Alex was already gone.

Maybe Alex wasn't so perfect after all. I knew something about mother's guilt. Maybe we had something in common. I couldn't help but feel sorry for her.

When it was my turn, I placed an order for two marionberry muffins and two large coffees. Fresh-baked dog biscuits were in a jar on the counter. I ordered one for Noah and one for Maya. A bit of a thank you gift.

Standing off to the side, I waited for my order to be ready. I spotted Austin sitting in the corner, having an animated conversation on his phone despite the **No Cell Phone Zone** sign behind him. So, he hadn't left town. I figured he must have heard the news about his aunt by now.

He gave a belly laugh. Huh? If he'd been told, he was sure taking it well. He disconnected the call and casually dropped his phone onto the table. I debated whether I should tell him I had Maya at the pet hotel, but decided I'd want to know if something happened to Noah. When I heard my name called, I picked up my order and walked over to Austin's table.

He stood when he saw me, and a smile lit up his face. "Hey, Charlie, how goes it?"

His accent lost its charm the minute he'd left Maya chained up. He didn't act like someone who'd received devastating news either. Not about his aunt or her missing dog.

I couldn't help myself. "Lose something?"

He scratched his head. "Excuse me?"

"Maya. She came back to the hotel last night."

He gave an *aw-shucks* chuckle. "That little devil. I was about to put signs all over town."

I didn't buy it. I would have been frantically searching for Noah if he were missing, not sitting in a coffee shop yakking it up on my phone. And if he'd yet to learn about his aunt's body being found, he should have been looking for her as well.

"I'll come by for her this afternoon, if that's okay," he said.

"Maybe you should leave her with us," I said. "She's not an outside dog."

He stuck his hands in his pockets and rocked back on his heels. "You're mad that I tied her up?"

I gave a heavy sigh. "I wouldn't use the word mad. It's just not what I would do." Maya had tried to warn me she didn't want to go with him in the first place. I'd be sure to listen next time—animals have better judgment of people than most humans. "We can't keep her forever, but we have plenty of room until we figure something else out." I knew the hotel had limited space, but I didn't mind keeping her with me while in town.

"Well," he said with a smirk. "As long as you're not mad."

I stopped myself from rolling my eyes, but it wasn't easy.

He motioned to the empty chair at the table. "Care to join me?"

"Sorry, but I'm on my way to visit someone. Don't want her coffee to get cold."

"Another time then?"

I forced a smile. "Maybe."

But I could think of a million things I'd rather do.

I stepped back outside in time to see Nick pull up on a bike. He wore sweats and a black T-shirt, the sleeves tight against muscular biceps. His waist looked narrow without his gun belt on. I caught myself staring and quickly forced myself to look into his smiling eyes. "Jersey," he said, leaning his bike against a tree.

"Hi, Nick."

Noah, unlike me, had no shame in showing how happy he was to see him. His butt wiggled furiously as he pulled me toward him.

Nick leaned down and gave Noah some attention. A man who was kind to animals melted my heart. *Down girl. He likes dogs, not you.*

"Noah doesn't look any worse for wear since the chocolate incident," he said, ruffling Noah's ears. "How's your foot?"

"Much better," I said. "Have you given Austin the news about his aunt yet?"

Nick stopped petting Noah and stood up. "Haven't been able to make contact."

I tilted my head toward the restaurant. "Well, he's inside. I just talked to him."

"About Lucy?"

"No. That's your job."

Nick awkwardly arranged his hands by his waist, seemingly missing letting them rest on his gun belt. "Next of kin notifications are my least favorite part of the job."

"I can imagine. But if I had bad news coming, I'd want it to come from someone like you."

He smiled. "That's nice, Jersey."

My face flushed hot. "I mean, some cops are just so gruff..." *Stop talking, Charlie.* I didn't know where I was going with this, but it was getting weird. "Anyway, I have to get going. Coffees getting cold."

Nick nodded. "Tell Jo-Jo I said hello. And I still need your statement from yesterday."

"I'll be around." I ushered Noah back to my car, conscious that Nick was watching after us. Why did I always become a bumbling idiot when I was around him?

Chapter Nineteen

Noah and I found Aunt Jo-Jo on the front porch of the rehabilitation center. I placed a muffin and a cup of coffee on the table next to her and settled on the swing across the way. Noah greeted her, standing on his back legs so my aunt could reach him for some serious loving. He had clearly forgotten his unfortunate morning event, as his tail wagged furiously.

My aunt took a satisfying sip from the to-go cup. "God bless you; this tastes like heaven."

"It's probably cold. I ran into a few people."

"It's perfect. And look at you, a few days in town and you already have people."

It had been a whirlwind of activity. I produced her cell phone from my pocket. "Look what I found."

"Thank you." She took it from my outstretched hand. Her face darkened as she took in the badly cracked screen. "How bad does the car look?"

I blew out a long breath, thinking how lucky I was that she was still with us. "You'll need a new one."

My aunt looked at her lap and shook her head. "I've had that car for twenty years. Your uncle bought it for me one Christmas. Never had any real problems with it."

"I'm sorry," I said.

"What about my things?"

"I went kind of late, and I wasn't able to get into the trunk, but I'll go back later and get the rest of your stuff. If you give me your info, I'll call the insurance company."

"Martha already took care of that." She leaned forward in her seat. "What about the box I told you to get?"

"Didn't see it, but I'll do a more thorough search of the car when I go back. Oh, and Clara says Hi."

She looked disappointed, but then shook it off. "Everyone's been so wonderful. I've lost count of the cards I've received, and I've had to turn some flowers away. I had the nurses give them to other patients. There are just too many."

I told her about Maya escaping Austin's attempt to leave her in the cold.

Aunt Jo-Jo laughed and slapped her good hand on the table. "That Maya is a hoot!"

I looked down at my lap. "Okay if she stays awhile?"

"Of course. Us girls need to stick together."

Thank God. I had no claim over Maya, or the right to give her free room and board, but I felt I owed her.

I took a sip of lukewarm coffee and a bite of my muffin. Then I leaned back on the swing and welcomed Noah, who jumped onto the seat beside me, no doubt hoping I was in the mood to share. I closed my eyes, trying to gather the courage to ask my aunt some questions before the police did.

But my thoughts were interrupted.

"When are you gonna fess up?" Aunt Jo-Jo said.

My eyes bounced open. The intense look on her face told me we were about to have a "Come to Jesus" moment. "Fess up about what?"

Her disapproving look became more... disapproving. It was the same expression she'd given me when I lied to her about breaking her favorite vase when I was in the fourth grade. And it was just as effective. I squirmed in my seat.

"I've known you since you were an idea in my sister's eye," she said. "I've loved you like the daughter I never had. I know something is up. You don't just leave the police academy. Leave something you've wanted your whole life. Not even for your favorite aunt."

I looked down at my unforgiving hands, clasped over my stomach. No one else seemed to notice, but their deformity screamed at me, and I didn't even recognize them as my own. I placed them under my thighs. A few minutes too late.

Aunt Jo-Jo shook her head. "Your grandmother had RA. I'd recognize her hands anywhere."

"So, you know."

"Of course, I do. But it would be nice to hear it from you."

I'd only talked about it with my doctor, a few friends, and my sergeant. Not with anyone who truly cared about me. I looked at the ceiling, blinking back tears.

"It's okay to cry," she said. "This is a safe place."

And just like that, the tears came. I swiped at them with the collar of my T-shirt, but they just kept coming. "It's just that…I really wanted to be a cop."

"I know, pumpkin."

"People have worse things happen," I said.

"They do. That doesn't negate what's happening to you."

I dropped to my knees and crawled over, placing my head on my aunt's lap. She stroked my hair. "You're grieving the life you almost had," she said. "But your strength isn't in your hands. It's in your mind, your heart. You will still do great things. We just have to figure out another path. You're not alone."

I sucked in a deep, shuddering breath. The comfort of her hand on me brought me back to the time when I was twelve and my mother didn't show to pick me up from camp. Luckily, my aunt was in town. The counselor called her, and she was there within minutes. She held me all night, quelling my fears of becoming an orphan until my mother surfaced the next morning, claiming she got swept up in an art project. But we all knew that was a lie. My aunt told her I wouldn't be going home with her and that she was taking me back to Orca Cove. My mother could use the time to address her issues. I never forgot how safe I felt, knowing my aunt would care for me and no strange men would come by, and I wouldn't have to make sure my mom ate every day and comfort her when she cried. I was tired of mothering my mother. At my aunt's house, I felt like a normal kid. I felt loved.

I was so involved in reliving the past that I almost forgot where I was. Then Noah trotted over and swatted me with his paw. I felt relieved, sharing my current plight with my aunt. Her love for me was never in doubt. I should have told her sooner.

I wiped my eyes dry, then stood and reclaimed my seat on the swing, encouraging Noah to settle in my lap. "Sorry," I said.

"Why are you sorry? You didn't ask for this. I just wanted you to know you don't have to go it alone."

My burning questions about Lucy and my aunt's connection to her seemed inappropriate at the moment.

Before I could wrestle too much with the idea, her physical therapist appeared. "Time for your therapy, Jo-Jo," she said.

I waved goodbye as they wheeled my aunt back into the building. I felt doused in love, but I couldn't shake the image of Lucy's dead hand holding onto my aunt's necklace in the surf.

Chapter Twenty

I drove through town on my way back to the hotel. My heart was full from my aunt's compassion and understanding. I felt the burden of my disease and its implications lifting from my shoulders after sharing my misfortune with someone who cared.

The guilt I felt for even considering for a split-second that my aunt had anything to do with Lucy's demise settled like a coffin lid over my good feelings. How could I have even had such a thought? No way she could be involved.

I loved her, and I knew how much good she had in her heart. As fond as Nick and the rest of the town were of my aunt, I didn't think they'd give her the benefit of the doubt like I did once they learned Lucy had held Aunt Jo-Jo's necklace in her dead hand. I'd have to find them another place to look before she became a suspect. I just had to figure out how to do that.

In a way, I was glad my aunt had sidelined me with inquiries about my health, and I wasn't able to pepper her with questions about her relationship with Lucy. I needed to think about how to do that without sounding like I was accusing her of anything. My aunt had my back, and by God, I would have hers.

It was a warm, sunny day and lots of people were out, having lunch at sidewalk cafes or popping in-and-out of quaint boutiques, arms loaded with colorful shopping bags.

I spotted Nick, taller than most around him, head down as he walked up the hill toward Wiggle Butt Manor. I pressed the lever and lowered the window as I slowed to a stop next to him. "Going my way?"

He leaned into the car, arms folded on the door. "In fact, I was coming to see you." He reached inside the car and stroked Noah's downy head.

I tried to stop the stupid grin that spread my lips, but my face seemed to have a mind of its own. I pointed to the backseat and gave Noah a gentle nudge. "Go on," I said. When Noah jumped in the back seat, I turned my attention back to Nick. "Hop in."

Settled in his seat, he said, "How's Jo-Jo today?"

I put the car in drive and started up the hill. "She's tired. I'm worried about her. I think this is taking a greater toll on her than she admits. It kills me to see her so vulnerable. She's always been my rock."

"She loves you to death," he said. "She always talks about you. Said if only you lived closer, we'd be perfect for each other."

Either my face turned crimson, or someone had lit me on fire. "She didn't!"

He laughed. "She did."

"I'm mortified."

"I took it as a compliment that she'd think I was good enough for her favorite niece."

"Just what did she tell you?" I almost added, "Don't answer that." I wasn't sure I wanted to know.

He bit his lip in a miserable attempt to stop a slow grin. He was toying with me, and I wanted to scream. "Enough to pique my interest," he said.

I'd just poured my heart out to my aunt. I didn't have the energy to do it again so soon. But I assumed she'd told him I'd been in the police academy. And like her, he'd be astute enough to realize one didn't take a vacation during the regimented training.

I was thankful we'd reached our destination, and I could cut the conversation short. I got out and opened the back door for Noah, who hopped down and followed me.

"Is there a place we can talk?" Nick asked. "I still need to get your statement."

There was a picnic table under a grand oak tree. "Step into my office," I said.

Nick laughed, and we settled at the table. He put down a recorder and turned it on. For good measure, he also took a small notebook out of his pocket and started writing. After announcing the date and time and who we were, he invited me to tell the story of finding Lucy's body. When I was done, he added, "Anything else?" and clicked his pen open and shut while looking at me with such intensity, I squirmed in my seat.

I thought about my aunt's necklace. This was my chance to share that little detail. To come clean, but the words stuck in my throat like cotton candy. "Nope," I said. "That's about it."

He nodded and shut the recorder off. "Well, if you think of anything, let me know."

Nick walked by my side to the hotel. Barking erupted as soon as I opened the door. The hotel didn't need a doorbell, that was for sure.

Martha came down the hall, yelling, "Pipe down!" as she passed the pet rooms. I opened the door to the first room, taking care of the loudest mouth in the place. Maya was happy to see me and immediately settled down. The other dogs followed her lead, and it became blissfully quiet. Maya strutted around me, tail swishing from side to side as she pranced into the lobby like she owned the place.

"Hey, scoundrel." Nick reached down to pat her head. Maya gave him a moment of attention and then went to sniff Noah, who wagged his tail in return, his usual indifference to the other dogs put aside. Well, Maya saved his life, and it seemed to earn her his respect.

"I see you're off duty," Martha said to Nick. "But any word on what happened to Lucy?"

Nick folded his arms across his chest. "Still waiting for Alex to get back to me on that. But I finally caught up with Lucy's nephew and gave him the news."

"How'd he take it?" she asked.

"Everyone's different," he said. "But he seemed detached. I'm guessing they weren't close."

"Yet he came up here the moment he learned his aunt was missing," I said.

"That's a good point, Jersey." He turned to Martha. "You and Jo-Jo knew her as well as anyone. I don't mean to get ahead of the autopsy results, but do you know of anyone who would want to cause Lucy harm?"

"I've been thinking about that very thing," Martha said. "She yelled at all the kids in the neighborhood if they even looked her way when they rode their bikes by her house. She was the type of person to give her opinion, whether or not you wanted it. I can't think of anyone who really liked her, but hating her enough to kill her is another story."

"Those were my thoughts, too," he said. "I dealt with her a lot because of Maya. Lucy often told me what she thought of the people of Orca Cove. Didn't see much good in anybody."

"What was her situation?" I asked. "Her house needs a lot of work, but her property must be worth a fortune with the view it has."

"I'm sure it is," Martha said. "The home has been in the family a long time. I think she inherited it. She's let the property go over the years. She was too damn old to keep up the place, but she was too cheap to hire someone to help out."

"Is Austin the only heir?"

Nick and Martha looked at each other. "As far as I know," Martha said. "He came to stay with her one summer when he was a kid. But I don't know how closely they stayed in touch after that. It was years ago. I don't remember her mentioning anyone else."

"Well, if he's the only heir," I said. "That might be a good reason to get her out of the way."

"Money's a good motive," Nick said.

"Did she still work at the library?" I asked.

Martha nodded. "She ran a tight ship. I always returned my books on time. Fines always came with a lecture about how selfish it was to keep a book too long when somebody else might want to read it."

Nick laughed. "Tell me about it. I kept a book one day past due when I was twelve, and just a week ago, she reminded me of it."

"Yet she put up with Maya and her shenanigans," I said.

We all looked at Maya, who was alert and seemed to listen. "She was one of the few who got a pass," Martha said. "The dog, Kyleigh, and her mom,

Jody. But that was a long time ago."

"I didn't know about that," Nick said.

Martha rubbed her chin. "I think it was after you left for college. Maybe you were even with Portland Police by then. Jody Boyce was raising Kyleigh by herself and struggling. Lucy took them in. They lived with her a few years. Then one day, Jody took off and left Kyleigh behind."

I thought about the room I'd seen in Lucy's house with the twin beds. It appeared that no one had touched the room for years. Like maybe she was waiting for the occupants to return.

"Lucy wanted to keep Kyleigh, but Ray Boyce, Jody's half-brother, wouldn't have it. I think the Boyces saw dollar signs. The state pays them to take care of the girl," Martha said.

I thought about the dilapidated trailer they lived in. "Seems like Lucy had a soft spot for the underdog," I said.

Maya barked as if she agreed.

We all laughed.

Martha got back to business. "I talked to the insurance company about Jo-Jo's car, and they authorized a rental for her. Because you'll be helping take care of Jo-Jo, I finagled the insurance company into letting you be a driver on the rental. If you return your car and pick up hers, you can save a few bucks, Charlie."

"That would be great," I said. "Can I get it this afternoon?"

"Anytime you're ready," Martha said.

"Will you watch Noah?" I knew I'd have to drive to the mainland, and that dogs weren't welcome everywhere.

"Of course," she said.

I looked at Nick. "I can give you a ride back to your Jeep."

"Or?" Nick said with a twinkle in his eye. "I could go with you if you don't mind some company.

I raked a hand through my hair. "Oh…. Um…. I don't want to take up your day off."

"Oh, for heaven's sake," Martha said. "Don't be dense. He wants to go with you."

Nick snickered. "Before it gets more awkward, let me just say that I do want to go. But if you want some space, it's okay to say so."

I didn't know what I wanted. I would head back to Red Bank soon, and I was enjoying Nick's company more than I should. I didn't need a broken heart on top of everything else.

Then I scolded myself for letting my mind run wild. Just because Nick wanted to bum around didn't mean he was romantically interested in me. And if he was, he wouldn't be when he knew it hurt to tie my shoes. I could be in a wheelchair someday. Plus, my aunt had told him I wanted to be a cop. He was expecting that. And that wasn't in the cards. Not anymore.

They were both staring at me like I was about to call the winner of a game. "Of course, you can come," I said. "I'd like the company."

I gave Noah and Maya some goodbye loving, then went with Nick to the car.

Chapter Twenty-One

As we started down the hill, and the bridge came into sight, I realized I was going to have to drive across it. The hair on my arms rose. Why didn't I think this through? Not only was I going to have a panic attack, but Nick would witness it. Twice!

I felt my freak-out would extinguish any flame between us. This wouldn't be pretty.

I racked my brain for a way to get out of my pending situation. But as I rejected each stupid reason why I couldn't cross the bridge that came to me, I realized I was too late. We were at the entrance with no way to turn around.

My hands became white as I death-gripped the steering wheel, and I slowed to twenty miles an hour. Nick was talking, but I felt like I was in a windstorm, and I couldn't decipher his words. My pitiful attempt at positive self-talk in my head drowned out any surrounding noise. *Think about puppies and rainbows, puppies and rainbows...* I focused on the ten feet in front of us. I thought I might throw up.

The car behind us blared its horn. But because my hearing was on vacation, it didn't have the effect on me it should have.

"Jersey," Nick said, his hand resting gently on my shoulder. "Are. You. Okay?"

I gritted my teeth. A memory burst like a bubble in my mind. I was in the backseat of our car. Mom was driving across a bridge. She was crying hysterically. *"I'm gonna do it,"* she said. *"I'll jump and end it all!"*

"Take a breath," Nick said calmly. "Come on, in and out."

I shook the memory from my mind, focusing on the here and now.

I did as he said. After a few breaths, my mind cleared, and I felt a little better. It was like waking from a deep sleep and slowly noticing the world around you. I continued deep breathing until flat ground welcomed us. The memory hung heavy in my mind. I pushed it back into the shadows. No time to deal with that now.

"Cripes," I said, accelerating to a normal speed once the bridge was behind us.

"Afraid of heights, are we?" he said.

"A little."

He laughed. "If that's how you act when you're a little afraid, I'd hate to see you when you're terrified."

I ignored him.

"Don't you have bridges in Jersey?"

"Of course," I said. "But I know how to avoid the big ones. This damn island gives me no choice."

"Well," he said. "How about I drive on the way back? That way, you can close your eyes."

"I just might take you up on that."

I was beyond embarrassed that Nick witnessed my weakness. I kept my eyes on the road, afraid to see him laughing at me.

"I'm afraid of chickens," he blurted.

Stopping for a traffic light, I turned to look at him. "You're kidding, right?"

"Nope. I always think they're going to peck me. Not fun when Maya chases them, and I have to stop her."

I let out a barking laugh, then held my hand over my mouth. "I'm sorry."

"It's okay," he said. "It's a stupid phobia, and I'm not proud of it. More likely to fall off a bridge than die by a poultry attack."

"Well," I said, grateful he was trying to make me feel less exposed. "Thanks for sharing."

"I'll make you a deal," he said. "I'll protect you from high places if you'll defend me if a wayward chicken crosses our path." He offered his hand, and I shook it.

"Deal."

When I went to pull away, he held on for a few extra seconds before letting go.

My heart started racing again for a totally different reason.

Nick's cell rang. I glanced over at the phone in his lap, where a photo of Alex lit up the screen. Nick sucked in a breath and seemed to struggle for a minute before he answered the call.

"Hey," he said.

I could hear her talking, but couldn't make out her words.

"Can't," he said. "I'm in the middle of something. Any autopsy results?"

He listened for a moment, then said, "Look, I gotta go. Call you later?"

He disconnected the call and dropped the cell back into his lap.

I chanced a glance at him. They sounded so familiar on the phone, I felt like I was spying on something private. But I had to know. "Any news about Lucy?"

"Not yet."

I turned my attention back to the road. They clearly had other stuff to talk about. Personal stuff. I wondered just what their relationship was.

Once I exchanged cars—the one available was a baby blue Subaru Crosstrek–I handed Nick the keys.

"You need to get back right away?" he said. "Because there's something I'd like to show you."

"As far as I know, all I have to do is walk the dogs before bed."

"I promise to have you home in time to do that," he said.

We got in the car and drove for approximately ten minutes before we took a turnoff that led us to an unpaved road deep in the woods. After about half a mile, we came upon a dead end. "You okay walking a bit?" he asked.

I nodded and followed Nick down a narrow trail through the trees, flashing back at the path that led us to Lucy. I tried to shake those memories. The small, pebbled beach at the end of the trail certainly helped. There was a gorgeous view of the water between the mainland and Orca Cove. No one was on the beach. "How is this place a secret?" I said. "It's amazing."

Although I could see the bridge, it didn't look so scary from so far away.

"Because it's on private property," he said. "My uncle owns it, so I have access. Most of the locals respect that it's private, but teens have been known to come down here and party at night. Most of the time, my uncle turns a blind eye."

I spotted the remnants of a bonfire a few feet away. Rocks jetted out into the ocean, and when the waves crashed against them, there was a magnificent spray. "Orcas come by here sometimes," he said. "There's a sheer drop off where the whales trap salmon against the rock. Of course, they probably won't show since I'm trying to impress you."

"Well," I said, tickled that he wanted to impress me. Especially since he'd witnessed my meltdown. "Regardless, this is a magical place. Thanks for sharing it with me."

He motioned to the craggy, enormous rock that jetted out high above the waves. "Take a seat."

I climbed up about six feet and found a flat spot. Nick sat by my side, close enough that I could feel the heat off him.

"I've been to the island several times over the years," I said. "Never been lucky enough to see an orca. I've missed them by minutes, according to those fortunate folks who managed to see them. It's a definite goal of mine."

"The trick is patience," he said. "Eventually, they come. First time I saw them, as big as a truck, yet slicing gently through the water...it changed my life. They can be so playful, spy hopping and breaching as if they're putting on a show. The resident pods who frequent the area are mellow souls. They survive on salmon and don't hunt larger prey. I've had them glide under my kayak, as curious about me as I am about them."

"Aren't you afraid they'll tip you over?"

"I have to admit," he said with laughter in his voice. "It's a heart-racing experience, but I know they won't cause me harm."

I jabbed him in the side with my elbow. "Not scary, like say, a chicken?"

He laughed. "I swear if you tell anyone about that, I'll get revenge."

I motioned like I was locking my lips. "Your secret is safe with me."

We stayed there about an hour, talking some, but mostly decompressing and enjoying the tranquility of the spot. No whales came, but Nick promised me we'd come back again soon.

As the sun sank into the ocean, he hopped down off the rock and offered me his hand, guiding me so I landed softly on the sand. Although he let go, the weight of his touch lingered all the way back to the car.

I let Nick drive us home, and we listened to a Joni Mitchell CD someone had left in the car. I liked that he didn't see a need to always fill the silence. It was comfortable being close to him.

My eyes closed as I listened to the mellow music playing on the stereo. I hadn't noticed we'd crossed the bridge until we came to a stop at the traffic light on the other side.

Nick looked over at me and smiled. "You did good, Jersey."

"Trick is to keep my eyes closed," I said. "Risky when I'm driving."

He reached over and touched my arm. "Anytime you need me to get you over the bridge without having a heart attack, I'm up for the job."

"A true gentleman."

He shrugged and took his hand away. "I try."

A warm spot remained where his fingers had brushed my skin. In my experience, gentlemen were few and far between, but he definitely qualified. He loved dogs, didn't judge me, and was hotter than the Mohave Desert sand in August. I knew he had to have faults, but so far, I couldn't find any. Except for a giant one. He lived across the country from me. And yes, he accepted my fear of heights, but how would he feel about a disability? I didn't want to ruin the moment and find out.

He parked the rental car behind his Jeep. "Well," he said. "Today turned out to be a nice surprise. Thanks for letting me tag along, Jersey."

"Thank you," I said.

We got out of the car, and I took his spot in the driver's seat. My heart fluttered as he smiled at me before walking back to his Wrangler.

I relished my thoughts of him, reliving the day as I drove up the hill to the pet hotel. A peaceful feeling enveloped me. It was a good day.

Chapter Twenty-Two

Martha had clocked out by the time I got home. I went straight to the hotel to walk the dogs, wanting to get it over with before I had dinner, and turned in for the night.

I grabbed two leashes and started with Noah and Maya. My head was still in the clouds from my time on the mainland with Nick. Could he really be interested in me? Hard to wrap my mind around the possibility. But if he wasn't, would he have spent the afternoon with me? Would he have taken me to such a romantic spot?

I walked further than I would have if I'd been paying attention. We came upon a small, but charming single-story bungalow where Riley was in the yard, raking leaves. "Hey, you," she said as we came upon her.

A white picket fence separated us as I stopped to chat. Other than my aunt and Martha, and maybe Nick, she was the closest thing I had to a friend on the island. I hadn't remembered she lived so close to my aunt, but I recognized the house from my childhood. Everything seemed bigger and further away when I was young.

We talked about the dogs, the weather and then she invited me to meet her at the coffee shop for breakfast sometime soon.

I was about to say goodbye and head back to the hotel when Ray drove by in his truck. He slowed as he passed Riley's house, giving us the stink eye. I braced for a confrontation, but he didn't stop.

"What a freak," Riley said.

I waited until the truck was out of sight and then said, "He seems to have it in for me."

"He's always been a jerk," she said. "He was even that way with his family."

"How so?"

"He has a half-sister, Jody. She left town years ago, abandoning her young daughter. I think Ray is the reason she ran off. I saw them fighting about something shortly before she left."

"How bad of a fight?"

Riley tilted her head. "I can't remember verbatim, but something about Jody's inability to keep a secret and how she didn't care if sharing it would affect others. The poor girl was in tears. I remember he told her that if she didn't toe the line, she'd pay the consequences."

"Every family has its secrets," I said. "And I can't imagine having Ray for a brother."

"Me either."

Noah tugged on the leash, and I looked down at the dogs. Maya was no longer at my feet. My heart raced as I looked around the immediate area, relieved to see her sitting, looking at us from several feet away. "What the heck?"

Her leash dangled from my hand. Chewed right through. "You rascal." I hadn't even felt her escape.

Riley shook her head. "You're something else, Maya."

I prepared to play the game of catch me if you can, but Maya let me approach her. We were coming to an understanding. Not trusting her completely, I grabbed her collar and then switched leashes with Noah, who I knew wouldn't run off. "I better get these dogs back," I said. "I still have several to walk."

"See you soon," Riley said.

We hurried back to the house where I secured the dogs inside, threw out the ruined leash and went back to the hotel to walk the other dogs. Down a leash, I went through the drawers of the dresser in the lobby for another lead. Not having any luck, I went back to the storage room where I knew Martha kept necessities.

I pulled the string hanging from the ceiling, and a single bulb lit the space. Shelves held plastic bins stacked from floor to ceiling. I pulled several out far enough that I could check the contents, finding treats, toys, and office supplies.

Crouching down, I pulled a container out from the bottom. Sure enough, there was a supply of well-worn leashes. They would have to do. I selected the one in the best condition and shoved the bin back into place, but it wouldn't quite fit. Something must have fallen behind it when I pulled out the basket.

I pushed the bin aside and got on my hands and knees so I could see what was obstructing the space. The light in the room didn't reach the dark corner, so I took out my cell phone and activated the flashlight.

A dark item, so far back, I had to lie on my stomach to reach it. Afraid it was a rat or some other undesirable thing, I held my flashlight as far into the space as I could. When I realized what it was, I grabbed it and settled back on my heels. A single black pump. Exactly like the one found by Lucy's body on the beach.

Instinctively, I pulled up Nick's number to advise him of my find. But I stopped short of pushing send. My aunt's necklace and her argument with Lucy would already lead the police to suspect Aunt Jo-Jo in Lucy's death. I didn't need to add another clue to the list.

I stuffed the shoe behind a smaller tote, hoping no one would notice it. Not until the investigation pointed to another suspect.

I turned off the light and closed the storage room door behind me, a sick feeling in my stomach.

I walked the last dog, a blind and deaf Chihuahua named Joe Pesci, before Noah, Maya and I shared yet another tuna sandwich I chased down with the last of the beers. As I relived the events of the day, I marveled at how I'd started the morning with tears in my eyes and ended it with hope in my heart. That was until I found the darn shoe.

And then there was the butterfly pendant in Lucy's dead hand. Once Nick connected it to my aunt, we would be on opposite sides for sure. Try as I might, I couldn't come up with a reason for it being there. I couldn't stop the scenario that played in my head of my aunt shoving Lucy into the ocean and Lucy reaching out and pulling the necklace off her as she fell. And then what? She kept the shoe as a memento? That just didn't make sense. I tried to shake the image from my mind, but it wouldn't budge even though I knew my aunt wasn't capable of such a heinous act.

I'd come full circle from that morning, back to desperate and depressed. I should go to bed and forget it all.

But then I saw a flicker of light through the hotel window.

My stomach pitched. Now what?

As soundlessly as I could, I got up and put my shoes on. Placing my cell in my pocket, I grabbed the baseball bat from its spot by the front door. I left Noah in the house but clamped the leash on Maya, who was happy to accompany me.

"Don't spaz out on me," I whispered as we crossed the yard between the house and the hotel.

Using my key, I unlocked the door, freezing as it clicked open, hoping I didn't expose my presence. I waited a moment, but no sound came from inside. In the darkness, I crept toward the back room where I'd seen the light.

When I'd made it to the office, it was so dark, I couldn't see more than a foot in front of me. Bracing myself, I clicked the lamp on.

It took a moment for my eyes to adjust to the light, but soon I noticed a heap of blankets on the sofa under the window. The mound moved so slightly, I could have imagined it.

I let go of Maya's leash and held the bat at the ready. "Who's there?" I said, trying for an authoritative tone.

The mound seemed to shrink. Whoever was under the blankets had flattened themselves.

"Nice try, but I can still see you." I pushed at the lump with the end of the bat. It was solid. I reached down and yanked the covering back, revealing a dark-haired person tucked into a ball. "Kyleigh?"

She looked up at me through the curtain of hair that obstructed her face.

"Jeez," I said. I lowered the bat to my side and felt tension release from my body. "What are you doing here?"

Kyleigh sat up and pulled her knees to her chest. I sank onto the couch beside her. I couldn't see her face. Instinctively, I reached out and pushed the hair off her cheek.

A dark bruise bled under her eye. "Oh, Kyleigh," I said.

She jerked away from me, and her hair fell, concealing her shame. Maya had climbed onto the sofa between us, and she lowered her head onto Kyleigh's lap. The girl absently stroked the dog, but she wouldn't look at me.

"Who did this to you?"

She lowered her head to her knees. "It's nothing."

"It's not nothing," I said. "I can help."

She gave a bitter laugh. "What do you know about my life? You're perfect. You've got it all."

Little did she know. But I guessed it was all perspective. I didn't have to break into a place to get a good night's sleep and avoid having the crap beaten out of me. I tried another tactic. "What can I do to help?"

She didn't answer, but Maya seemed to be the best medicine. She looked up at Kyleigh and licked her chin. The girl tightened her hold on the dog.

I sighed, remembering how comforting Nick's silence had been for me. So, we sat quietly together. Eventually, Kyleigh lay back down with Maya's head on her chest. I sat there until I could tell she'd drifted off, and Maya gave me a look that said; *I got this*. I clicked off the light and left the hotel as soundlessly as I'd arrived.

Chapter Twenty-Three

I woke to loud voices outside my window. I recognized Kyleigh's, but the other, a male, was unfamiliar. The words were indistinct. I couldn't understand what was being said, but the anger was deafening.

It was still dark outside. I looked at the bedside clock. Just after 4 a.m.

Sliding out of bed, I pulled on a pair of sweatpants, stuffed my feet into my shoes, and grabbed my new best friend—the baseball bat—before stepping outside.

Motion sensor lights switched on as I moved onto the porch, Noah on my heels.

Kyleigh and the man she quarreled with were so immersed in their argument, they didn't notice me walking toward them. As I got closer, I realized the man was Kyleigh's uncle Ray. Maya, who was circling them, gave me a brief glance, but her attention quickly returned to Ray, who now had Kyleigh by the arm. He pulled her toward his dingy pickup truck.

Kyleigh tried to dig her heels into the dirt, and she swatted his arm, but he was much stronger than she was, and she was no match for him.

"Let her go," I said.

They both looked at me with surprise. "Back off, Stretch," Ray said. "This ain't your business."

"I'm making it my business. Let go of her or I'm calling the police."

He was half-a-foot shorter than me, but he was agile. And determined. Ignoring me, he shoved Kyleigh toward the truck, and she reluctantly got inside.

"Don't," I said. "You don't have to go with him."

I wished I had my phone with me so I could make good on my threat to call the cops, but it was inside on the charger.

Before I could come up with my next move, Maya lunged at Ray, and he stumbled back, landing against the truck. As she prepared for her second strike, he kicked her, and she let out a yelp. He drew his leg back to deliver another kick, but I ran over and pushed the end of the baseball bat at his throat. "Do not hurt her."

He looked at me, eyes bulging with hate. I reached down and grabbed Maya by the collar, and we slowly backed away, the bat still raised and ready to do damage if necessary.

Ray rubbed his throat and pointed at me as he moved around the truck and got behind the wheel. "I'm not done with you."

Kyleigh rolled down the window, and I jogged alongside the truck as it headed out of the lot. "Please, stay," I begged.

"It's okay," Kyleigh yelled. "I'm sorry."

Ray swerved the truck toward me, and I had to jump out of the way, so I wasn't hit. Dust rose behind his tires like the wake behind a boat as he hightailed it down the driveway and onto the main road. I dropped to my knees in front of Maya. "You okay, girl?"

She licked my chin and wagged her tail. I squeezed my eyes shut, thankful that she didn't appear to be injured, but I was angry that he'd tried to hurt her, and I was worried sick about Kyleigh.

I ran inside with Maya behind me. Noah watched us from the bed. Plucking my phone off the charger, I dialed 911.

I waited for the police to arrive on the porch swing with both dogs. I'd examined Maya several times, looking for signs of injury, but I couldn't find a tender spot.

I cradled her to my chest. "We tried to stop him, girl. I'm glad to have you on my team." Jealous, Noah climbed between us. I hugged him, too.

The three of us sat together while I relived the sequence of events in my mind, wondering what I could have done differently. Kyleigh got into the truck on her own, so it wasn't exactly kidnapping. And he was her uncle and her guardian, as far as I knew. But someone had given her a black eye, and if I had to hazard a guess, I assumed it was Ray Boyce, nice guy that he was. I hoped it wasn't because he'd seen me on the property. Kicking Maya had been the last straw. I was pretty sure that if I hadn't intervened, Maya would have won that fight, but I wasn't about to risk her getting injured to find out.

About twenty minutes later, the police cruiser came up the driveway.

Nick got out and walked over. I'd never been so happy to see someone. I stood and crossed my arms against the chilly morning air, meeting him on the porch steps. He leaned down to pet each dog before settling his attention on me. "You okay?"

I nodded. But the adrenaline dump I'd experienced was fading, leaving me nauseous.

"I stopped them in town," Nick said. "Kyleigh denied any wrongdoing on her uncle's part."

"He hit her, I'm sure. Did you notice the black eye?"

Nick put his foot on the step in front of him. "Did you see him do it?"

"No."

"She had some BS story about walking into a door. I separated them, tried to get her to talk, but she seems to hate me more than she hates him."

I rubbed my arms. "She doesn't trust cops."

"I got the message."

"Ray kicked Maya," I said. "That I did witness."

Nick tapped his thigh, calling Maya over. Noah was a bonus as both dogs vied for his attention.

"She seems okay," I said. "Can't you arrest Ray for animal cruelty?"

Nick ran a hand through his hair. "I'd love to. Kyleigh denied that it happened, too. So, it's your word against theirs. Since there's no apparent injury, it makes it even harder to prove. I'm sure Ray will say he was protecting himself. I'll take your statement and submit a report, but I doubt the DA will file charges. Even if she does, it's a misdemeanor. Not much will happen."

I shook my head. "I'm mad that people don't take animal abuse more seriously. Can we at least try? He can't just get away with what he did."

Nick took out a stack of cards and jotted down my telling of events. When he was done, he stuffed the pack back in his vest pocket.

The sun had risen, and it cast an orange glow on the horizon. "I can make coffee," I said. "Unless you have someplace to be."

Nick smiled. "I'm not even supposed to be working. I monitor the radio when I'm off. Don't have much of a life, as you can tell. It's usually quiet overnight. But when I heard you called in, I threw on my gear and headed out. Didn't even take time to put on my uniform."

I took a closer look. He had on jeans and a tee shirt under his tactical vest. I wanted to hug him in thanks, but then I remembered we weren't a "we."

"I'll put on a pot." I headed inside.

I brought out two mugs of coffee and found Nick rubbing Noah's belly as he lay on his back, tongue hanging out of his mouth, perfectly relaxed. Dog heaven. It warmed my heart to see Nick loving on my pup.

Nick had shed his vest and had put a light jacket on. He looked like any civilian except for the gun clipped to his belt.

When he saw me standing there, he gave Noah a final tummy rub and then stood and accepted the mug.

"Do you want cream?" I asked. "Because there's some in the fridge."

"This is fine."

We settled on the porch step, watching the sun brighten the sky. I told him about finding Kyleigh sleeping in the hotel. "I don't think she's safe at home."

"I made a referral to Child Protective Services," he said. "Hopefully, they'll investigate her black eye. Meanwhile, maybe you could get close to her. See what's going on. Would be nice if she found a good female role model."

I blew on my coffee before taking a sip. "Don't think it should be me. I won't be here that long. Doesn't she have anyone? A teacher? School counselor?"

"I have no idea," Nick said. "I can ask the principal."

"That would be good," I said.

"Just when are you heading back to Jersey, Jersey?"

I shrugged. "I haven't decided yet."

He took a sip of coffee. "Your aunt told me you were in the academy. That not work out?"

I stiffened. I wasn't ready to have a heart-to-heart about that.

Nick's eyes locked on mine. It was as if he could see into my soul. I felt the tears come as my sadness of losing my dream bubbled out of me. I wiped them away with the back of my hand, then took a deep breath and placed both hands on my knees.

He reached over and patted my arm. "It's okay," he said. "I'm here whenever you're ready."

We sat in the quiet of the early morning, his hand on mine. I didn't need to share my story. He knew. And he still sat there with me. Knowing. And that made me feel a whole lot better.

Chapter Twenty-Four

After Nick left for work, I walked the dogs and gave them treats. I still had the special ones I'd bought at the bakery and decided this was the perfect time for a reward. Both dogs snarfed them down so quickly, I could have fed them cardboard and made them just as happy. After a quick shower, I dressed in jeans and a hoodie. The usual.

Heading to the hotel, my cell buzzed in my pocket. Caller ID told me it was my mom. I declined the call. Maybe it was passive-aggressive, but I was tired of our one-way relationship. She rarely came through for me, yet I was supposed to drop everything when she reached out. The last time she'd called in a tizzy, I cancelled a date to help her, and she stood me up.

Even so, I felt guilty and almost called her back. I told myself I had things to do, and I would call her later, but I felt like a jerk.

I found Martha emptying bags of dog food into plastic bins.

"I'll walk the dogs before I head over to see Aunt Jo-Jo," I said. I flashed back to Lucy's shoe and wished I would have hidden it better. But I couldn't do anything about it now.

Martha shook the last few pieces of kibble out of the bag, then flattened it and put it in the trash. "Kyleigh's on the schedule to do that."

I bit my lip. "I doubt she's coming in today."

I updated her on the excitement from that morning.

"If he hurts Kyleigh or any of these dogs, he's going to have to answer to me," Martha said, her hands balled into fists.

She was so angry; I was afraid she'd have a stroke. "Maya seems to be alright," I said. "But I'm hoping the DA presses charges."

"That would be nice."

We were down to five hotel guests. I walked them in two batches, then secured Maya in an empty room with Noah. They'd bonded after the attack at the dog park, and I no longer feared Maya would cause Noah harm. Better for him to have a buddy than to be in the house alone. I had stuff to do, and I didn't want to leave him in the car that long.

It was after nine, and I figured the impound lot would be open and I'd have plenty of time to gather my aunt's belongings.

I parked in the visitor's lot and, noting the **Open for Business** sign in the window, I let myself inside. When I saw the woman behind the desk, I came up short. It wasn't the friendly lady who'd been there the day before, who'd been so kind.

The woman on duty today greeted me with a narrow-eyed stare. Her grouchiness overwhelmed what would have otherwise been an attractive face. It seemed to take her a moment to place me, but I recognized her from the dog park right away. Mary Boyce. This day kept getting better and better.

I plastered a fake smile on my face, hoping she wouldn't remember me from the run-in between her dog and Maya the day before. No such luck. "You," she said.

I gave up on pretending and wiped the grin off my face. "Is Clara here?"

"Nope."

I shoved my hands in my pockets and rocked back on my heels. "Well, I told her I'd come back today to get stuff out of my aunt's car."

"Who's stopping you?" Dismissing me, she turned her attention back to the magazine on the counter in front of her.

I hurried outside and opened the passenger door, gathering everything off the floor and laying it on the seat. I used the keys I found at my aunt's house to open the trunk. Inside, I found a few shopping bags, which I placed on the ground, then filled them with whatever else I could find. Not seeing the green box my aunt specifically asked me to get, I gave one more look under the seats. Nothing. Maybe she hadn't left it in the car after all.

Gathering my bags, I went back through the office. Mary still sat at the counter. She gave me a quick glance.

"Something appears to be missing from the car," I said. "Any idea what could have happened to it?"

Her eyes narrowed. "What are you accusing me of?"

"I wasn't," I said. "Just asking if you might know what happened to it."

Her silence told me I would not get an answer from her. I'd almost made it to the door when she cleared her throat. "You really need to mind your own business."

I stiffened and turned to face her. "I don't know what you're talking about."

"Putting ideas into my niece's head."

I wasn't sure what ideas she was talking about, but I guessed it had something to do with Kyleigh not wanting to have the stuffing beaten out of her and coming to what she thought was a safe place. I didn't want to make things worse for Kyleigh at home, so I opted not to engage her. "I don't know what you're talking about."

"What happens in our family is our business."

"Not when it happens on our property."

"When you harbor a runaway, you get what you get," she said, snapping.

"And when you abuse a child, you get what you get," I shot back.

"I suggest you watch yourself," she said, pointing her finger at me. "Ray ain't no one to mess with."

The Jersey in me was about to erupt. It wouldn't be pretty and would come out in a torrent of cuss words that would even make little miss sunshine here blush. But that would probably lead to a brawl, which wouldn't do any of us any good, least of all Kyleigh. So, I put a cork in it and flashed a condescending smile instead. "You have a nice day." I backed out the door.

Sometimes kindness took the wind out of the devil's sails. It worked. Mary's mouth fell open, but she didn't deliver a comeback.

Chapter Twenty-Five

I stopped for coffee and bagels on the way to visit Aunt Jo-Jo. Austin was at the same table he'd been at the day before. He intercepted me before I could pay for my order. "Please," he said. "Let me get this. It's the least I can do since you're helping with Maya."

"Not necessary," I said.

Before I could get to my wallet, he reached around me and laid a twenty-dollar bill on the counter. The cashier took the money and handed Austin his change. He stuffed a dollar bill in the tip jar. "Join me," he said.

I sighed. He was like an annoying gnat who wouldn't go away. "I have to be somewhere."

"Then meet me for dinner tonight," he said. "You're the only friendly face I've found around here, and I'm going through a rough time, losing my aunt and all."

If my face was friendly, I hated to think how awfully others treated him. "I'm sorry about your aunt," I said.

He hung his head, and his shoulders sagged. Oh, boy. I didn't see any way out of this without being a total jerk. And I could use the opportunity to pump him for information about his relationship with his aunt and find out if he was a money-grubbing opportunist wanting to cash in on Lucy's demise. "What time?"

He stood tall and smiled. "How about seven? There's an interesting-looking bistro down the street."

"Okay, see you then."

Scooping my order off the counter, I turned and left. Austin's eyes remained on me, burning a hole in my back.

When I walked into the rehab center, the receptionist greeted me with a welcoming smile. I made a mental note to bring cookies for the staff to thank them for caring for my aunt. She watched as I signed in. As I gathered up the tray of coffee and bagels, the woman stood and looked at my signature. "Oh, Charlie, I thought that was you. I'm supposed to tell you that the social worker wants to talk to you."

"Sure thing. Just let me give my aunt her breakfast before her coffee gets cold."

"Take your time," the woman said. "Her office is just a few doors past your aunt's room."

"Thanks."

I found Aunt Jo-Jo in bed, which I thought was odd since it was almost ten o'clock. When I walked in, she shut off the TV.

"How are you today?" I placed her coffee and bagel on the tray table and then wheeled it in front of her.

She shrugged. "Any news on Lucy?"

"You mean cause of death? No, not yet. The social worker wants to talk to me. I imagine it's to make plans for you to go home."

"Thank God. Did you get my stuff out of the car?"

I nodded. "It's in the rental. I'll bring it home and put it in your bedroom."

She leaned forward. "Did you find the green box?"

"Sorry, no. It wasn't in the car."

My aunt raised her eyebrows. "It has to be."

"I went through everything. It wasn't there."

She scratched her head. "What could have happened to it? I need that box." She looked panicked.

"Do you really not know what's in it?"

My aunt lowered her voice even though we were the only two people in the room. "Lucy asked me to hold onto it for her. Said it was important. And now that she's gone, I just wonder…"

"Did she give you any inkling what the contents are?"

"No," Aunt Jo-Jo said. "Like I told you before, I don't have a clue."

"I'm sure it will turn up."

My aunt looked skeptical, but she didn't push the issue.

Leaving my bagel and purse on her chair, I took my coffee with me as I wandered down to the social worker's office.

A woman in a wheelchair sat behind a desk, talking on the phone. Platinum blonde hair curled around a sweet face, and her oversized, pink-framed glasses gave her a doe-eyed look that I assumed helped her gain the trust of her patients. I hovered in the doorway until she registered my presence and waved at me to take a seat.

I sat across from her desk and sipped my coffee while she wrapped up her conversation. Once she hung up the phone, she offered me a warm smile. "How can I help you?"

Leaning forward, I gave her my hand. "I'm Charlie Calderbank, Jo-Jo McMullen's niece."

She shook my hand. "Pleasure to meet you. I'm Lilly Foster, the director of social services. Actually, I'm the only social worker here, so the title seems silly."

I liked her right away. "Nice to meet you. The receptionist said you wanted to see me."

"I did. We need to do some preliminary discharge planning. The doctors think your aunt will be able to go home early next week. She signed a release of information, so I'm allowed to talk to you about her care."

I nodded. "Good. I'll do anything I can to help."

"I'm worried about your aunt. She doesn't remember the accident, which isn't all that uncommon. But she drove into a tree. Tests don't show anything wrong with her brain, no sign of a stroke or anything, but I'm wondering why she would do that. Aside from a medical reason, or say, swerving to avoid a squirrel, or just being plain distracted... I mean, there are a lot of reasons that could happen."

I leaned forward in my seat. "Yet, you're worried it was something else."

"Not really," she said. "But I don't want you to overlook the possibility."

I straightened. "Possibility of what?"

She leaned her elbows on the desk and placed her chin on folded hands. "That it was a suicide attempt. Older people sometimes have depression. She did seem down this morning."

I felt like I'd been slapped in the face. To even consider such a thing horrified me. "I don't think... I mean, Aunt Jo-Jo is a pretty upbeat person. And she's really not that old." Plus, her car had damage to the front and back. It wasn't like she just drove into a tree. Someone probably pushed her. I needed to get the accident report.

The social worker nodded. "Of course. I just wanted you to keep an eye out. You know, just in case."

A chill ran through my body, and I had a sudden case of Deja vu. My mom had depression. But Aunt Jo-Jo was the opposite of her sister—wasn't she? "I'm sure it was something else," I said.

"Most likely," Lilly said. "I would feel bad if I didn't mention it, though."

"Understood."

"I'll work on the discharge plan and go over it with you and your aunt at the end of the week. Home health will come to the house to do an assessment. They inspect the living space for safety reasons and so they can make accommodations for showering and daily living. And we'll get her a wheelchair and a walker."

"Thank you," I said. "I appreciate everything you can do to help. I've never dealt with anything like this."

"It's why I'm here," Lilly said. "Have a nice day, and let me know if you have any questions."

Taking my coffee, I walked back to my aunt's room. The conversation had left me unnerved. I was relieved when I saw Aunt Jo-Jo leaving the room with her physical therapist. I needed some time to process what the social worker said.

I drove back to town, my mind on my conversation with Lilly. My aunt hadn't been her usual upbeat self that morning, and I worried that maybe the social worker was on to something. I didn't know much about the wreck Aunt Jo-Jo had, except that no one else had been injured. Since the police investigated all accident scenes, I figured Nick could shed some light on what had happened. I felt bad bothering him when he was working, so I drove by the police station instead to see if I could get a copy of the accident report, like any member of the public could do.

There was one police cruiser and a handful of civilian cars in the parking lot of the small brick building that housed the Orca Cove Police Department. I left my car in a visitor's spot and entered through the double glass doors. A woman sat behind a desk on the other side of a partition.

"Good morning," I said, checking my watch. "How do I go about getting a police report?"

"Good morning to you, too," she said in an overly cheerful voice. She reached into a bin on the desk and pulled out a form she slid my way. "Just fill this out. There are clipboards and pens on the table over there." She pointed to a small waiting room with two chairs and a coffee table.

I took a seat and balanced the clipboard on my knees as I filled out the form. Once done, I handed it to the woman.

"There's a ten-dollar charge," she said.

"That's fine."

She looked over the form and then started typing. "I know just about everyone in town," she mused. "Don't think I've seen you before."

Would I ever get used to how everybody knew each other's business? Red Bank wasn't the biggest town, but its proximity to New York made it feel more worldly.

I introduced myself. "Jo-Jo McMullen is my aunt."

"Oh dear," she said. "How is Jo-Jo? Her accident sounded just terrible."

"That's why I want the accident report," I told her. "I'm curious how it happened."

"Probably will help with the insurance company, too," she said.

The copy machine sprung to life and spit out the report. I paid the ten dollars with my debit card, and she stapled the document together and handed it to me. "Anything else I can help you with?"

"This will do, thanks."

I thought about asking if Nick was in, but I'd taken up enough of his time.

I didn't want to be a pest. I took the report back to my car, rolled down the windows, and then read the statement.

The accident happened on a warm, sunny day, so the weather wasn't a factor. The diagram showed my aunt's car hitting a tree head-on. The lack of skid marks indicated that she hadn't tried to stop, making Lilly's theory more plausible. I studied the attached pictures. Even though I'd seen the car in person, seeing it smashed into an unyielding oak tree made my heart race. The mild damage to the rear bumper didn't seem like enough to send her into a tree. Why didn't she brake? Had my aunt tried to commit suicide? I couldn't imagine such a thing, but I wondered what other explanation there could be.

The rear-end damage indicated there was another car involved. My eyes shot up to the top of the report. It read: Accident Report—Hit and Run.

Why had no one mentioned this? I scanned the page for more information. K. Moore was listed as the officer who took the report.

I hated to bring Nick into this, but I needed answers. I sent him a quick text message. *U busy?*

Waiting for a reply, I turned back to the accounting of events. No witnesses to the accident. My aunt sat injured in her car until another motorist drove by and called for help. The report said Aunt Jo-Jo was confused and unable to give a telling of events.

I sat back in my seat and blew out a long breath. Something wasn't adding up.

My phone buzzed, and I snatched it off the passenger seat. Nick. *What's up?*

I have some questions about my aunt's accident.

Bubbles indicated he was typing, but then they stopped. I pressed the heels of my hands against my eyes. A headache threatened.

Then the message came through. *I'm in court. Should be finished around 5. How about dinner?*

I almost typed yes. But then I remembered I was meeting Austin at 7. If I had his number, I'd cancel, but I had no way of getting a hold of him.

Sorry, can't do dinner. But I could meet you after court for a drink.

CHAPTER TWENTY-FIVE

More bubbles. *Ok. 6 at the Bistro.*

C U then. I added a smiley face and pressed send. I was about to toss my phone back on the seat when the message I'd transmitted caught my eye. "No, No, No!" Instead of the emoji I'd meant to send, I'd sent a heart.

How the heck was I going to walk that one back? Any justification I gave would seem like an excuse. I decided it would be better to explain my mistake in person.

Chapter Twenty-Six

Back at the hotel, I brought Noah and Maya into the house with me, then changed into a nicer pair of jeans and a flowery blouse, the dressiest things I'd packed from New Jersey. Exchanging my sneakers for ankle boots and swiping on a bit of mascara elevated my look from college student who had rolled out of bed late for class to someone who gave an iota of a damn.

Martha had left for the day. Her note stated that all tasks were complete except for the dogs' final evening walk. Something I could do when I got home after dinner.

My phone rang. The ring tone made me sweat—the theme for the movie *Halloween* that I'd assigned to my mom. I couldn't put her off forever, so I answered.

"Hello, Kim," I said flatly.

"You know I go by Gabriella," she cooed. "How are you, baby?"

"I'm fine, Kim."

She sighed but seemed to choose her battles and moved on. "I went by your apartment, but you weren't home."

"I'm in Orca Cove," I said. I didn't tell her about her sister's accident because I knew Aunt Jo-Jo wouldn't want her rushing out and pretending she cared.

"Oh," she said. "How is my sister?"

"Fine. Look, I've got to be somewhere. What do you want, Kim?" The annoyance in my voice was even too much for me to digest.

But she didn't seem to notice it. In a sweet baby voice that made me gag, she said, "could you spare a few bucks? Just for a few days, weeks, maybe. I'll pay you back."

If I'd kept a tally, I was pretty sure I could buy a new car if she paid me back. Of course, she never did. "How much?"

"Three hundred should cover it," she said.

"And what's it for?"

Her sigh traveled the three thousand miles between us. "Don't you worry about that. You can just route it through the app like you've done before. It's kind of time sensitive."

"I'm not bailing what's his name out of jail again," I said.

"I don't know why you don't like Ben," she said. "You barely know him."

Ah, so it **was** bail money. "My finances are kind of tight right now," I said. "Look, Ma, I have to go." I disconnected the call before she could ask for anything else. In my mind, if Ben was in jail, he belonged there.

I put on a light jacket and gave the dogs a last look. "Behave," I said on my way out the door.

I swear Maya laughed at me.

I walked down the hill to town. My sore heel complained about my footwear choice. I wasn't sure who I'd dressed up for, but bistro and running shoes didn't seem to go together.

Rounding the bend into town, I came upon bustling activity. Leaves had fallen, blanketing the sidewalk in red and yellow. Streetlights illuminated darkening streets, giving the town a snuggly feel.

People spilled out of boutiques as they closed for the night. I nodded at them in greeting as I passed by. I spotted the bistro sign a block away and checked my watch to see if I'd be on time to meet Nick. It was barely six o'clock. My heart fluttered in anticipation. Inwardly, I scolded myself. Lost in thought, I came up short when scuffed boots appeared on the sidewalk in front of me. I almost lost my balance trying not to barrel into the man who wore them.

Face-to-face, I looked into the beady eyes of Ray Boyce.

He crossed his arms and stared up at me. A gentle breeze blew his scent in my face—a mixture of marijuana and cheap cologne. If he wore the perfume to mask the scent of weed, it wasn't working.

"Excuse me." I attempted to step around him. But he moved to the side with me, blocking my exit.

"You called the police." He spat on the ground next to my shoe. "You gonna make me teach you how to mind your own business, or you gonna get with the program?"

I struggled not to react. There were enough people around that I doubted he'd try anything, yet I was unnerved. But I didn't want him to know that.

I stood my ground and looked him in the eye. "I have nothing to say to you."

Ray looked around him. People were staring at us. "I'd watch your back if I were you," he said.

"Is that a threat?" I asked loud enough that I'd have witnesses if needed.

"It's a promise." He puffed out his chest to drive the point home.

A family pushing a stroller came along, and I moved around Ray and fell into step behind them. My heart pounded. Halfway down the block, I dared a glance over my shoulder. Ray no longer stood where I'd left him. I put my back against the brick wall of the bank and took a minute to steady my breathing, searching the street to see where Ray had gone. I had to strain in the near darkness, but eventually I spotted him getting into the driver's seat of a yellow cab before it drove away.

Outside the bistro, people stood in huddles, some of them jostling in place to keep warm as they waited for their table. Nick wasn't among them, so I thought he might be inside already. I squeezed through the crowd and into the restaurant, where I spotted Nick sitting at a booth in the back corner, his back to the wall so he could keep track of what was going on around him. Typical cop move. I walked over and slid into the seat across from him.

"Jersey," he said. "You okay? You're shaking."

I looked at my vibrating hands and lowered them to my lap so he could no longer see them. "Just had a run-in with Ray Boyce."

Nick glanced around the restaurant. "He here?"

"No, outside. He's gone now."

"What did he say?"

"Something about not wanting me talking to police."

Nick leaned back in his chair. "Yet here you are."

I shrugged and attempted a smile. "What can I say? I'm a risk taker."

The waitress appeared. "What can I get you, Hon?"

I looked at the draft beer in front of Nick. "What he's having is fine."

"Sure thing." She moved back to the bar.

"I'll have a talk with Ray," Nick said. "Tell him to stay away from you."

"I appreciate that, but please don't. I'm afraid he'll take out his frustration on Kyleigh. I'll be careful." The waitress returned with my beer, and I took a grateful drink. "Anyway, that's not what I wanted to talk about."

He folded his hands on the table and leaned forward. "I'm listening."

He'd changed out of his uniform and into a long-sleeved gray Henley shirt. He wore it well.

Concentrate, Charlie.

What do you know about my aunt's car accident?"

He tilted his head to the side. "I wasn't on duty that day. Why do you ask?"

"I got the report, and some things don't add up. Who's Officer K. Moore?"

"Karl? He's a reserve officer. Mostly works when we can't cover a shift because we're on vacation, tied up in court, or in training."

"The report listed the accident as a hit and run."

"Really? That's strange. Usually, we share that information with each other so we can work the case. Do you have the report?"

I pulled it out of my bag and handed it to him.

He spent the next several minutes reading the document. I used the time to ease my nerves by almost finishing my beer. I spotted Austin sitting at the bar, talking to a woman in a red dress. I checked my watch. I still had a few minutes before I was supposed to meet him.

Nick slid the report back my way.

"She didn't brake," I said.

Nick drummed his fingers on the table. "Where's her car?"

"Impound lot."

"A mechanical inspection should have been done. I'll check with Karl and see if he got one."

"The social worker at the rehab wonders if my aunt hit the tree on purpose."

Nick pursed his lips. "Jo-Jo? No way. What does your aunt say?"

"She doesn't remember much about the accident."

Nick took a long drink. "Makes sense. The lots closed for the night. I'll talk to my sergeant in the morning to set up an inspection if one hasn't already been done. Nice catch, Jersey."

So, why did I feel so unsettled? I should have looked into the crash sooner, but I'd assumed it was a regular car accident, and I hadn't wanted to force my aunt to regale me with the gory details. They had to be somewhere in her memory, and I wondered if, in time, she could recall more.

I glanced at my watch. It was almost seven. The woman in the red dress was getting up from her stool. She turned and looked our way. It was Alex. Her face brightened when she noticed Nick, but when she saw me, her mood visibly darkened. I wondered if it was because of the conversation with her mother that I witnessed or that I was with Nick. She strode toward the back of the restaurant without Nick noticing her. Austin sat alone, his attention on his phone. I wanted nothing more than to continue my conversation with Nick, but I'd committed to dinner with Austin.

"You hungry, Jersey?" Nick asked. "They have a great pasta dish."

I sighed. "Sorry, I have other plans. Raincheck?"

He nodded. "Of course."

I took a last tug of my beer, shoved the police report back in my purse, and pulled out my wallet. I extracted a ten-dollar bill, but Nick held up his hand to stop me.

"I got this," he said.

"No, it's okay. I like to pay my way."

"You won't let me buy you breakfast or dinner. I was starting to think you don't like me, but then you hearted me, you shameless flirt," he said with a cheeky grin.

Remembering my gaffe made my cheeks burn. "That was in error. I meant to send a smiley face."

Mischief danced in his eyes. "So, you don't like me?"

CHAPTER TWENTY-SIX

Boy, it was getting hot in here. "I....I..."

A shadow drifted over the table. I looked up to see Austin standing there. He was nicely dressed in khakis and a button-down blue shirt. "I didn't see you come in," he said. "You ready for our date?"

My mouth dropped open. "Date?" I wished I'd been upfront with Nick. What a crappy way for him to find out I had dinner plans with Austin.

Nick gave me a look that said, *seriously?* But he stood and shook Austin's hand. "I was going to call you. If you can come to the station in the morning, the M.E. report should be in. We can go over it."

Did Austin know he just had drinks with the coroner? Or, excuse me, medical examiner.

If so, he kept it to himself. "Sounds good. I keep imagining how she died. I hope whatever caused it, she went quickly. I hate to think of her suffering."

"None of us want that," Nick said. He looked from Austin to me. "Enjoy your date."

He walked back to the bar with his wallet out. I was speechless as I watched him settle the tab while Austin took his place at the table.

"This isn't a date," I said. *Now you find the words!*

"We'll see about that. Don't you ever relax?"

I finished my beer. I'd need a few more if that were going to happen.

Austin ordered the pasta dish Nick had talked about. For some reason, it felt like I'd be disrespectful to Nick if I ate it without him, so I ordered a Caesar salad. I was having a hard time concentrating on Austin's velvety voice as he commented on the food and about how he was an actor in his local theater back home. My mind was still on my conversation with Nick, and I wanted to kick myself for how I'd handled it.

"Charlie?" Austin said, jarring me from my thoughts.

I looked up from my plate.

"You're a million miles away, and you're picking at your food. Is there something wrong with the salad?"

"No," I said. "Sorry, just a lot on my mind."

He dropped his fork. "Okay, let's talk about the elephant in the room."

I gave him my complete attention.

Austin leaned back and folded his hands across his chest. "I feel like we got off to a rough start."

"I'm not sure what you're talking about."

"The whole Maya thing. When I grew up, a dog was a dog, and they belonged outside. Of course, in the south, it wasn't as cold at night. Looking back, I realize it's an archaic opinion. Can you forgive a guy who's willing to learn from his mistakes?"

I hadn't expected an apology, and it took the wind out of my sails. But it would take more than his newfound awareness to let me trust him with the care of any dog. Still, long ingrained good manners made me want to make him feel better. "Sorry if I've been judgmental."

He laughed. "Maybe just a little."

I laughed with him. "I have a few flaws myself."

He went back to eating. The mood was lighter, and I felt less like a hostage and more like a dinner companion. Yet something still bothered me about him beyond his leaving Maya outside. The dog and I both had a gut instinct about this guy, and it was hard to ignore.

Apology aside, I wasn't ready to scratch Austin off the suspect list for Lucy's murder. I didn't want to come straight out and ask him about his motive, so I tried for a gentler approach. "Do you have any family who can help you settle the estate?"

Austin shook his head. "I'm afraid not. It's just me. Don't suppose you know any good local realtors? I'll need to put the house on the market."

"Sorry, I don't," I said. "I can ask around, though."

"I'd appreciate that. I don't know anyone in town."

I looked at my watch. It was getting late, and I needed to walk the dogs. Yet I had gotten no real information out of Austin, yet. "Had you seen your aunt recently?"

He shook his head. "Afraid it's been a few years. I feel bad about that now."

"Did you have a falling out?"

"No. Nothing like that. I just know she wasn't happy with me because it had been so long since I'd come to see her. She joked about taking me out of her will."

Joked? I remembered Martha saying Lucy had talked about changing her will and leaving her money to the library. "Yet she was coming to visit you. Do you think that's what she wanted to talk about?"

"I guess we'll never know," he said.

"I don't really know how wills work. Do you have a copy? How do you find out what it says?"

"I'm meeting with her lawyer tomorrow afternoon," he said.

I made a mental note to check in with him tomorrow and learn what the will said. If she was going to change her mind, or if she already had, or was she just blowing smoke and planned on leaving her estate to her nephew all along? If she was going to change her heir and he knew about it, having her die before she could do so would be the perfect motive for murder.

When the waitress came with the check, I once again reached for my wallet. Austin swooped in for the bill before I could get my hands on it. "My treat," he said.

I struggled not to argue. "Thank you."

While we waited for the waitress to return with Austin's change, I said, "I'm sorry about your aunt. Aunt Jo-Jo means the world to me. I don't know what I'd do without her."

Austin's shoulders slumped. "Thanks. I'm dreading the coroner's report tomorrow."

"I'm sure. If you want to talk after, I'll be around the hotel." I was dying to hear the news about what happened to Lucy.

He looked up and smiled. "Thanks, Charlie. I just may take you up on that. I can beg Maya for forgiveness while I'm there."

"I can't speak for her. She's got her own agenda, but it seems like you've learned your lesson: Don't mess with Maya."

He held up his hands. "Message received, loud and clear." The waitress returned. We put on our jackets and left the bistro behind. Outside, the air was brisk, and golden leaves fell like rain. Austin walked me to my street, and then we stood awkwardly, chilled hands stuffed in our pockets. "I can walk you home," he said.

I looked at his car, parked just feet away, and noticed the Georgia plates. "That's okay. It's just up the hill. Thank you for dinner."

"You're welcome," he said, his drawl strong. "I enjoyed your company."

"Good night," I said.

"See you tomorrow."

I started up the hill, unable to ignore that little voice in my head. Austin wasn't so bad tonight. He'd told me he was an actor. Was his demeanor nothing more than a display of his acting skills, or had I misjudged him? I supposed time would tell, but if Lucy had met with foul play, and Austin remained her only heir, he was at the top of my suspect list.

Chapter Twenty-Seven

One thing about living with a "real" dog was that sleeping in was a thing of the past. Maya was an early riser, while Noah could stay in bed all day long. My mom often referred to Noah as a "duman"—part dog, part human. If he were human, he'd have a stash of weed and a love of video games.

I was coming to learn that Maya was one hundred percent dog, and she wasn't having this whole "waste the morning away" thing.

She scratched at the door four times before I relented and got out of bed. Throwing on a pair of sweats and a hoodie, I snapped her leash in place, coaxed Noah out of bed, and took them both for a walk.

After letting each dog do their thing, I brought them to the hotel where Martha was sweeping the floors.

"I thought that was Kyleigh's job," I said.

She took off her glasses, letting them hang from the chain around her neck, and wrinkled her nose.

"Let me guess, she didn't show up."

"That's two days in a row," Martha said. "I told you she wasn't dependable."

"Has she ever missed this many days before?"

Martha scratched her head. "No. But she's been late."

"I'm worried about her," I said. "Her home situation is not the best."

"Knowing the Boyces, I'm sure it's not," Martha said. "And I want to be understanding, but we have a business to run. I can't have clients picking up their dogs and seeing the place a mess."

"I'll walk the dogs," I offered. "I'm meeting Riley for breakfast. Then I'm going to check on Kyleigh. Not only do her aunt and uncle give me a major case of the creeps, but she just found a dead body. That has to weigh heavily on her."

Martha nodded. "How about you? You also found Lucy."

"Trying not to think about that," I said.

Truth was, my thoughts were a jumbled mess. Not only was I reeling from finding a drowned woman, but I had questions about my aunt's accident and was fighting off my growing feelings for Nick that were getting harder to deny—unless having dinner with Austin ruined that. Add to that my suspicions about the Boyces and Austin and there was a lot to think about.

The only upside was that those thoughts made it easier to ignore my personal problems. A silver lining, I supposed.

After walking the dogs, avoiding the place where we'd found Lucy's body, I got in the Crosstrek and started toward town. Riley was waiting outside the coffee shop. She wore scrubs that were raining cats and dogs, holding umbrellas. Vet techs had the cutest uniforms. I parked and joined her in line.

"Morning," she said. "Thanks for meeting me."

"Happy to," I said. "I've often wondered about you over the years. I should have known you'd end up working with animals. Our love of dogs was something we bonded over."

She laughed. "Yeah, it was a no-brainer. I always thought you'd do something ballsy, like be a cop."

She really knew me. But I didn't want to go into how that had almost happened. "Still trying to find my way."

We both ordered coffee and then settled at a table in the corner. "Its weird being back here," I said. "I think I recognize someone, but then I'm not sure."

"Well," she said after taking a sip. "That makes sense. You were what, fourteen, the last time you were here for any length of time?"

"That sounds about right." Although I'd visited my aunt since, it wasn't all that often. My mom had a few years where she'd gotten her act together, and then I was eighteen and on my own. So, I'd only come for a few days here and there, not the few months' breaks I had from Kim before that.

Riley filled me in on her life. She was engaged and living with her fiancé, Matt. She asked if I remembered him. I racked my brain. "Wait, was he that kid who always had his nose in a book?" I remembered the other kids picking on him.

Riley nodded. "Yeah, and he still does. But he's more confident now that he has returned from college. He works at the local paper."

"Well, I'm happy for you."

"Thanks," she said. "I saw you talking to Nick the other day. Looked like you two were hitting it off."

Something deep inside me tingled at the mention of his name. "He's working on Lucy Masanova's case. I found her body, so it's strictly work-related."

"I heard you found her. How horrible."

We fell quiet for a moment, and I tried not to let the memory of finding Lucy come to the front of my mind.

"Anyway," she said. "Do you remember Nick from our childhood?"

"No."

"I'm not surprised. He's a few years older than us. We really didn't have much interaction. When I was a freshman, he was a senior. I remember thinking he was so cute."

"That would have been about the time I stopped coming here so much." I leaned forward and lowered my voice so no one at the surrounding tables would hear. "What's the deal with him and Alex? Are they a couple?"

Riley leaned forward as well. When she spoke, there was a twinkle in her eye. "On and off. You are interested, aren't you?"

I sat back and gave a tight smile. "Just wondering. I'm leaving in a few weeks, not something I could pursue even if I wanted to."

Riley laughed. "Of course you can. You should always follow your heart."

For a moment, that sounded like a good idea. But so far, my heart had led me to nothing but dead ends. I was sure this time would be the same.

Riley and I parted ways with plans to get together again soon.

Next on my to-do list was checking in on Kyleigh. I hoped I could remember how to get to the Boyces' property. I thought about bringing Maya along for protection, but I didn't want to subject her to further abuse if Ray was around. Both dogs were safer at home.

I wasn't completely crazy, and I had somewhat of a plan. My cell was at the ready in case Ray or Mary were there and unhappy to see me again. I also didn't intend to proceed if Ray's truck was parked out front.

Turned out, I drove by the property twice, circling back after I realized I must have gone too far and missed the turnoff. Ray probably purposely chose the location so no one could find them.

It was about 10 a.m. by the time I found the one-lane driveway. It felt like the forest was swallowing me as I drove down the narrow path between the trees. Memories of my previous encounters with Ray made my pulse quicken. Thick woods concealed the trailer until I came to a clearing, and it was right in front of me. There was no way to camouflage my arrival. My nerves were frazzled, but I tried not to think about what could go wrong. I was worried Kyleigh might be in danger. I could have called the police for a welfare check, but I had the feeling I'd used up Nick's last bit of patience with me when he thought I'd chosen a date with Austin over spending time with him.

When I reached the trailer, I was relieved to find that Ray's truck was nowhere in sight. It dawned on me that Mary could be home even if Ray was gone. Although there was no love lost between us, I felt I could handle whatever she threw my way.

I backed my car up to the trailer, allowing myself a path for a quick getaway, then pocketed my cell phone and walked to the front door.

The slant of the front stoop had me off balance. I listened before knocking, hoping for a clue of what I was about to walk into.

The TV was on low, and I could hear Cesar Millan's voice as he tried to calm an out-of-control dog. I'd seen the show enough times to realize he was training the owners more than the dogs. I'd bet Maya would test his skills in a way he hadn't seen before. There were no other sounds besides the TV.

I held my breath and lightly rapped on the door. When no signs of life occurred, I knocked again.

A moment later, there was a rustling from inside, and the door popped open. Mary Boyce did not look happy to see me. "What do you want?" she barked, a cigarette dancing between her lips.

She blew a breath into my face, and an intense fog of smoke choked me. I could barely make out Kyleigh sitting on a chair a few feet away through the haze.

After giving me the stink eye, a gravelly coughing fit overcame Mary. She doubled over for a moment, and I made eye contact with Kyleigh. I tilted my head to the side. "Talk to you a minute?"

Kyleigh froze, then slowly got to her feet. Mary straightened and went to the kitchenette, where she turned on the tap and filled a glass with water. The liquid seemed to quell her cough, and she immediately reached for a pack of cigarettes and lit another. I noticed the large kitchen knife on the counter and hoped my sore foot wouldn't hinder a quick getaway if needed.

As Kyleigh crossed the room toward me, on a cluttered table I spied a small flat emerald green box about the size of an egg carton. Next to that, a handgun.

Between the gun and the knife, I knew that if Mary wanted to chase me off her property, she could easily do so. But she seemed more interested in puffing her way to dependence on an oxygen tank than getting rid of me.

Kyleigh stepped outside and pulled the door shut behind her. Wrapping her arms around herself to shut out the cold, she walked with me to my car. "Can we talk with the heat on?" she asked.

"Sure thing." I got inside and started the engine, pointing the heating vent toward Kyleigh as she settled into the passenger's seat.

"You're shivering," I said.

"My aunt's stingy with the heat in the trailer." She slouched in her seat. "What are you doing here?"

I checked the rearview mirror, making sure Mary hadn't changed her mind and decided to run me off the property, but the door to the trailer remained closed. "You up for a ride?"

Kyleigh shrugged. I took that as a "yes" and started down the driveway. I prayed Ray wouldn't come home and box me in, as only one car could fit down the bumpy road. But we made it to the main road without a problem.

As we headed toward town, I relaxed a little. But I knew from experience that Ray could pop up anywhere. And if he found me with Kyleigh, he wouldn't be happy.

Chapter Twenty-Eight

We headed through town to a drive-up coffee stand the size of a toolshed and shaped like a coffee mug. I pulled up behind one other vehicle. "My treat," I said. "What would you like?"

Kyleigh played with the tear at the knee of her jeans. "Chai tea."

"Anything to eat?"

"I wouldn't mind a snickerdoodle cookie."

When it was our turn, I pulled up to the window. A bubbly teenager appeared on the other side. "What will it be?" she asked in a sing-song voice.

Kyleigh and the girl exchanged a knowing glance, and Kyleigh slouched in her seat like she wanted to disappear. I rattled off our order and waited while the super cute barista prepared our drinks. Once I nestled our teas in the center console cup holders, and we each had a cookie in our lap, I pulled ahead and parked where we had a view of the ocean.

"You know the barista?" I asked.

"She's in my class," Kyleigh said, breaking off a piece of cookie and holding it before her like a prize. "Don't let her fake smile fool you. She's mean."

I felt for Kyleigh. The popular kids always looked down on me in high school because we moved so much, and my mom was always a bit of a kook. I wanted to tell Kyleigh it would get better, but I knew from experience that my sixteen-year-old self wouldn't have believed it if someone were to offer that advice, so I kept quiet.

We ate our cookies in silence while our teas cooled. Once we both had a few sips, I chanced conversation. "How you holding up?"

"Fine. Why wouldn't I be?"

"You discovered a dead body."

She gave me a sideways glance. "So did you."

I nodded. "And I'm a little freaked out. Thought we could talk about it."

She took another drink, then dared a look at me. "We don't even know what happened yet."

Austin was getting the news at this very moment, and I was eager to hear the details. "Not yet, but I think we'll know soon."

Kyleigh held her warm cup between her hands. "She was old. Probably just fell over and died." Although her words were cold, I noticed a single tear streak down her cheek before she wiped it away. I wanted to reach out and comfort her, but I didn't know how. So, we just sat there watching the waves lap at the shore.

"I was told that you lived with Lucy for a while."

Kyleigh kept her gaze straight ahead. "It was a long time ago. I don't remember it well."

"Was she nice?"

The girl shrugged. "I guess. My aunt said she wasn't out for my best interests. Stuck her nose where it didn't belong. After my mom left, they didn't let me talk to her; I remember that."

"Tell me about your aunt and uncle," I said. "How long have you lived with them?"

Kyleigh fidgeted in her seat, and I knew I'd hit a nerve. I racked my brain for a way to backtrack, but then she tucked her hair behind her ears and pursed her lips.

"I was eight."

I knew I was walking a tightrope. Push too hard, and this conversation was going to fall to its death. But I really wanted to know her situation. "Guessing there are problems," I tried.

She snorted. "Doesn't matter. Nothing I can do about it."

"Still…" I let the rest hang in the air.

Kyleigh turned her head to look out the window, and I thought I'd lost her, but then she spoke in almost a whisper. "My mom was alright. We didn't have much money, and she worked two jobs to put food on the table. But she loved me. She always read to me at night and stayed with me until I fell asleep."

"She was a good mom."

Kyleigh nodded. "Until…"

"She left," I said bluntly.

"Yeah. She didn't even say goodbye."

I let that settle in. "I'm sorry."

She shrugged and wiped her nose with the back of her hand. "It's okay."

"No," I said. "It's not. Any idea where she went?"

Kyleigh let out a sigh that was way too heavy for someone so young. The weight of the world was on her shoulders; no wonder she always slumped them. I wished there was a way I could take her pain away. Make it mine instead.

"No," she said, finally. "My aunt said she was an addict."

"Do you believe that?"

She looked me dead in the eye. "No. But what can I do about it?"

"I don't know," I said honestly. I supposed we could look into things, but I didn't know where to start, and I was fairly certain the Boyces wouldn't want me digging into their business. And I reminded myself I wasn't here for long. I shouldn't offer the poor girl any hope if I would not be here to see things through.

We drove back to the trailer in silence. I said an internal thank you that Roy's truck was still not there when we parked out front.

Kyleigh unbuckled her seatbelt, then put her hand on the door. She sat still for a minute, then looked back over her shoulder at me. "Can you come in? There's something I want to show you."

I bit the inside of my cheek. "I don't think your aunt would like that."

"She should be gone," Kyleigh said. "She's working this afternoon."

"And your uncle?"

"Same thing."

With a deep breath, I got out of the car and followed Kyleigh to the door. As soon as she opened it, stale smoke wafted out to greet us, and I found it hard to breathe. We stepped inside, and I took in our surroundings. The space felt cramped and outdated. The top of my head skimmed the ceiling, and claustrophobia threatened an incoming panic attack. High places and small spaces gave me the Willys.

Built-in furniture was wood-paneled seventies, olive green fabric torn and fraying. Dirty dishes overflowed in the kitchen sink, and cereal boxes, small appliances, and junk food wrappers cramped the Formica counters. I tried not to think about what must have been crawling amongst the trash and absently scratched imaginary bugs off my arms. Okay, I wasn't fond of creepy, crawly things either. I looked back to the place where I'd seen the handgun, but it was gone. I figured Mary had taken it with her and was packing. I assumed Ray was, too.

The scary knife, however, was still there, as was the green box.

Could this be the box my aunt was so intent on locating? When Kyleigh walked toward the back of the trailer, I slipped my phone out of my pocket and quickly snapped a photo of the box while her back was toward me.

She came back to the main living area and held out a photo. The rolled-up corners and wrinkled image showed it had been well-viewed. In it, a young woman stood next to a little girl. "My mom," she offered as an explanation.

"She's very pretty," I said. "Just like you." But there was no resemblance. Her mom was blonde and tall, and her features were much more severe than Kyleigh's.

Kyleigh looked at the floor. Her shoulders sagged. I wondered if she'd ever received a compliment before. Having met her aunt and uncle, I doubted it.

"Is Ray her brother?"

"Half-brother. They have different moms."

"Do you have any other family?"

She gave a sarcastic laugh. "If I did, do you think I'd live in this dump?"

Good point. I decided this was probably the best moment I'd get to push the issue. She was opening up to me and I couldn't let the opportunity pass. "You know," I said, "if he hits you, you can report it. He shouldn't be able to get away with that."

She rolled her eyes. "Only other place for me is foster care. Do you know how much fun that is?"

"No. But I can imagine." Aunt Jo-Jo kept me out of foster care, but without her, I surely would have experienced that life. My problems paled compared to Kyleigh's, and I felt guilty for having wallowed in them earlier.

I could see a veil of protection dropping over Kyleigh, as if she'd shared too much. Who was I to understand her circumstances?

"If my aunt hadn't been around to rescue me, I would have been in foster care myself," I said.

She looked up at me, interested.

"My mom is a bit of a disaster."

"Really?"

"I was lucky to have an aunt who believed in me. Don't you have anyone?"

Kyleigh hung her head.

"What's your number?" I asked, taking out my phone.

She gave it to me, and I added her to my contact list, then sent her a message. "Now you have my number. I won't be in town much longer, but even from New Jersey, I can be an ear. Call or text me anytime. We could have a code word. Even if you can't say much, just text me the code word and I'll do what I can to help."

Kyleigh smiled at this. "How about pickle?"

I laughed. "Like I'm in a pickle? I like it."

She looked up at me through thick lashes. "Thanks."

"No problem. I—" The sound of a car approaching interrupted my thoughts. I moved to the window and looked outside. My heart was in my throat as I prepared myself for yet another run in with Ray Boyce. But it was an unremarkable white sedan I didn't recognize.

I glanced at Kyleigh, who looked over my shoulder out the window. "Do you know her?"

Kyleigh sighed. "It's a social worker. I can spot one a mile away."

I remembered Nick saying he'd made a referral to Child Protective Services after Kyleigh showed up with a black eye. Kyleigh opened the door before the woman could knock. She'd obviously been through this before.

The woman introduced herself, and she was, in fact, a social worker with the Department of Social and Health Services. She quickly made it clear that she didn't want me there.

"Let me know if you need any pickles," I said with a wink on my way out the door.

Back at the hotel, I parked behind Martha's Cherokee. Austin was waiting in the parking lot, leaning against his car.

"You said I could come by," he said.

I tilted my head toward the house. "Come inside."

He followed me to the house. Noah and Maya were excited to see me—Austin, not so much. Maya's tail rose like a flag.

Austin tried to approach her, but she snarled at him.

"Maybe give her space," I said. "She may need some time."

Austin held up his hands in surrender. "No problem."

I got us each a glass of water, and we settled in the living room chairs across from each other. "So," I began, "what did the M.E. have to say? I don't mean to be nosy, but I feel invested in the case." As soon as the words were out of my mouth, I felt horrible for referring to his aunt's death as a "case." Of course, it was more to him than that.

Thankfully, Austin didn't seem put off by my remark. He stroked his chin and looked up at the ceiling. "Cause of death was strangulation. Who would do that to a sweet old lady?"

Sweet wasn't a word I'd heard used to describe Lucy Masanova, but who knew what his relationship with her was. "I'm sorry. That must be hard news to digest."

He nodded and let out a long breath.

"Do they have any leads?"

"Officer Sabato said there were some things they knew that they'd kept from the public. He asked me about a necklace."

I leaned forward. "What about a necklace?"

Austin took a drink. "Showed me a photo. Asked me if I'd seen it before."

"And?"

"I didn't recognize it."

I tried not to react. But it was only a matter of time before someone traced it back to my aunt. I had to figure out who the Number One Suspect was before their attention turned to her.

He fidgeted in his seat and drummed his fingers on the tabletop. "I don't even know where to start with planning a funeral."

"Is there even a mortuary in town?" I asked.

"On the other side of the bridge. I have an appointment this afternoon. I'd invite you to come along, as I could use someone with a clear head. But I understand it's probably not the way you'd like to spend your day." He gave me sad puppy-dog eyes.

I bit my lip. Unfortunately, I had some experience in the matter when my stepfather, who was a step up from Ben, died a few years ago, and my mother was useless. It was the last thing I wanted to do, but Austin looked lost, and I figured I might learn more details about Lucy's death and their relationship. I couldn't say no. Even if it meant crossing that damn bridge again.

I checked my watch. It was almost eleven. "I need to swing by and see my aunt. But I can meet you afterwards."

Austin smiled. "Thank you."

I watched him walk back to his car, then I started toward mine.

"Charlie," he called after me.

I turned back.

"I can't tell you how much this means to me."

I gave a tight smile and got back in my car. Hopefully, I wouldn't regret it.

Chapter Twenty-Nine

At the rehab center, I found Aunt Jo-Jo fresh from a shower, her hair still damp. For the first time since I'd been in town, she wore lipstick, making her look lively, more like her old self. She was in the hallway when I found her, making her way to the dining room for lunch. I felt guilty for not bringing her something good to eat, but Austin had sidetracked me. I fell into step beside her wheelchair, and she smiled up at me.

"I met with the social worker this morning," she said. "Just a few more days in this place."

"That's great news," I said. "It will be nice to have you home."

The cafeteria was bustling with activity. Wheelchairs were parked at tables around which an assortment of patients of all ages gathered. Chatter filled the space as they recounted the accidents or surgeries that led them to their current predicament.

A group of women in my aunt's age category sat at a table by the window. One waved my aunt over when she saw us enter the room. "Those are my peeps," Aunt Jo-Jo said. "Come sit with us. I'll introduce you."

I pulled up a chair and wedged it between my aunt's wheelchair and a woman who introduced herself as Bertie. "So, you're the famous Charlie Jo-Jo always talks about."

"That would be me."

"I remember you when you were knee high to a grasshopper," another one said. "My, you've grown into a stunning woman!"

I felt myself blush and looked at my lap, but I stopped myself from telling her she was wrong. One thing I'd read in a self-help book was learning to take a compliment. It was tough, but I was getting better at it.

The waiter brought over trays of roast beef sandwiches and a colorless soup. The women rolled their eyes at each other as they fingered their food, declaring that they'd seen more meat on a lemon tree. When the waiter asked if I wanted a plate, I politely declined.

"Coward," my aunt said, elbowing me in the ribs.

After listening to a meek, petite woman named Marjorie talk about how her daughters would rather put her in a home than let her recuperate with one of them, the talk turned to Lucy Masanova.

"She used to walk that beach every day," Bertie said. "She probably had a heart attack. I wonder how long she lay there before someone found her."

I fought the urge to share what Austin had told me. It wasn't my place. If it was just Jo-Jo and me, I would have spilled the beans, but I wasn't about to stoke the fires of the town gossips.

"Weren't you the one who found her?" the woman across from me asked, leaning forward in her seat, holding her sandwich like a dead fish.

I nodded.

"Well, what did you see?" Bertie urged.

"Not much," I said.

"You know," Marjorie chimed in. "I saw her in the library a few days before you found her. She was in a tizzy."

Bertie, who didn't seem to mind the food, took a big bite of her sandwich and wiped her mouth on her napkin. "Well, I didn't want to say anything, but she was at City Hall a few days before she disappeared. She asked for some records."

"What kind of records?" Marjorie asked.

"I don't know. I think she knew I was listening. She gave me the stink eye before lowering her voice so I couldn't hear."

"That sounds like Lucy," another woman said. "She didn't like people in her business."

"I would ask Stu," Marjorie said.

I looked at my aunt. It wasn't like her to be so quiet. But she just sat there staring at her plate. I wondered if Lucy's death had hit her harder than expected.

"Who's Stu?" I asked.

"The clerk at City Hall," Bertie said.

My aunt reached over and squeezed my arm. "Let's go back to my room. I need to lie down."

"Are you feeling okay?" Even I could hear the panic in my voice.

"Just tired," she said.

I stood and took control of her wheelchair. After bidding goodbye to the ladies, I wheeled Aunt Jo-Jo back to her room.

Once we got there, she sat up straighter. "Close the door," she said.

I shut it and offered her my hand. "Want me to help you into bed?"

She swatted my hand away. "Don't be silly. It's only noon."

"But you said–"

"Never mind that. Did you find the green box?"

I scratched my head. "Funny you should ask." Slipping my phone out of my pocket, I pulled up the photo I'd taken inside the Boyces' trailer and showed it to her.

My aunt patted her chest. "So, you have it," she said with a breath of relief.

"No. I took this at Kyleigh's trailer. I went over to check on her, and I saw it on the table."

"How the heck did they get it?"

I shrugged. "You said it was in your car. Your car was towed to a lot where Mary Boyce works. Maybe she took it."

My aunt tapped her good foot. "You need to get me that box."

I plopped down on the chair across from her. "You're asking me to commit a felony. I think it's time you tell me what's inside that box that you're so desperate to have."

She gave me a wide-eyed stare, and her mouth fell open. "It's not a felony if they stole it in the first place."

I slumped in my chair. "What's inside?"

"I'm not exactly sure, but I know it was proof of something big. Lucy said she had information that was going to shake up the town."

"Did you tell the police?"

"I promised Lucy I wouldn't tell anyone."

I crossed my arms. "Lucy is dead. Someone murdered her. I don't think you need to keep any secrets at this point."

Her eyes got even bigger. "Murdered? How do you know?"

I told her about my conversation with Austin.

"Strangled? Who would do such a thing?" She patted her hand over her heart.

"I don't know. But I have something to share with you that's delicate."

"Let me have it," my aunt said.

"Your pendant, the one I made for you, the one you never took off…" My aunt's hand shot up to her neck, and she felt for the necklace that wasn't there. "I saw it in Lucy's palm when Kyleigh and I found the body."

"That can't be."

"Do you have any idea how it got there?"

She shook her head.

"I haven't said anything to the police," I said. "I don't think they've figured out that the necklace belongs to you yet, but they will. Someone is bound to recognize it."

Her eyes grew wide. "Do you think they'll suspect me?"

I sighed. "I don't know. Hopefully, you were already at the hospital when she was murdered. Then you'll have an alibi." I thought about the shoe hidden in the hotel, but I felt I'd upset her enough.

"So, you don't know when the murder occurred?"

"No, but it's probably part of the M.E. report. I'll try to find out from Nick or Austin. Meanwhile, I'm trying to figure out who the killer was. A few people come to mind."

She leaned forward. "Who?"

"Something is going on with Ray and Mary Boyce. They don't want me nosing around. And they have the green box.

"Then there's Austin. As far as I know, he's the only heir. Did she tell you why she was going to see him?"

"Something about her will. But she didn't share more than that. Lucy is, I mean was, a very private person."

"Well, something is off with him. I don't trust the guy."

"I need you to get that box," Aunt Jo-Jo said. "I know it has something to do with what happened to Lucy. It's locked, and she didn't give me the key. It might be at Lucy's house. Maybe it's time to talk to Nick. He's reasonable."

"But he's a cop," I said. "And so far, everything points to you as a suspect."

"Everything?" Her voice squeaked. "You mean besides my necklace?"

"Clara saw you and Lucy arguing. And according to your planner, you've been meeting with her."

"I assure you," my aunt said. "Those things are innocent."

"I believe you," I said. "But the cops might not see it that way. Not with your necklace lying in her dead hand."

My aunt blew out a long breath. "We need that box."

"I wonder if the records she got at City Hall have anything to do with it. Like they were in the box. What's this Stu guy like? Will he talk to me?"

Aunt Jo-Jo rolled her eyes. "He'll talk to anyone with boobs."

I looked down at my chest and immediately felt self-conscious. I would need a better bra.

Chapter Thirty

City Hall sat across from the town square. In the green space, people occupied benches, soaking up a bit of sunshine before the forecasted rain would fall in the afternoon. I hoped to get a walk-in with Noah and Maya before the weather turned. But first, I wanted to talk to Stu and see if he would tell me what document Lucy Masanova had been after shortly before her murder.

The door to the small brick building was ridiculously heavy. I had to shove it with my shoulder to get it to budge.

An older man stood behind the counter, flipping the page of a newspaper. He glanced up at me, looking over half-moon glasses, eyes narrowing as I let the monstrosity of a door bang shut behind me.

The whoosh of air from the slamming door caused the newspaper to billow and dance across the counter. The man swatted it down with both hands, irritation clear on his face.

I wasn't off to a good start. I would need more than boobs to win him over. "Sorry about that," I said. "I'm looking for Stu."

"Well, you found him."

"Hi." I plastered a smile on my face, hoping he would smile back, but he looked as grumpy as a drunk cut off at the bar. "I'm Charlie Calderbank."

"And?" he said, folding the newspaper and tossing it on the desk behind him.

"I'm Jo-Jo McMullen's niece." I hoped that would earn me a few points as it usually did in this town.

But he didn't seem to soften. "And?"

"I understand Lucy Masanova was here a few days ago."

An eyebrow shot up, but he didn't respond.

Time to call out the big guns. Well, guns at least. I unzipped my hoodie, hoping to confirm that I was a girl and to remind him he was nice to girls. But he didn't seem impressed.

"I was wondering if you could tell me why she was here."

"And why would I tell you that?"

I swallowed hard. I needed to work on my charm. Until I sharpened those skills, honesty was all I had. "I'm trying to piece some things together. I think whatever document Lucy was after might explain some things."

Stu shook his head. "Sorry, dear. That's privileged information."

"But documents are public record, right?"

Stu crossed his arms. "They are, but my private conversations with the public and their requests are not." The phone rang on the desk behind him, and he turned his back to me to take the call.

I sighed and walked in circles in the small lobby while I waited. A table against the wall held a jar of those minuscule pencils government buildings always had and a pad of paper. I picked up the pad and studied it. It was a request form with a menu of documents one could request. It listed marriage licenses, death certificates, and birth certificates. I tore a page off, folded it, and placed it in my bag.

When Stu hung up the phone, I turned back to him. "But if the police ask, you'd share that information?"

Stu stared back at me. "Of course," he said. "If it was part of a police investigation, I would talk to them."

I'd pass the information on to Nick. Boobs or no boobs, there was no way Stu was going to talk to me. "Thank you for your time," I said. Not that I'd gotten anywhere.

I stepped back into the square. In the few minutes I'd been inside, the sky had clouded over, and a whopper of a raindrop smacked the top of my head. I zipped up my hoodie and jogged to my car.

Chapter Thirty-One

I passed the time between my two o'clock trip to the mortuary with Austin and my miserable attempt at sleuthing by helping Martha at the hotel. I thought about moving the shoe, but I figured it was as safe where it was as it would be anywhere. Walking the dogs under the protection of a large umbrella took up much of the time. Noah was not fond of the rain, and he stayed inside, curled up on a chair while Martha inventoried the supplies. Kyleigh hadn't shown for work. It didn't surprise me. That kid had a lot on her plate, and her family wasn't exactly subtle that they didn't want her hanging out with the likes of me.

I hated to leave Kyleigh in an abusive situation. If they were involved in Lucy's murder, solving the case to protect her was even more critical. Maybe it was my paranoia, but it seemed like Nick had pulled back since my dinner with Austin, and I feared any information he would have shared with me would now be impossible to get.

For now, I filed my suspicions about the Boyces in the back of my mind and focused on the suspect in front of me. Putting the last dog back in her room, I grabbed two bottles of water and walked out to Austin, who waited behind the wheel of his Mustang.

He had his phone to his ear and gave me a nod in greeting as I settled into the seat beside him.

"I told you not to worry," he said. "I got it covered." Disconnecting the call, he dropped his phone in his shirt pocket. He accepted the bottle of water I held out for him. "Appreciate you coming along. I've never done this before."

I buckled my seatbelt as Austin maneuvered his car out of the parking lot. "It's overwhelming," I said. "But the folks at the mortuary should talk us through the process. It's what they do."

"Still," he said. "I'm grateful for the company."

I cradled my water bottle between my palms. Going with him was my good deed for the day. He didn't need to know that I had an ulterior motive. And he didn't need to know that the most stressful part of this for me would be crossing that darn bridge. I was determined to keep it together this time.

I turned my head toward the window so Austin wouldn't see me close my eyes as we drove over the bridge. I blocked out his rambling about all the things he had to do and imagined Nick's soothing voice in my head urging me to take deep breaths.

Opening one eye, I saw that we'd made it across the water. I relaxed in my seat and gave Austin my attention. "I'm sorry. What were you saying?"

"I was saying this is a close-knit town. I feel like everyone is watching me like I'm some exotic species. A foreigner."

I laughed. "At least you're not from New Jersey."

"There's that," he said, laughing. "Why does Jersey get such a bad rap?"

Him saying Jersey made my heart tug for Nick, and the way he'd playfully made that my nickname. I didn't like Austin using it. It was like Nick had laid claim on the word. I flashed back to the hurt on Nick's face when he'd realized I couldn't do dinner with him because I had plans with Austin. Maybe it was for the best—I had no business developing feelings for anyone, at least not in Orca Cove. Problem was, I was having a hard time convincing my heart of what was clear in my head.

Back to Austin's question. "Because people only know what's around the airport. They don't realize it's called the Garden State for a reason."

"That's probably true," he said. "Never been there. Maybe someday you could show me around."

Whoa, cowboy, slow down. Not gonna happen. Not only was I intent on keeping Austin at arm's length, but as the days wore on, my home state was feeling like a distant memory. I reminded myself that I'd soon be back there and picking up the pieces of my life.

"Can I ask you a question about your aunt?"

He glanced at me and then concentrated on the road. "Fire away."

"Did they tell you when she was killed?"

He nodded. "Wednesday."

I swallowed. My aunt's accident occurred on Thursday. Being in the hospital would not be an alibi. And Austin wasn't even in town yet. From what Nick told me, he came here after I had reported Lucy missing, days after her death.

Austin pulled into the mortuary parking lot, an old Victorian House that had been converted into a business. I knew that years ago, people moved out of downtown and flocked to the suburbs and abandoned these character-filled homes as they did in most cities across the country. Many of the old homes had become law offices, medical centers or bed and breakfasts. I longed for a time I didn't even know. My aunt always told me I was an old soul.

Austin put the Mustang in park and turned to look at me. "Here goes it."

I braced myself and got out of the car. The rain had slowed to a drizzle. We ran to the front door, jumping over puddles. At the door, I lowered my hood and shook the water off my shoulders, then ducked under Austin's arm as he held the door for me.

Inside, I dried my hands on my jeans, hanging back while the mortician and Austin exchanged pleasantries. "I'm so sorry for your loss," the doughy man said, sliding his glasses up his nose.

Austin nodded, then looked to the floor.

The man stepped forward and held out his hand to me. "I'm Sergio," he said. "It's nice of you to accompany Mr. Masanova."

His handshake was firmer than I liked, given my arthritis, but I powered through it. "Charlie," I said.

He led us into an office where two leather chairs faced a desk. Sergio settled on the other side and folded his hands on a Kelly-green blotter. His desk was immaculate, as was the rest of the room. My gut tightened as my thoughts returned to the time three years ago when we planned my stepfather's funeral. My memories were hazy, but they threatened to make an appearance like a dream you can't fully remember. The feeling is there, but you can't quite recall the event. Perhaps it was because my mother's dramatic wailing had drowned out everything the funeral director had said.

I cleared my throat. Both men looked at me. I waved them away. "I'm sorry, go on."

"As I was saying," Sergio said, pushing a packet toward Austin. "This is our price list. Do you know what you want for your aunt?"

Austin glanced at the list and went white. "Ah, nothing fancy," he said. "My aunt was very humble, laid back. She wouldn't want anything grand. Just the basics, please."

Sergio nodded. His demeanor instantly changed. He wouldn't cash in on a family's grief this time. I was glad Austin made it clear from the start, and I wouldn't have to step in. I hated to see people taken advantage of.

Sergio reviewed the basics—pine coffin, minimal flowers, the in-house minister to say a few words. "How many people can we expect?"

Austin shrugged and looked at me.

"Orca Cove is a tight community," I said. "I imagine a lot of folks would want to pay their respects."

From what I could tell, Lucy didn't have an abundance of friends, but everyone knew her, and people usually forgave one's misgivings once they passed. I was pretty sure my aunt and Martha and the gang at the rehab would attend if they could.

Sergio nodded and moved along. "I'll need a deposit to get the ball rolling."

Austin reached into his wallet, removed a credit card, and placed it on the desk. Sergio picked it up and handed it to a secretary who had appeared from out of nowhere. She took it and left the room.

"While I work on things here," Sergio said. "If you could bring me an outfit for your aunt to be buried in, that would be a huge help." He then suggested he would set up a table where we could place photos to document her life and asked if there were any bible verses Lucy was fond of that he could incorporate into the ceremony. Austin looked lost, and I wanted to rescue him. "I can help," I said. "Maybe pick a dress from her closet."

Austin gave a tight smile. "Thank you. I don't know the first thing about choosing a dress to be buried in."

Neither did I, but I was sure I'd figure it out.

We stood to leave when the secretary came back in and handed Austin's credit card back to him. "I'm sorry," she said, wringing her hands. "But your card was declined."

Austin's mouth dropped open. "That can't be." He offered it back to her. "Run it again."

"I did," she said. "Three times."

"Do you have another form of payment?" Sergio asked.

Austin opened his wallet and flipped through the cards inside. From my seat next to him, I could see what looked like other credit cards in the stack, but Austin closed his wallet without taking one out. "Sorry, I don't have one with me. Can I get back to you on that?"

Sergio nodded. "Of course. We will need payment within the next day or two."

Austin nodded and pocketed his wallet as he stood. "I understand."

I followed him out the door. If he had a tail, it would have been between his legs, for sure.

We drove through town in silence. Austin reached across my lap, opened the glove box and grabbed a CD. Otherwise, papers and insurance cards filled the box. Not being a fan of country music, I tried to keep an open mind, but my thoughts drifted, and the music became background noise. It seemed apparent that Austin was broke. His credit card was maxed, and I was guessing the other cards in his wallet were also out of credit. An inheritance from his aunt would surely solve that problem.

My radar cranked up a notch. I didn't trust him.

As we rolled past a nice hotel, I spotted a man and woman embrace in front of a highly polished black BMW. The woman had a super short skirt on, which didn't fit given the crazy weather and the laid-back atmosphere of the town. Most people wore sweats or jeans. She looked trashy with bleach blonde hair that hung to her waist and an overly made-up face. When she gave the man a kiss and pulled back, I clearly saw the face of Ray Boyce.

I sat up in my seat and craned my neck to keep them in my sight. But Austin drove on.

Had I imagined it?

"Can you turn around?" I asked. "I think I saw someone I know."

Austin glanced over at me and turned down the volume on the radio. "Sure."

He turned at the next intersection and drove about two hundred feet to a bank parking lot where he turned around. But by the time we got back to the hotel parking lot, the BMW was gone.

"Never mind," I said. "I guess I was mistaken."

But I knew what I saw—that was Ray. And the woman in his arms was not his wife.

We arrived back at Lucy's house as the sun skimmed the tree line. My stomach growled, and I tried to remember the last time I'd eaten. A well-timed cough covered up the sound, as it didn't seem right to be concerned about such things at a time like this. And I didn't want him to suggest we go out to dinner again, not that he could pay for it.

Austin had been silent on the drive home, and tension was thick in the air. He tossed his jacket on the sofa. "I could use a drink. You like whiskey?"

I cringed. "Sorry, I can't handle the hard stuff. I'll take some water, though."

He laughed. "Guess I'll drink alone." He moved into the kitchen and returned with a bottle of water. He handed it to me and then went to a cabinet in the dining room and retrieved a bottle of whiskey. Pouring himself a glass, he leaned against the dining room table and took a long drink. "I appreciate you coming today," he said.

I took a sip of water. "Not a problem."

I walked over to the dining room table. Someone had picked up the mail from the floor and piled it haphazardly in the middle of the table.

"She was a hoarder," Austin said, watching me. "Not going to be fun to purge everything."

I nodded and resisted the urge to offer to help. I was here for my aunt, not some new guy I'd met.

"Mind if I go upstairs and have a look at her dresses?" I asked. "Hopefully, I can find something appropriate for the burial."

Austin held his glass up toward the stairs. "Have at it."

I took the steps to the second floor and the bedroom I remembered from the first time I'd been in the house. The suitcase was still on the bed. Half-packed or unpacked. I guessed Austin had been sleeping on the couch or in the other bedroom. The room had been disturbed since the last time I'd been in it—probably done by the cops when they searched the place. I wondered if they'd found anything that would help them solve the case.

A photograph sat on the bedside table. In it, an older woman stood with a teenage boy in front of a red Mustang. Was it the same car Austin now drove? A sick feeling came over me. I'd thought it was a rental, not even occurring to me that rental companies had new cars, not vintage ones, although I assumed such a place that rented them existed. The abundance of insurance cards in the glove box suggested it was his personal vehicle.

I'd assumed he'd flown up after Nick had told him his aunt was missing, arriving the next day. But he drove. And I didn't care how fast he went. It would have been impossible for him to make it from Georgia that quickly. Had Austin already been in town when his aunt went missing? What reason would he have had to be here except to kill his aunt?

I picked up the framed photo and opened the latch on the back. The picture slid out, and I took a closer look. The photo was slightly faded, and I imagined it was at least several years old. I turned it over. Lovely cursive handwriting said, *With Austin, Oregon coast, August 2000.*

If she kept this photo next to her bedside, they must have been close at some point. I flipped the picture back over and studied the image, searching for any likeness to the man downstairs. The skinny, knobby-kneed kid had outgrown his awkward teenage body, but I could tell it was him.

I put the photo back where I'd found it and turned to the closet. It was stuffed with clothing. A knee-length sweater hung on the door. Not appropriate for a burial garment. I pushed it aside, and it fell off the hanger. Bending down, I picked it up and tossed the sweater on the bed. A folded envelope fell to the floor.

I retrieved it, ready to stuff it back in the pocket, but then I noticed the same exquisite handwriting from the photo addressing the envelope to: Ralph Watson, Attorney at Law. There was a stamp on it; it was ready to drop in the mail. I turned it over. The envelope wasn't sealed.

Sucking in a breath, I slipped the letter out of the envelope and unfolded it, aware that reading someone's mail crossed an ethical line.

> *Dear Mr. Watson,*
>
> *Per our discussion, I am putting this in writing until we can do the paperwork to make it official. I wish to remove my nephew, Austin Masanova, from my will and leave my estate to someone else.*
>
> *I will travel to Georgia to discuss it with him in person. He is terrible with money, and I don't want my legacy to disappear at the racetrack.*
>
> *When I return, I will come by the office, and we can prepare the necessary documents to make this a reality. If something should happen to me in the meanwhile, I wanted you to be aware of my wishes.*
>
> *Sincerely,*
>
> *Lucy Masanova*

There was a creek on the stair floorboard. Austin would be in the room in seconds. Stuffing the letter in my back pocket, I moved to the closet and had my hand on a purple dress by the time Austin made it to the door. He leaned against the doorframe and took a drink from his whisky glass.

"Find anything?"

The letter felt like a brick in my pocket, and I worried he could read the fear of him finding it in my eyes. I pulled the dress from the closet and held it at arm's length. "I'm guessing she was fond of this color," I said. "Given that her house is lilac, as is half her wardrobe."

Austin nodded. "It's perfect."

I laid the dress on the bed and then found a pair of black pumps, much like the one found by her body. All the while, my heart pounded in my chest, and an uneasy feeling swirled in my gut. If Austin knew he was going to be cut out of the will, how far would he have gone to stop that from happening?

CHAPTER THIRTY-ONE

And why hadn't he shared that news, instead of insisting he was the only heir?

"Bring these to the mortuary," I said.

"Thank you." He took a step forward. He was uncomfortably close, and I could smell the whisky on his breath.

"I have to go," I said.

He didn't budge. We were face-to-face. Austin eyed me up and down. "Do you have to? I have some steaks I could put on the grill."

"Nice of you to offer," I said. "But I have to get back to the hotel." It wasn't exactly true, but it was as good an excuse as any. Under the best of circumstances, dinner with Austin two nights in a row was one time too many. But I had to think. Austin was probably in debt, his credit cards maxed. He needed the inheritance. And his aunt was going to take it away from him. And I now had good reason to believe he'd been in town longer than I originally thought. Had he stopped his aunt before she could make her wishes official? My Spidey senses were on full alert. He reached out to touch my arm, but I ducked away and squeezed past him.

Bounding down the steps, he followed on my heels. "Did I say something to offend you?"

He came up behind me as I grabbed the front doorknob.

"No," I said. "I just need to go."

I scooped my bag off the table near the entrance and wrenched the door open. Standing there, I watched the heavy downpour for a moment, then pulled up the hood of my sweatshirt, like that would help.

He laughed. "At least let me drive you. It's miserable out there."

"Not necessary," I said. "The hotel is just a few blocks away."

I stepped out into the storm, jogging down the steps, my Converse sneakers instantly waterlogged. I didn't care. I needed to put some distance between me and Lucy's little house of secrets.

Chapter Thirty-Two

Drenched, my clothes were instantly glued to my body. My heel ached and I could barely see a foot in front of me as my eyes burned from the rain that blurred my vision.

I quickly realized I was disoriented. Lucy's neighborhood was unfamiliar to me, and I'd missed the turn that would have taken me down the hill and back to the hotel.

I came up short at a dead end, almost losing my footing on the gravel. Teetering on the abrupt edge of an embankment, I fought gravity so as not to topple over and into the forest below. Over the trees, I could barely make out the lights on the bridge, at least two miles away. If I fell into the abyss below me, I might never be found.

I turned, backtracking. It was dark, and there were no streetlights. Panic weighed me down, and I felt sluggish moving through the deluge back to where I thought Lucy's house stood. I'd have to swallow my fear and my pride and ask Austin for a ride after all.

But as I tried to retrace my steps, I realized I was hopelessly lost. Lucy's house was not where I thought it would be. Just more rain-battered pine trees swaying like a macabre gathering of ghosts at an ancient ball.

My foot caught on something unforgiving, and I fell to my knees into a wading pool-sized puddle. On all fours, I took a minute to catch my breath, then struggled to my feet.

I thought about using my cell phone to call for help, but I had no idea where I'd tell them to find me. I doubted the Orca Cove police department could ping my phone for my location as a big-city police department could do.

It all seemed so hopeless, but then I saw a set of lights coming my way. I held up my hand to shield my eyes, making out a pickup truck. My pulse quickened. Wouldn't it be my luck that Ray Boyce would be the one to rescue me? He'd probably run me over before he'd help.

The truck passed, dousing me with a wave of water, then came to a sudden halt. The rear lights lit as the truck slowly backed toward me.

The driver's side window rolled down, and I made out the sole occupant, the driver. Expecting to see Ray's angry face, I was relieved to see it was Alex, the medical examiner.

"Charlie, is that you?" she yelled above the howling wind.

I stepped closer to the truck. "Alex, thank God. I was trying to go home. I got turned around."

"Get in." She leaned over and unlocked the door with a flip of her finger.

I ran over to the passenger's side of the truck and got inside, sloshing water on the floorboard and the seat. I lowered my bag onto the spot next to me and pushed sopping wet hair out of my face. "Thank you so much. It's hard to tell which way is which in this storm."

Alex took in my disheveled appearance and gave me the once-over. One perfectly tweezed eyebrow raised. "What are you doing out here?"

"Just trying to find my way back to the pet hotel."

She put the truck in reverse and turned it around. "Where were you coming from?"

I didn't want to admit that I'd run off on Austin or that I had a bad feeling about him, but I couldn't come up with a better reason for being in the area. "I was at Lucy's house," I said, shivering.

Alex aimed the vent at me and turned up the heat. I noticed a peeling pro-life sticker on the dashboard. Otherwise, the truck was in pristine condition.

"What were you doing there?" she asked.

The warmth choked me and felt good at the same time. Steam rose off my clothes. "I was helping Austin pick a dress for his aunt to be buried in."

"I didn't know you knew each other."

"We don't," I said. "Not exactly sure how I got myself involved."

"Well, it was nice of you to help."

As Alex started down the pothole-covered street, I spotted Lucy's house in the distance. I was almost there. I was relieved Alex rescued me before I had to turn to Austin for help.

We bounced past the house, and she took the turn I'd missed, driving halfway down the hill before she took a left toward the hotel.

"How long are you staying in town?" She kept her eyes on the road.

My teeth were clattering now like a jackhammer, making it hard to talk. "Not long," I managed.

"A few days? A week?" She glanced my way.

"A little longer," I said. "Until my aunt can manage on her own."

She came to a stop outside the hotel. "I hope you plan to leave things as you found them."

My hand was on the door handle, but I stopped and looked back at her. "I'm sorry?" My voice went up an octave.

She smiled, but it lacked warmth. "Nick. Sometimes people misinterpret his kindness."

I tilted my head. "I'm not sure what you mean," I said, but Riley's words played in my head. They had a past.

She stared me down. It was the same look Aunt Jo-Jo used to give me when I swore I wasn't the one who forgot to put the milk away, even though only two of us were there.

"Are you and Nick a thing?"

She gave a tight smile. "It's complicated. But it would be better if you left him alone."

"I... I don't even know what you're talking about. There's nothing going on between us. I'm just visiting."

"Of course," Alex said, not breaking eye contact. "I just don't want to see my friend get hurt."

"There's no reason he'd get hurt," I said. "Not by me. I'm merely a witness in an investigation. Nothing more."

"Sure," she said.

Picking up my bag, she held it out for me. It was as clear a signal as if she'd said, take your lying butt and get the heck out. I took my backpack and got out of the truck, barely closing the door before she gave me a last look of warning and drove away.

Chapter Thirty-Three

The rain had slowed to a drizzle by the time I got back to the house, but the damage had been done, and my sneakers squished out water with every step. I felt fifty pounds heavier and knew I'd have to wring out my clothes before I put them in the wash, or the machine would overflow.

Noah greeted me at the door as if I'd been gone for days. Despite how uncomfortable I was, I took the time to bend down and give him some attention before I kicked off my shoes and rolled my saturated socks off my feet. I carried them to the basement laundry room, where I left them like two wads in the sink. Peeling off my clothes, item by item, I tossed them in the washing machine. Before I turned it on, I remembered Lucy's letter to her attorney that I'd stuffed in my pocket. It fell apart in my hands as I pulled it out in pieces. Cringing, I tried to separate the remnants, but the ink was washed away, and all I had left was a clump of wet paper.

I felt sick. In my haste, I'd destroyed the only evidence that Lucy was going to write Austin out of her will. I prayed the lawyer could back up my claims, as the letter indicated that Lucy and he had already discussed the matter.

Noticing a substantial puddle on the floor, I threw a dry towel over it and stomped on it until it soaked up most of the moisture.

Shivering in my underwear, I made it back upstairs to the bathroom, where I ran the water hot. The damp cold made my hands throb. I waited until the temperature got to where I could barely stand how it scalded my skin when I stepped under the spray and let my bones glory in the warmth.

As I stood there, I tried not to wallow in my angst over destroying the letter. That would come soon enough, as I'd have to share the information with Nick. I tried to focus instead on my newfound knowledge about Austin. His apology the night before almost had me thinking I'd misjudged him, but my gut had told me differently the moment he'd left Maya tied up in the cold. I was back to trusting my gut. Although the Boyces were despicable people, they didn't have the motive to kill Lucy that Austin did. I had felt desperate to get away from him, but I shouldn't have taken the letter with me. I wasn't looking forward to admitting my screw up to Nick.

And fleeing in a torrential storm and getting lost was probably not the best idea I'd ever had. And to be rescued by Alex. I hadn't known she had a grudge against me. I'd met the woman for five minutes, for goodness' sake. I tried to remember what I could have said or done to make her think I had designs on Nick. I'd just discovered a dead body. Doubtful, I'd drooled over Nick at that moment. Was she really looking out for Nick's best interests, or her own?

And about Nick. For days, he was there every time I turned around. And suddenly, radio silence. Ever since my dinner with Austin. Oh well, it was better this way. I'd be leaving soon.

So then, why did my heart feel so tight in my chest?

Shutting off the water, I dried myself with a giant towel before slipping on sweats and a long-sleeved T-shirt. It was still drizzling, and I dreaded going back outside, but I knew I had to walk the dogs at the hotel. I pulled a beanie over my wet hair, borrowed my aunt's rain jacket, and persuaded Noah to join me. He didn't enjoy getting his paws wet, so it took some doing, but eventually he trotted by my side to the hotel.

Martha had gone home for the night. We were down to seven guests, if you counted Maya. I walked them, three at a time, then took Maya for a quick stroll before bringing her back to the house with us.

Still chilled to the bone, I lit a fire and heated some canned chicken noodle soup. While it cooled, I retrieved the request form I'd lifted from City Hall from my bag. I smoothed it out against my thigh. My fingers felt an indentation. Holding it to the firelight, I could make out marks on the paper.

Whoever had filled out the form on top of this one had pressed down hard with their pencil. Jumping to my feet, I almost tripped over Noah, who'd been lying at my side. I stepped over him and brought the form closer to the flames. I could make out the signature at the bottom of the page and the now-familiar handwriting. *L. Masanova.*

At the top of the form, under the name slot, was a "K," but I couldn't read the rest of it. The last name was easier to see. Boyce. Kyleigh Boyce? I couldn't determine which box someone had checked, but it couldn't have been a death certificate because Kyleigh was very much alive. It could have been a name change request, but a birth certificate seemed most likely.

Why would Lucy want Kyleigh's birth certificate?

Maya's head jerked up, and her ears raised. She listened for a moment, got up, and started barking at the door.

Laying the form on the table, I walked over and looked out the window. Austin knew where I lived and, for a moment, I feared he had come to confront me about my quick departure. But it was Nick's Jeep parked out front, not Austin's Mustang. I watched him get out and walk toward the door. He wore jeans and a light jacket.

Alex's warning echoed in my mind, tightening my throat.

I grabbed Maya by the collar and told her to hush. As usual, she didn't listen. No one was going to sneak up on us, that was for sure.

I opened the door before he could knock.

"Hey," he said.

I smiled and let Maya go. She placed her paws on Nick's chest, thumping her tail to say hello. He gave her a few pats before turning his attention to Noah, who'd finally come forward to see what all the commotion was about.

"Sorry to show up unannounced." He looked past me into the living room. "You alone?"

I was about to make a joke about usually being alone, but I felt the tension between us and surmised he was talking about Austin. "Just me and the dogs." Stepping back, I invited him inside.

We stood there, waiting for the dogs to settle down. Once they did, an awkward silence ensued.

"I'm off duty," he said. "But I thought you'd want this information as soon as possible."

"Oh?"

"Can we sit down?"

"Of course, sorry." I pointed to a chair in front of the fire. "Can I get you something to drink?"

"Water would be nice."

"Right." I headed to the kitchen and filled two glasses with water. When I came back into the room, I noticed Nick had taken off his jacket and hung it over the back of the chair. He looked stiff and unsure of himself. Like we'd had a fight. I longed for the easy banter that had once flowed between us.

Placing a glass on the table next to him, I settled in the chair across from him. The pups were curled up on the dog bed next to the fire. The logs crackled, but otherwise the room was uncomfortably quiet. I tried to gather the courage to spill my guts.

Nick took a long drink, then folded his hands in his lap. "You were right to ask questions about your aunt's accident."

I leaned forward. "Go on."

"She didn't just drive into the tree. Someone cut her brake line. The curve she was navigating is tough. It looks like a tap from behind would have sent her off course. It would have been impossible to avoid the tree if she couldn't slow down. Why Karl didn't have her car checked for mechanical problems, I don't know. I turned the matter over to my Sergeant."

Stars danced before my eyes, and I thought I'd pass out. "Who would do such a thing?"

Nick pursed his lips. "That's what I intend to find out. You said your aunt doesn't remember the accident?"

"No." I felt like I'd been punched in the stomach. Pulling my knees up, I hugged them against my chest.

"Do you think she's well enough to talk to me? I'd like to ask her some questions."

I sighed. "She's not that fragile. But I'd like to be there if you don't mind."

He nodded. "Sure. I can pick you up in the morning."

He placed his hands on his knees and stood. Grabbing his jacket, he slipped it on. I knew if I didn't tell him about the letter, I'd be withholding evidence. Well, more evidence, but I didn't want to think about that. At least the letter had nothing to do with my aunt. "Please don't go," I said. "I have something to tell you."

Nick looked up at the ceiling and sighed, then crossed his arms. "If it's about Austin, I'm not sure I want to hear it. I can see you like him."

"What? No…" I stood and paced. Maya's head jerked up, and she watched my every move. "I needed to tell you about a letter I found in the pocket of Lucy's sweater."

He gave a little moan. "Go on."

"It was from Lucy to her attorney. She was going to write Austin out of her will, and Austin knew about it."

"And where's this letter?"

I picked the sopping mess off the end table and held it out to him in my open hands.

Nick took a step forward, so we were inches apart, and looked down at my offering. "What happened?"

I told him about the storm, leaving out the part about Alex rescuing me and telling me to keep my distance from him.

Nick glanced away and then held my gaze. I couldn't tell if he felt sorry for me or was angry. Maybe a combination of both.

"I'm sorry," I said. "I panicked when I found the letter. I should have left it there and told you where to find it."

Nick ran his hand through his hair. "Who was the attorney?"

I thought for a moment. "Watson," I said. "You know him?"

Nick nodded. "He's here in town. Mostly retired, but I think he's kept a few clients. I'll talk to him." Nick turned to leave.

"There's more." I followed Nick to the door.

He stopped and turned to face me, his hands clasped in front of him.

"I went with Austin to the mortuary. His credit card was declined. I'm wondering if he's having financial trouble."

Nick exhaled a heavy sigh. "Anything else?"

CHAPTER THIRTY-THREE

"You seem annoyed with me."

"I'm just confused," he said. "You seem drawn to this guy. At least you're spending a lot of time with him. Yet you suspect him of murder?"

I shrugged. I couldn't tell him I was invested in finding the killer to steer them away from looking at my aunt as the murderer. Not without giving him reason to suspect her in the first place. "Right place at the right time, I guess."

"Well, be careful around him," Nick said. "He has a motive to kill his aunt for the inheritance. Especially if he was so close to being written out of the will. But please leave the police work to me."

I nodded. "I will." It didn't seem like the right time to add to my suspicion that Austin had been in town earlier than we'd thought. That would just give Nick more reason to be annoyed with my sticking my nose into his investigation.

"I'll pick you up around nine unless I'm needed on a call," he said.

"I'll be ready." I wanted to ask him to stay, but the chill in the air was not from the autumn weather. Nick barely looked at me. I got to my feet and followed him to the door.

I watched him walk back to his car, then closed the door and leaned against it. Both dogs looked at me with worried eyes. His news about my aunt's brake line being cut was not what I'd expected. Could Lucy's murder be connected to what happened to Aunt Jo-Jo? Suddenly, my quest to find Lucy's killer seemed even more personal.

Chapter Thirty-Four

Sleep didn't come easy, as I couldn't stop my mind from going down rabbit holes. What if Lucy's killer had also targeted my aunt? What if my aunt was still in danger? What if Austin realizes I read Lucy's letter to her attorney, and he comes after me? What if Nick hates me? I played the "what if" game until fatigue won, and I fell into a fitful sleep.

Not trusting myself to get up on my own, I'd set my alarm for seven-thirty, so I'd have time to walk the dogs and have breakfast before Nick picked me up. But when it went off, blasting Taylor Swift's latest hit, I groaned and rolled over, pulling the covers over my head. I would have given my last dollar for twenty minutes more, but I knew I didn't have that luxury.

Opening one eye, I met Maya's expectant stare. Noah snored at my feet. At least it was sunny out.

I walked both dogs, munched on a granola bar, and then went to the hotel where Martha was already hard at work mopping the floors. "Good morning," she said, scrubbing one spot so hard I thought the handle would snap in two.

"Good morning." I took a leash off the hook, ready to take the pooches for a stroll.

"Kyleigh actually came to work this morning," she said. "She's out walking Joe Pesci and Marlon Brando. You don't need to walk anyone."

"Who comes up with these names?"

Martha leaned on the mop and looked at me. "The dog's owner, Tim Tuple, used to work in Hollywood. He actually knew these people."

"Interesting." I checked my watch. I still had half an hour before Nick would pick me up. I filled Martha in on his visit the night before. Not the part about how he hardly looked at me and acted like he wanted to be anywhere else, but in my company, but the part about my aunt's brake line being cut.

"I was wondering why she'd drive into a tree," Martha said. "She's not the most cautious driver in the world, but she's not crazy. Who would do such a thing?"

"I don't know. Nick's taking me to talk to Aunt Jo-Jo in a few. See if she can shed any light on the situation."

"Unless her memory has come back, she doesn't remember the accident," Martha said.

I wasn't sure how much I should share with Martha. As much as I trusted her to have my aunt's best interest at heart, I knew how easy it was to be sucked into the town gossip. "I'm just wondering if it's related somehow to Lucy's death."

"I don't see how," Martha said. "But it would be strange if two killers were targeting the old folks of Orca Cove."

"Indeed. Something troubles me, though. Cutting a brake line is a hands-off kind of killing, if you know what I mean. Strangling someone is so…well, so up close and personal."

"The whole thing just makes no sense to me," Martha said. "Lucy's murder has me locking my doors at night. I can tell you that much."

I thought of the flimsy barrier between the sleeping porch and the outside world. "Sounds like a smart move."

The door bounced open, and Kyleigh came in with Joe Pesci and who I assumed was Marlon Brando. Marlon was a bulldog, who did remind me of the movie star. Something about his demeanor made him seem like a mob boss. All he needed was a cigar and a handgun. He trotted over to me, and I rubbed his nubby head. "You gonna make me an offer I can't refuse?"

"What's that supposed to mean?" Kyleigh said.

"The Godfather," I said.

She gave me a blank stare.

Martha laughed. "Kids."

Kyleigh put the dogs away and got two more. I followed her outside. "Can I ask you something?" I said, jogging to catch up to her.

She stopped to wait for me.

"Did you request your birth certificate recently?"

She gave me another dumbfounded look.

"At City Hall? Maybe with Lucy signing for it?"

She narrowed her gaze. "Why would I do that?"

"Do you have a birth certificate?" I asked.

"Duh," she said. "Doesn't everybody?"

"I mean, do you have it in your possession?"

She stopped walking and made a show of checking her pockets. "Must have forgotten to bring it today."

My turn to roll my eyes. "Okay, smarty pants. Funny. I mean, at your house."

She shrugged. "Don't know. I guess. My aunt and uncle probably have it somewhere."

"Can you find out?"

Her eyebrows raised. "Why?"

"I think Lucy requested a copy before her death."

"Why would she do that?"

"That's the million-dollar question." The police cruiser pulled into the lot. "I have to go," I said. "But please see if you can find your birth certificate. Take a picture of it and send it to me, okay?"

Kyleigh sighed. "I still don't see what my birth certificate has to do with Lucy, but I'll look for it."

"Thanks," I said. "And maybe don't share this with anyone just yet. Not until we understand what's going on."

"Roger that," Kyleigh said. With a salute, she turned and headed off down the street, letting two yellow labs lead the way.

Chapter Thirty-Five

The ride to the rehab was awkward. Nick glanced at me and then kept his eyes on the road. What I wouldn't give to have him call me Jersey again.

I wrestled with the idea of telling him about the birth certificate, but I didn't know if that was important to the case yet, and I didn't want him scolding me again for looking into things when it was his job. And I didn't want him riling the Boyces up if it wasn't necessary. I'd give Kyleigh a chance to find the document first. Why make things harder on her than they already were?

So, I kept my mouth shut. It was the longest ten-minute drive of my life.

Aunt Jo-Jo sat on the front porch. Her silver hair was in a neat bun, and she wore lipstick for the second day in a row. I took that as a sign that she was feeling better.

"Hello, Nicky," she said, a bright smile lighting up her face.

He leaned down and gave her a kiss on the cheek. "How's my favorite Orca Cove citizen?" he asked.

"I bet you say that to all the girls," Aunt Jo-Jo laughed. "I'm itching to get out of this place, otherwise I can't complain."

Once Nick stepped back, I bent down and gave my aunt a gentle hug.

"Glad you two are getting acquainted," she said. "Isn't Charlie fabulous?"

Nick ran a hand through his hair and looked out at the water like he'd never seen it before.

Internally, I moaned and wished the deck would open and swallow me.

After a few uncomfortable moments of silence, Nick leaned against the railing, his back to the water. He crossed his feet at the ankles and his arms across his chest. I took a seat next to my aunt.

"I'm afraid this isn't exactly a social visit, Jo-Jo," he said. "I've got some upsetting news for you."

My aunt reached over and grabbed my hand. "Let me have it."

Nick cleared his throat. "Your accident wasn't exactly an accident. Someone cut your brake line."

"What?" She leaned forward. "You've got to be kidding me."

"I wish I was," he said. "What do you remember about that day?"

She squeezed my hand and let it go. "Not much," she said. "I know I was on my way to the mainland to get supplies. But I don't remember the actual accident."

"What about before that?" I pressed.

"Well, it was a normal day."

"And the day before that?" I asked.

"I worked at the hotel. Lucy brought Maya by. She was getting ready to head out of town."

"To see Austin?" I asked.

"Yes." She held up her cell phone. The message was hard to see on the shattered screen, but as I made out the words, I read them aloud. "I need to see Austin and explain things before the inevitable happens."

Nick and I looked at each other.

"Inevitable?" he asked.

Aunt Jo-Jo shrugged her good shoulder. "Beats me," she said. "There's more."

I scrolled to the next page and read the text.

"When I get back, I need to see Albert about my will. New information has me second-guessing my decision to leave my money to the library."

"What new information?" Nick asked.

My aunt shook her head. "Don't know, but I think the answer to your question might be in that green box. She was adamant that I keep it safe."

"What green box?" Nick asked.

My aunt and I exchanged glances. "Lucy asked me to hold on to a box for

166

her."

"It went missing after the accident," I added. "It was in the car."

Nick scratched his chin. "Why didn't you show me the message before?"

Aunt Jo-Jo shrugged. "I had no idea what it meant. Maybe she was going to leave the money to Austin after all. If that was the case, he certainly wouldn't kill her."

"If that was the case," Nick repeated. "That's the question."

We walked back to Nick's car in silence.

Settled behind the wheel, Nick rubbed the back of his neck. "Mind if I stop by and see if Albert Watson is home?"

"Not at all." More like I'd be thrilled.

Albert Watson lived in an old Victorian rambler that probably had one of the best views on the island. On the west side of the cape, it showed an endless ocean with a few smaller islands scattered about.

The man who opened the door was not who I expected. To me, retired meant old and weathered, but the man who greeted us was in tip-top shape. Lean and quick, with black hair and bright eyes, he wiped his hands on a towel. "I've got a pot of spaghetti sauce on the stove," he said, moving away from the door and inviting us down the hall with him using a tilt of his head.

A long, dark hallway opened to a bright white kitchen where, in fact, an enormous pot bubbled on the stove, the scent of sauce wafting through the air. From the kitchen window, I could see a carpet of perfect sod meeting the shimmering sea. "Aren't you going to introduce me to your friend, Officer?"

"This is Ms. Calderbank," he said. All business. "She's a witness in the Lucy Masanova case."

Ouch. So not a friend.

"Nice to meet you, Ms. Calderbank," he said, stirring the pot.

"You as well," I said.

"Was wondering if you could tell us about Lucy's will," Nick said. "Seems like there were some changes in the works."

Albert nodded. "I'd love to help you, Nick. You know that. But attorney-client privilege survives death."

"Yeah," Nick said. "I was afraid of that. But her nephew is looking like a prime suspect, and he seems to think he's the sole heir."

"That I can confirm, as Mr. Masanova and I will read the will this afternoon," he said. "But if someone were thinking of changing their successor and didn't get around to it before their demise... and I'm speaking generally here...the existing will would stand."

"So, Austin gets everything."

He pursed his lips. "Unless there is something I don't know about."

"What if there was a letter," I said.

"Sorry." He scooped sauce on a wooden spoon and took a taste. "Perfection," he said. "That wouldn't do it."

Well, that was a relief. At least I didn't ruin the only thing standing between Austin inheriting the estate and Lucy having her wishes recognized.

Back in the car, Nick said, "Well, that was pointless."

"It still seems Austin had the most to gain by Lucy dying. But you didn't think he was in town at the time of her death, did you?"

"I called him when we learned his aunt was missing, but I talked to him on his cell phone. He could have been anywhere."

It was time to come clean. Well, cleaner. I told him about my suspicions that Austin's car wasn't a rental and that if he drove from Georgia, he had to have been, at the very least, close to Orca Cove when he got Nick's call.

Nick cleared his throat and gave me a quick glance. "Good point."

At least he wasn't mad at me. Still, a chill ran through me. Austin was at the top of the suspect list, and I'd been alone with him. "He trusts me," I said. "I can try to get some information out of him."

"No." Nick pulled into the hotel parking lot. "Keep out of this. If he killed his aunt and he thinks you're nosing around, as much as he digs you, he might go after you as well. Your aunt knew something, at least someone thought she did, and they cut her brake line."

My throat tightened as anger replaced my fear. No one messed with Aunt Jo-Jo.

Nick dropped me off at the hotel. Martha was working on the books, Bruce lying on his back beside the desk while Martha absently rubbed his belly with her foot.

I slumped in the chair across from her.

"You look like you lost your last friend," Martha said.

With Nick being all business, I felt like I'd lost my best hope of having a new friend. And then there was Austin. "Just wondering if I had dinner with a murderer," I said.

My phone vibrated in my pocket. I pulled it out and checked the incoming message. It was from Kyleigh. "Come outside."

I got to my feet. "See you later," I said to Martha.

She looked like she had questions, but kept quiet as she watched me leave.

Slipping outside, I found Kyleigh sitting on a swing hanging from a grand oak tree. With scuffed Doc Martens, she dragged them through the dirt, making little puffs of smoke.

"Hey," I said, coming to stand before her.

She looked up at me through limp strands of hair. "I checked the entire trailer," she said. "Couldn't find my birth certificate. I found the folder where they keep those kinds of things, but it wasn't there. Maybe my mom never gave it to them."

"Maybe. How about we head to City Hall to get a copy?" I asked. "It may or may not tell us anything, but you should have a copy, anyway."

"Doesn't it cost money?"

I shrugged. "No worries, I'll pay." What was one more thing?

Stu was back at the desk. He quickly folded his newspaper and secured it under the table while glaring at me. Like I controlled the wind.

I waited while Kyleigh filled out the request form. She laid it before Stu, and I added a ten-dollar bill to cover the cost.

"I need to see your ID," he said.

Kyleigh snorted. "You've known me all my life, Mr. Casimo."

"Just following the rules," he said.

She reached into her wallet and laid her student ID on the counter. Stu studied it like she was trying to pass a counterfeit twenty-dollar bill. Satisfied that Kyleigh hadn't been the victim of a body snatcher, Stu folded his hands in front of him. "There is no birth certificate for you on file, my dear."

"So, there's no record of my birth?" Kyleigh asked, wide-eyed.

"Not in Orca Cove. Are you sure you were born here?"

Kyleigh looked at me and then back to Stu. "I guess I don't really know. I just assumed so."

He shrugged. "Sorry, I only have access to our city. I can't help you."

My cell vibrated in my hand. Another text from my mother. *Don't leave me hanging...*

I started to answer. *Sorry, can't do it this time.* But I didn't have the guts to send the message. I erased my reply and stuffed my phone back in my pocket.

"So, Lucy didn't get what she came for either," I said.

Stu cocked his head to the side. "Obviously not."

I grabbed my money off the counter, thanked Stu for his time, and we went outside, where there was a break in the weather.

"That was weird," she said.

"Don't you have to provide a copy of your birth certificate to the school?" I asked.

Kyleigh shrugged. "You'd think so."

As far as I could surmise, the identity of Kyleigh's father was the only missing piece the birth certificate could provide.

Was someone willing to kill to stop us from knowing that information? The only people who had something to gain by keeping that secret were the Boyces, as far as I could tell. I didn't think the state would pay enough to maintain custody of Kyleigh to justify murder. But if their living situation was any indication of their financial status, they might just be desperate enough to keep that income coming.

We walked to the Subaru and settled inside. I started the engine. "Are your aunt and uncle home?"

Kyleigh checked the time on her phone. "Shouldn't be."

"I saw something when I was there yesterday. A green box. Length of a shoe box, but thinner."

She pursed her lips. "I saw my uncle trying to open it last night. He had a blowtorch."

"Did he succeed?"

"Yeah."

"Did you see what was inside?"

"A book," she said. "Thin. Blue with red hearts on it. He told Aunt Mary that he'd hit pay dirt."

Chapter Thirty-Six

We went to the trailer, anyway. Sure enough, the box sat open and empty on a bench in front of a fire pit. An empty bottle of Jack Daniels lay on the ground beside it. The book that had been in the box was long gone. Ray Boyce had what my aunt had almost died to protect. No way he'd share it with me.

I thought about the birth certificate. Without Jody Boyce around to ask, the only way to know would be to see it. If the birth certificate even listed a father. I knew that was sometimes the case, as my father wasn't listed on mine—another source of contention between my mom and me. The next source of information stood beside me. I knew it would be a sensitive topic, but Kyleigh might hold the answer to the question of the day.

"I have no idea who my father is," I said. "My birth certificate lists him as unknown. Sometimes I wonder about him. If he even knew my mother was pregnant. Or if he just didn't want to be involved."

Kyleigh looked at her shoes and shrugged. "I've never seen my birth certificate."

I tucked my hair behind my ear and gave her a minute. "Did your mom ever tell you anything about your father?"

"Not that I remember, but she's been gone half my life."

"Understand," I said. "It's a small town. People talk. Anyone ever tell you anything?"

"No. My aunt and uncle always tell me how lucky I am that they stepped in to care for me when my mom took off. I sometimes wonder if I would have been better off being adopted out. I'm a big inconvenience to them."

I wanted to reach out and touch her, offer support. But hugging Kyleigh would be like hugging a cactus. Not that I was so huggable myself. So, I let the silence simmer and hoped she got the vibe. She wasn't the only one with a crappy upbringing. Sometimes it felt like everyone in the world had a sitcom family, while mine was an episode from a daytime talk show.

"How old was your mom when she had you?" I asked.

Kyleigh shrugged. "About sixteen. Same age I am now."

"That was a lot of responsibility," I said. "I'm thirty and I can't imagine being a mom yet."

She nodded and looked at the ground. I patted her back, and she froze, but then looked up at me with tears in her eyes.

"Sucks," I said.

Kyleigh sniffled and wiped her nose with the back of her hand. "It's fine," she said. And she turned and walked back to the trailer.

I left her at home with a sick feeling in my gut. Getting off the Boyce property without a confrontation was a win, so that relaxed me a bit. But I still felt uneasy. I needed to think things through. There was a reason Lucy had wanted Kyleigh's birth certificate, and shortly afterward, she was dead.

The math I'd done told me Jody Boyce would be about thirty-two years old now, wherever she was. I wondered if people from her class would know who her friends were and who Kyleigh's father might be.

I would start with the best source of information in town. Martha.

I found her eating lunch at her desk. Bruce sat to her side, eagerly awaiting a handout.

I patted his head, and he chanced a glance at me before his focus was once again on the sandwich in Martha's hand.

"What can you tell me about Jody Boyce?" I asked.

Martha tossed the last bit of her sandwich to Bruce and folded her hands across her stomach. "What makes you ask about her?"

Settling in the seat across from her, I propped my feet up on the ottoman and watched the ceiling fan go around. I told her about Lucy requesting Kyleigh's birth certificate. "Why would anyone kill over that? Maybe the father didn't want to be found, and whoever he was, he killed Lucy to keep the secret. I'm hoping that if we can figure out Jody's circle of friends, we could narrow down who that could be. If she even finished school. She was pregnant with Kyleigh when she was sixteen."

"Let me think," Martha said. "I remember Jody was a quiet girl. The schools here are so small, there were maybe thirty kids in the graduating class. I remember her hanging out with Lindsey Hanson."

"Where can I find Lindsey?"

"She lives on the north end of the island. She's married and has a baby now. I remember her being upset when Jody ran off." Martha scribbled a crude map on a Post-it Note and handed it to me. "Maybe share your thoughts with Nick. If someone killed Lucy and cut Jo-Jo's brake line, this could get even uglier."

I looked at the map and blew out a long breath. "Sure," I said. "As soon as I have something more than a hunch, I'll tell him."

"Well, be careful," she said.

"I will."

What harm could a few questions cause?

I drove through town and headed north. In minutes, I'd arrived at a house perched on a bluff, with a gorgeous ocean view. The home was a Cape Cod, white with black shutters. Lindsey had done alright for herself. I parked in the driveway, walked up to the door, and pressed the doorbell.

It sounded like wind chimes.

A few moments later, the door opened, and a plain woman greeted me, bouncing a baby on her hip. She looked me up and down. "Can I help you?"

She wore sloppy sweats, and her hair was pulled back into a tight ponytail. Just looking at her gave me a headache. "I hope so," I said. "My name is Charlie. I'm Jo-Jo McMullen's niece," I added, hoping to erase the skepticism from her face.

"Oh," she said. "I heard about her accident. How is she?"

"She's good," I said. "Getting stronger every day."

"Good to hear." Lindsey flicked some food off her daughter's face, then wiped her hand on her leg. "What can I do for you?"

"You're Lindsey, right?" When she nodded, I added, "I was wondering if we could talk."

Lindsey looked past me at my car. She seemed to be weighing a polite way of getting rid of me.

I smiled. "It won't take long."

She held the door open and stepped back. "Come in," she said. "I could use some adult company. You caught me in the middle of feeding Chrissy."

I followed her to a bright kitchen in the back of the house that had a view of the sea. The baby in her arms would grow up thinking such a view was normal. So unlike how Kyleigh and I had grown up.

Lindsey slid her daughter into her highchair, where she squished macaroni and cheese between chubby fingers before shoving a fist full into her mouth. "I just made a pitcher of iced tea," she said. "Would you like some?"

"That would be great."

Lindsey poured two glasses and set them on the kitchen table. I settled into the seat across from her. "Sorry about the mess," she said. "With a baby, there are never enough hours in the day."

I took in the piles of laundry on the great room sofa, and toys spewed across the floor. A cartoon I didn't recognize played on the television in the background.

"So," she said, sneaking a forkful of something green into her daughter's mouth. "What brings you over?"

"I wanted to talk to you about Jody Boyce."

Her gaze darted to mine. "What about her?"

"I understand you two were friends."

Lindsey bit her lip and sat back in her chair. "We were."

"Have you heard from her since she left town?"

"No. Not a peep. Why?"

I hadn't come up with a ploy, so I opted for a bit of honesty. "I'm just trying to help Kyleigh figure some things out."

Lindsey nodded. "That poor girl. What exactly do you want to know?"

"Anything you can tell me. What about Jody's parents?"

Lindsey shifted in her seat. "Her dad was in prison for an armed robbery for most of Jody's life. He's probably out now, but I haven't seen him since I was a kid. Her mom was an addict. She overdosed and died a few years ago."

"Wow, sounds like a troubled family. Did anyone care when Jody left town?"

"Only family she had was her mom, who was so deep in her addiction, she was just trying to survive, you know what I mean?"

"What about Ray and Mary?"

"Useless."

"What about friends?"

"I'll be right back," Lindsey said, rising. "Can you watch Chrissy for a moment?"

My heart raced. I knew nothing about babies. "Sure," I said, but I wasn't convincing, not even to myself.

Lindsey seemed excited to have a few minutes of freedom—she was gone before I could say anything more.

Alone, I looked at Chrissy, who was wide-eyed. She seemed suspicious of me, and rightfully so. I tried a smile. She blew raspberries back at me, then slapped her hands on the tray of her highchair, sending macaroni fragments into the air. I jumped up and grabbed a few paper towels, mopping the mess off the floor.

"Wah," she said, slinging another wad of pasta at my head.

This better be worth it.

Lindsey came back, finding me at the sink, washing the slop out of my hair. She didn't seem concerned. It probably happened to her every day. Settling back at the table, she laid a large book before her. I returned to my seat.

"It's our yearbook," she said. "From our junior year. Jody dropped out after that because she already had the baby."

She flipped through the pages, turning the book my way when she found what she was looking for. She pointed to the photo of a heavy-set girl with a tight smile. "Was she pregnant in this photo?" I asked.

"She must have been. But she didn't share that with me."

"Did you find that odd?" I asked. "Being her friend?"

Lindsey wiped her daughter's hands with a rag and then set her on the floor. Chrissy took off, scooting across the tile like there was a cupcake at the other end of the room.

"Jody always wore baggy clothes, so no one noticed her baby bump. And we weren't so close about then. She started hanging out with the popular kids. She no longer had time for me."

I flipped through the pages of the yearbook. "Any idea who the father is?"

Lindsey looked over her shoulder to check on her daughter, then leaned forward and in a conspiratorial tone said, "She wouldn't say. It was odd because she didn't exactly attract boys. I was the same way before I got my teeth fixed and my skin cleared up. We were wallflowers, for sure. But when she started hanging out with the in-crowd, she would go to parties I wasn't invited to. She probably got knocked up then."

I froze when I came upon a photo of Nick a few pages later. His hair was shorter, but other than that, he hadn't changed much. "Officer Sabato was in your class?"

"A year ahead of us. Not that he gave us the time of day."

"Did he have a girlfriend?" I didn't know why that mattered, but I wanted to know.

"He did." She took the book back and jumped forward a few pages. "There," she said. "Nick and Alex. She was even more stuck up than he was."

I took the book back and studied the photo. Alex sat on Nick's lap; her arms looped around his neck. They looked like they were in love. Their relationship went way back. No wonder she hated me.

"How long did they date?"

"I think until they went to different colleges," she said. "She came back as the big shot medical examiner, and he came back as a cop. I saw Alex recently, and she looked right through me. Like she always did. But back in the day, she developed a soft spot for Jody."

"Were Nick and Alex part of the popular crowd Jody started hanging out with?"

Lindsey nodded. "Them and a few other kids."

Interesting. "Back to Jody," I said. "How was she as a mom to Kyleigh?"

"She seemed unsure of herself. I thought it was odd at the time, like having a baby would make mothering intuitive. Now that I have Chrissy, I can see that isn't true. Anyway, her mom's house wasn't a good place for a baby. Jody and Kyleigh stayed with my family for almost a year, but my parents wanted our lives back, and eventually they asked her to leave. She had nowhere to go."

"Is that when Lucy Masanova stepped in?"

Lindsey got up and followed Chrissy into the other room, then came back with the kid in her arms. "That was a surprise. Ms. Masanova was the librarian, and she was less than friendly. But she let them live with her for a few years. I went off to college, and me and Jody pretty much lost touch. But I saw her the week before she took off."

"How was she?"

Lindsey's forehead crinkled. "Distracted. I could tell something was wrong, but she didn't want to talk about it."

"Any idea where she went?"

Lindsey shook her head and leaned back when Chrissy stuck her finger in her mother's ear. "No."

"Did you find it strange that she left Kyleigh behind?"

Lindsey shrugged. "I could tell that being a mother was hard for her. She'd lost weight and was getting male attention. She told me she felt stuck, and she wanted something different. She said she had a plan."

"Any idea what that plan was?"

"No. But a few days later, she was gone. I figured she was out chasing the life she wanted."

"And Kyleigh went to live with her aunt and uncle."

"I heard Ms. Masanova wanted to keep her, but the Boyces insisted she live with them. Rumor is, they do it for the money. Ms. Masanova got even meaner after that."

And dead.

The Boyces inched back up toward the top of my suspect list.

Chapter Thirty-Seven

A tightness spread across my chest as I headed back toward town. Alex and Nick had a long history, which explained why they were so familiar with each other. But how was their relationship now? Had I misread things between me and Nick? I was pathetic. I wanted so badly for him to like me, that I hadn't even seen what was now so obvious.

I had to forget about my childish crush. I was going back to New Jersey soon, anyway. Long-distance relationships never worked—not that he seemed interested in me anymore. I'd thought it was because of Austin, but maybe Nick and Alex had been together all along.

I still had questions about Kyleigh's father. All signs pointed to Alex and Nick having information about that time period and who Jody had been friends with. I hated to bother Nick with my questions, but between him and Alex, my best bet was Nick. Alex had made it perfectly clear she wanted nothing to do with me unless it was driving me to the airport.

I found a spot in front of the coffee shop, parked, and went inside, where I ordered an iced tea and found a table on the patio in the shade of a giant oak tree. It gave me the perfect vantage point for people watching.

Some deep breathing calmed me a little. Laying my phone on the table in front of me, I summoned the courage to send Nick a text. I'd composed at least five different versions before I came up with the right mix of casual and interesting. *Hey, Nick. Wondering if you have some time today to chat. Worried about my aunt and that whole attempted murder thing.*

As soon as I hit send, I regretted it. He was not my personal cop.

Before I could fret too much, my phone pinged a reply.

Was just about to take a lunch break. Where R U?

Coffee shop.

And just like that, I had a date.

I was on my second iced tea by the time the police cruiser pulled up to the curb, parking several spots ahead of my rental car. Nick got out of the car, in uniform, and a baseball cap with a badge embroidered on the front. He turned when he heard his name called.

Alex strutted toward him, and he stopped to wait for her. They were far enough away that I couldn't hear their conversation, but Alex was laughing and touching his arm the way couples do. They looked good together. Damn it.

When they parted company, Nick strode toward the coffee shop, with Alex watching after him. When her eyes met mine, the smile evaporated off her face.

Nick came to stand before me, blocking her from my view. I smiled up at him, hoping to mask the jealous monster that was bubbling inside of me.

"Hey, Jersey," he said.

His use of the nickname he'd given me warmed my heart. I was getting whiplash from my changing emotions.

"Gonna grab a sandwich. Can I get you anything?" he asked.

"No, I'm good."

When he went inside to place his order, I looked back to where Alex had stood. She was gone, thank God, but her message to stay away from Nick echoed loudly in my ears.

Back at the table, Nick took the chair that was across from me and moved it closer. I would have liked to think he wanted to sit by my side, but I knew having his back to the street made him nervous. He settled with a to-go coffee cup and a cellophane-wrapped sandwich on the table and sat down.

"What's up?" he asked.

"Anything new about the cut in my aunt's brake line?"

He sucked in a deep breath. "No fingerprints found where someone would have touched it to sever the line. Whoever did it was smart enough to wear gloves. Some paint transferred to your aunt's car at the point of impact.

Yellow, which narrows it down if we find a yellow vehicle with front-end damage. So, I'm keeping an eye out for that."

"Ray drives a yellow cab."

"I know. I'll check it for damage as soon as I catch up with him."

"Was there a surveillance camera at the hotel?"

He nodded. "But it doesn't capture the spot where your aunt parked. I watched the tape going back a few days and up to the accident. In the early morning hours, someone in a hoodie darted across the yard toward where Jo-Jo parked her car. I blew up the image as much as I could, but can't tell who it is."

He brought the video up on his phone and handed it to me.

The picture was grainy in the pre-dawn light. It could have been me, except I was in New Jersey when the recording was made. "Might have been Kyleigh," I said. "I caught her sleeping in the motel the other night. She seeks refuge from her aunt and uncle. Remember the black eye?"

"I do. You don't think she cut your aunt's brakeline, do you?"

I quickly shook my head. "No. But I wonder if she was there, and she saw something. Maybe it meant nothing to her at the time."

Nick sighed. "The kid hates me. I'll never get anything out of her."

I took a long drink. "I'll try. We're coming to an understanding."

Nick took a bite of his sandwich and wiped his mouth with his napkin. "Well, let me know if she tells you anything. I really want to catch this person."

Nick had finished his sandwich, and I'd gulped down my second glass of iced tea, and we still had unfinished business to discuss. When Nick glanced at his watch, I knew I was running out of time.

"Speaking of Kyleigh," I began. "How well did you know her mom?"

"Jody?" He leaned back in his seat and took off his cap. "She was a year behind me. Small town, so not a lot of kids in my age category. I remember her being quiet. Kind of sweet."

"Was she dating anyone?"

Nick raised an eyebrow. "Why all the questions?"

I crossed my arms and leaned forward, resting my elbows on the table.

"Like I said, I've been talking to Kyleigh, and there are so many unknowns about her mom. I don't know my dad, so I know how that feels."

He tossed his cap on the table and ran a hand through his flattened hair. "I don't think she was dating anyone. I mean, she must have been, knowing how babies are made, but no one I was aware of. But I was a bit wrapped up in my own journey. Sports, getting ready to go away to school, and all."

"And dating Alex."

He laughed. "How do you know that?"

"It came up," I said. "I was talking to Lindsey. She said Alex had a soft spot for Jody. Do you think she would know who Kyleigh's father was?"

"Doubtful. She went away to school at the same time I did. Different schools. We broke up, and I lost touch with everyone except my family until I came back to work here five years ago."

"Did you and Alex ever get back together?" I held my breath.

He scratched his head. "Now and then. We aren't a good fit."

"Seems like she disagrees with that."

Nick sighed. "She can think what she wants, doesn't change things."

So, he wasn't arguing. He saw it too.

"Anyway," he went on. "What does my love life, or lack thereof, have to do with anything?"

A cool breeze moved his hat a few inches across the table, and I felt suddenly chilled. He was available, after all. I tried not to let my voice show how excited that little piece of news made me. "Just trying to figure out who Kyleigh's father was and what made Jody leave like that. I feel bad for Kyleigh having to live with her aunt and uncle. They're obviously in it for the money."

"Maybe," he said. "It's a rotten thing to do, but there's no law against it."

"But if she could at least understand why her mom left her behind, it might bring her some peace."

"I get that." Nick looked at his watch again.

I assumed he'd need to get back to work soon. It was time to take a leap of trust. "Shortly before her murder, Lucy requested Kyleigh's birth certificate. Why do you think she would do that?"

Nick looked at the sky like he wanted someone to intervene and save him, then gave me a hard stare. "And how do you know that?"

I gave him the details.

Nick massaged his chin. "So, you think this ties Kyleigh to the murder somehow?"

"Not directly. But for some reason, Lucy wanted to know who Kyleigh's father was."

"That's easy enough to find out. I can get the birth certificate."

"If only," I said. "Kyleigh and I tried. It seems to be missing from City Hall."

"You've been busy," Nick said.

The mic clipped to his shirt crackled. He leaned down for a minute, then keyed it and said, "On my way."

Grabbing his hat, he stood. "Got a lead on a necklace found on Lucy when she died. I circulated a photo amongst her group of friends. Someone recognized it."

I swallowed hard and hoped the shade from the tree would conceal my face turning white. I'd have to get to Aunt Jo-Jo before he did.

He started to leave, but then turned back. "You can talk to Kyleigh about what she saw at the hotel, but otherwise, I wish you'd stop nosing around. Especially where the Boyces are concerned. Someone in town is a killer. I don't want you added to the body count."

"So, you suspect the Boyces," I said.

"They're on the list," he said. "Promise me you'll stay away from them."

I smiled. "Ah, so you do care about me."

Adjusting his cap, he said, "Of course I do. It's my job to protect the citizens of this town."

Ouch. The elation I'd felt burst like a bubble as I watched him walk away.

If he was cold now, wait until he found out that the necklace belonged to my aunt, and I had said nothing about it.

Chapter Thirty-Eight

I analyzed Nick's comment on the walk back to my car. So, I wasn't special. Just another resident of Orca Cove, and a temporary one at that. Point taken.

What was Nick going to think when he learned the necklace Lucy had clutched in her dead hand belonged to Aunt Jo-Jo? He would at least have to question her. But would he believe her when she told him she didn't know how her prized possession had fallen into Lucy's hands?

Stopping at a light, I turned on my blinker to make a right turn and head up the hill to the rehab. Just then, my phone pinged. I grabbed it out of the center console and checked the message. It was from Kyleigh. One word.

Pickle.

Where R U? I responded.

Meet me where we found Ms. M.

I turned off my directional and drove toward the hotel, breaking into a cold sweat.

I parked at Wiggle Butt Manor and jogged toward the path and down to the ocean. My foot still ached, and I favored it, slowing my stride. It felt like forever since I'd had the chance to think. Pickle was our code word. Did that mean Kyleigh was in danger, or did she just need to talk? What exactly was I going to find in the same place we found Lucy Masanova?

It was midday, still light, but the darkening clouds made it feel later in the day. A giant raindrop plopped on my head when I stepped out from the cover of trees and onto the beach.

Kyleigh stood with her back to me, her curtain of dark hair swept behind her as a gust of wind moved along the shore. She was alone. She crossed her arms and kept her gaze on the surf as I came to stand beside her.

At least she wasn't in immediate danger.

"Pickle," I said.

She nodded and wiped at her eyes with the back of her sleeve.

I put my arm around her shoulders and guided her to a log where we sat.

The ocean seemed angry as waist-high waves crashed ashore. Gray clouds swirled above us. I half expected a seaweed-covered monster to emerge from the swell.

"There's a tree," she said. "On my uncle's property. I climb up sometimes. It's the perfect spot to sit. You can see everything, but for some reason, no one ever looks up and sees me. It's like I'm invisible up there."

She took a shuddering breath.

"What did you see, Kyleigh?"

"My uncle. He was on the phone, pacing."

"What did he say?"

She turned and looked at me. The pain on her face made me want to look away, but I held her eyes with mine.

"He said: I might have cut the brake line, but I didn't kill Lucy, you did, and I can prove it." She wiped her nose with the back of her sleeve. "He went on to say he would take the journal to the cops unless whoever he was talking to made it worth his while not to."

A journal. Is that what Lucy stored in the green box? But whose journal was it, and what secrets did it hold? I rubbed Kyleigh's back. She was looking out to sea now. It seemed that sharing her burden gave her some relief.

"Do you know who he was talking to?"

"No."

"We have to go to the police," I said. "They need to question your uncle and find out why he sabotaged my aunt's brakes. He could have killed her."

"I think that was the goal."

"I know."

"Can't you tell the cops?" she asked, wide-eyed. "I just can't…"

"I can go with you," I said. "But only you can attest to what you heard."

"Aunt Mary will be so mad at me. It's us against them, she always says. If I betray her..."

I wanted to assure her that everything would be okay, that she didn't have to go back to her aunt's care. But I knew I didn't have the power to make such promises. "I'll do what I can to help." It was the best I could offer.

Kyleigh was shaking. I wasn't sure if it was her fear of talking to the police or the fact that the temperature had dropped about ten degrees. I pulled the sleeves down on my hoodie, so they covered my raw, red hands. I'd always heard people complain that cold weather was not good for arthritis, and now I understood why. I'd need a good pair of gloves.

"Let's go," I said. "I'll drive you to the station."

The woman behind the counter didn't look happy to see us. It was just about five o'clock. Minutes before closing time. In this small town, the desk wasn't manned twenty-four seven. There was a sign to call 911 in case of after-hours emergencies. She had one arm in the sleeve of her jacket when we walked in.

"What do you need?" she asked, a tinge of annoyance in her tone.

I walked up to the desk while Kyleigh lingered behind me. "We need to talk to a detective," I said.

She chortled. "We have officers. Orca Cove isn't big enough for detectives."

"Okay," I said. "Can we speak with an officer?"

"Captain Sanders is in back. I'll grab him for you."

She disappeared for a minute and then came back, gathering her purse and a book as she moved past her desk. "The captain will be with you in a few. Sit and make yourselves comfortable." She flipped the Closed sign in the window, and she was gone.

I looked at Kyleigh and shrugged. I debated calling Nick and letting him be the one to break the case, but I knew Kyleigh didn't trust him. Plus, he'd be busy adding my aunt to the suspect list by now. I hoped for a gentle female detective, but it didn't seem Orca Cove had such a thing.

A few minutes later, a middle-aged, chalky pale guy came out, scratching his gray beard. His white uniform shirt stretched across an ample belly. The buttons looked about ready to give up the fight and pop. He was the reason people joked about cops spending too much time in doughnut shops. But he had a friendly face, and I hoped that would put Kyleigh at ease.

"What can I do for you ladies?" he asked.

"I'm Charlie Calderbank," I said. "Jo-Jo McMullen's niece. Kyleigh here has some information about my aunt's accident."

He looked from me to Kyleigh, who leaned against the wall, checking her cuticles. "Come on back," he said.

We followed him to an office at the rear of the building. Dark wood paneled the office, and it had a well-worn, probably 1970s-hip look. When Captain Sanders settled behind his desk, we sat on the cracked green leather chairs across from him.

I looked at Kyleigh and tilted my head toward the captain. "Tell him," I said.

"I heard my uncle say he cut Mrs. McMullen's brake line," she said so softly, I could barely hear her.

Captain Sanders leaned forward in his seat. "What? You're gonna have to speak up, Miss. My hearing isn't what it used to be."

Kyleigh gave a heavy sigh. "My uncle was the one who cut Mrs. Mc-Mullen's brake line," she said in a louder voice.

"And how do you know that?"

"I heard him on the phone to someone. He said he cut the brake line, but he didn't kill Ms. Masanova. Whoever he was talking to did."

"I see," the captain said. Picking up a pen, he clicked it open and started making notes on a legal pad.

Over an hour later, Kyleigh had answered a barrage of questions. The same information looked at from every angle, backwards and forward, and inside out. Ray Boyce admitted he'd sabotaged the brake lines on my aunt's car; he had a journal that held Lucy's killer's secret, and he was using it to frame them.

"I'll have Officer Sabato pick Ray up so we can question him," he said. "Are you going to be okay with your aunt, Kyleigh?"

Kyleigh shrugged. "I guess."

"I have an idea," I said.

I had Kyleigh send her aunt a text saying that we had asked her to spend the night at the pet hotel because one dog needed several doses of medication throughout the evening.

Her response: *You better get paid double time!*

I got Kyleigh away from the police station before Nick could bring Ray Boyce in for questioning. If he saw his niece ratting him out, I was sure he wouldn't take it well.

We stopped at the rehab on our way home. I asked Kyleigh to wait in the car while I checked in with my aunt for a minute. She didn't need to witness another conversation.

I found Aunt Jo-Jo in her room, sitting in a recliner, and watching the news.

When she saw me, she muted the sound. I shut the door behind me and sat on the edge of her bed. "Nick knows about the necklace," I said.

She nodded. "Yes, he came by."

"What did he say?"

She fussed with the blanket over her knees. "Oh, you know, the usual questions when your belongings are found at a crime scene. I told him the truth. I have no idea how my necklace got there."

"Do you think he believed you?"

"Nick and I go way back. He can't possibly think I murdered Lucy with my bare hands. But he said he would look at all leads, no matter how much I meant to him."

I thought back to his comment about protecting me like all citizens. "He can be all business at times."

She nodded. "I imagine it's a tough job in a small town, where you walk the tightrope between having friends and upholding the law. Anyway, your aunt is now a suspect in a murder investigation. It is what it is."

I filled her in on Ray Boyce being the one who cut her brake line.

She raised an eyebrow. "Ray? Well, I'll be darned. I wonder just what I could have done to make him want to kill me."

"The box Lucy gave you had a journal inside. Apparently, that journal is the key."

"And Ray has it?"

"Last I heard. Hopefully, Nick will get his hands on it when he brings Ray in for questioning."

"And we can put this whole miserable chain of events behind us."

"That would be nice," I said. "I'm sorry, I can't stay longer, but Kyleigh's waiting for me in the car."

"I'll be fine," she said. "I need to sit with this information for a while. It's a lot to digest."

I gave her a hug and kissed the top of her head. She squeezed me with her good arm, and I left the room.

Kyleigh and I stopped at the market for groceries and then headed home.

Back at my aunt's house, we made a salad and grilled cheese sandwiches. The storm had rolled in, making it feel like the middle of winter. I lit a fire, which we sat in front of while we ate.

She was quiet, and I battled fleeting thoughts that scared the bejesus out of me. Would Ray go with Nick peacefully? Thoughts of Nick getting hurt made me sick. I was relieved that Kyleigh was safe for now, but just how far would Ray go to keep his freedom?

Even though reason told me not to, I sent Nick a text message after we'd put the dishes away. *Dying to know how things went with Ray and that you're safe.* I didn't care if it sounded too familiar, since I was just an ordinary resident of Orca Cove. He wasn't just another resident to me.

I made up a bed for Kyleigh on the couch and she quickly fell asleep with Maya at her feet. I changed into a pair of sweats and a T-shirt and brushed my teeth, then closed myself inside the sleeping porch so I wouldn't disturb her slumber, knowing Maya would protect her and that her biggest threat was probably in police custody.

Noah jumped onto the bed and curled into a ball. I checked my phone for the millionth time, but no response from Nick. Maybe I'd overstepped the boundaries he'd been trying to set. With Aunt Jo-Jo as a suspect, he'd have even more reason to distance himself from me. But I was going out of my mind with worry.

Turning out the light, I stood in the dark and looked out the window. My heart caught in my throat when I saw the police cruiser pull into the driveway. I could see Nick sitting in the driver's seat. He made no motion to get out, but looked up at the dark house. I turned to grab a jacket, but by the time I put it on and pulled the door open to rush out to him, he'd backed down the driveway, and all I could see were the taillights of the cruiser as it drove slowly down the hill.

I shut the door. Noah stood, waiting for me. I reached down and patted his head. My phone lay on the bedside table, the screen lit, the only light in the room. I picked it up and checked the message.

Sleep tight, Jersey.

I held the phone to my chest and climbed under the covers. It was the closest I could get to a hug.

Chapter Thirty-Nine

I stopped in front of the school and put the car in park. Absorbed in our own thoughts, Kyleigh and I had driven in silence. She hugged her backpack to her chest but made no move to get out of the car.

"I imagine it will be hard to concentrate today," I said.

She let out a long breath. "I have a test first period. I didn't study at all."

"Pick C," I said. "When in doubt, always pick C."

She laughed.

"I was wondering," I said. "Your school should have a copy of your birth certificate. Do you have time to see if they'd give you a copy?"

She shrugged. "Why are you so focused on my birth certificate?"

"If Lucy tried to get a copy before she died, she must have had a reason."

"I guess."

We got out and walked to the office. The lady at the counter greeted us with a smile. "Good morning," she said.

"Good morning," I said back. I nudged Kyleigh with my elbow.

"Hi, Mrs. Matheson," Kyleigh said. "I need a copy of my birth certificate for a class project. I can't find mine. Do you think I could get a copy of the one you have on file?"

Mrs. Matheson tilted her head to the side. "I don't see why not. I'll be right back."

She disappeared into a back room. "I'm nervous," Kyleigh said.

"Why?"

"What if it lists my father? It's going to open a whole can of worms."

"But won't it be good to know?"

"What if he's a loser?

"I can look at it first," I said. "You only have to look if you want to."

She nodded.

Mrs. Matheson had a paper in her hand when she came back into the room. She stopped at a copy machine and made a copy, then handed it to Kyleigh. Kyleigh held it for a moment, but then handed it to me. "Thank you," she said.

At the door, we let two students in before we exited into the hall. Kids filled the hallway, hanging out at lockers or walking down the wide space. Chatter was deafening. I hated high school, and for a minute, I felt like I'd stepped back in time. The clothing and hairstyles might have been different, but it still felt the same.

"Do you want me to look now?" I asked.

"No," she said. "Go do it in private. I'll talk to you about it later." She started to walk away.

"Good luck on your test," I called after her.

She waved at me over her shoulder, and then the mass of teenagers engulfed her. I couldn't get out of there fast enough.

It wasn't until I was safe in my car that I unfolded the paper and read the document. It listed Jody Boyce as the mother. The father was unknown. Nothing I didn't expect. What was surprising, however, was the place of birth. Orca Cove.

So, how come Stu said Kyleigh wasn't born here?

I drove three blocks and parked in front of City Hall.

Stu Casimo stood behind the counter. Like the last time, he didn't look all that thrilled to see me. "What now?" he said.

I laid Kyleigh's birth certificate on the counter in front of him.

He put his glasses on and looked down at the paper.

"We got this from the school," I said.

"A photocopy."

"Well, yeah. You should have the original. Place of birth *was* Orca Cove."

He held it up for closer inspection. "It's fake," he said. "The seal isn't right." He laid the paper back on the counter and pushed it toward me.

"Are you sure?"

He rolled his eyes, then pointed to the insignia on the wall behind him. It had four pictures in the middle. The one on the birth certificate had the same amount, but they were not in the same order.

"Ah, thanks," I said.

I left with more questions than answers.

Chapter Forty

My head spun as I stopped by the coffee shop for breakfast to go. Why did the school have a fraudulent birth certificate in Kyleigh's folder? It didn't give any real information. We already knew that Jody was Kyleigh's mother. We knew the date of birth. And I always suspected the father's name would be listed as unknown. Was the actual place of birth the secret?

I'd have to do some thinking. But for now, I was stumped.

I arrived at the rehab equipped with coffees and mini breakfast quiches.

My aunt was in her room with a plate of fake eggs and rubbery bacon untouched before her. She held out her hands, eager to see what treats I'd brought her.

"How are you doing since we found out about Ray?" I asked, settling in the chair across from her.

"I can't stop thinking about it," my aunt said. "I never got along with Ray. Nobody does, but I never thought he'd want me dead."

"Hopefully Nick picked him up and was able to crack him," I said. "It seems he knows who killed Lucy. Maybe he'll work out a deal for cutting your brakes by giving up the killer."

"As long as he gets some time," Jo-Jo said. "I don't like him being around Kyleigh."

Not that living with Mary was much better, but I didn't know what I could do about that.

"Do you remember when Kyleigh was born?" I asked.

My aunt swallowed her food and took a drink before she answered me.

"Kind of. I remember seeing Jody pushing her in a dilapidated stroller she must have gotten at a thrift shop. I took up a collection and a bunch of us threw her a baby shower, getting her a decent stroller and some other baby things."

"That was nice of you."

She shrugged. "In Orca Cove, we take care of our own."

"Do you remember Jody being pregnant? Or where Kyleigh was born?"

She took a minute. "No, I don't. I assumed it was a secret because she was young and unwed. And I assumed Kyleigh was born in the town hospital."

"According to Stu at City Hall, she wasn't born in Orca Cove."

My aunt tilted her head. "Well, that I don't know anything about. Her family had their problems. Maybe she went to stay with a relative. What does that have to do with anything now?"

"I'm not sure," I admitted.

I had a mouthful of quiche when Nick came through the door. He was in uniform. He looked tired, and he sported a black eye. "What happened?" I gasped.

"A brief scuffle with Ray." He perched on the corner of my aunt's bed. "The guy's a Pitbull."

"Is he in custody?" my aunt asked.

Nick nodded. "Unfortunately, he denied saying what Kyleigh overheard before he lawyered up. Trying to get his phone records, but that will take a few days or more. Good thing he assaulted me, or we'd have nothing to hold him on."

"He's his own worst enemy," my aunt said. "I just don't know why he'd try to hurt me."

"He probably thought Lucy told you more than she did," I said. "He was after that box and most likely thought you knew what was inside."

Aunt Jo-Jo shook her head. "I wish I knew. If it was worth Lucy dying over and me almost meeting my maker, it must be something big."

"And Ray has it," I said. "Can't you search his place?"

"I drew up a search warrant," Nick said. "Waiting for the judge to sign it. We only have one judge, and she's at a conference. She said she'd read it as soon as she could. We held onto his cab so we can check for any paint transfer from your aunt's car, but I couldn't see any damage that would indicate he'd shoved your aunt off the road."

He checked his watch and stood. Tilting his head toward the door, he said, "Walk me out?"

I placed my half-eaten quiche on my aunt's tray and followed him to the door. Once outside, standing next to his car, he turned to me. "Look," he said, running a hand through his hair and then tucking one side behind his ear. "About what I said the other day…"

Here we go… I crossed my arms.

"I think you know I like you a bit more than the average citizen."

A smile spread my lips; I hadn't expected an apology. "That's nice to hear, Nick. And I like you more than the average Orca Cove cop."

He laughed. "Thanks. I know the competition is tough, since I'm probably the only one you know."

We stood there awkwardly. It wasn't exactly a profession of love, but at least he admitted he liked me a bit.

"I gotta know one thing," he said, finally. "You found Lucy. I'm guessing you saw your aunt's necklace in her hand. Yet you never mentioned it. Why?"

I kicked at a pebble and put my hands in my pockets. "Sorry about that. I just didn't want you focusing on my aunt as a suspect and turning your back on Ray and Austin."

"I wouldn't have done that. I've known Jo-Jo all my life. She's a suspect, but if anything, I'd work to clear her."

"I'm sorry," I said.

He nodded. "Anything else you're keeping from me?"

"No."

"I need you to trust me," he said. "I'll figure this out."

My heart was full when I waved goodbye. I tried not to think about the shoe I'd found hidden in the storage room of the pet hotel.

Chapter Forty-One

After Nick left, I spent a little more time with my aunt, but I could see she was getting tired, so I gave her a hug and promised to visit the next day.

For the first time since I'd been in town, I didn't really have anything to do aside from cleaning the house. I was having a moderate pain day, and physical labor was as appealing as having my legs waxed. Sleuthing was much easier on my joints.

As far as finding Lucy's killer and the connection to Kyleigh's birth certificate, I was at a dead end. Nick was getting a search warrant for Ray's place. Hopefully, he could recover whatever Ray had found in Lucy's box. I doubted it. Ray didn't seem like the brightest bulb in the chandelier, but even he couldn't be that stupid.

It still seemed like Austin was the most likely suspect in the murder of his aunt. He had the most to gain. Did he know his aunt wanted to change her will? It wasn't like I could admit to him I'd seen the letter that no longer existed and ask Austin what he knew. If he was the killer, he would keep any incriminating information to himself. Besides, Nick was up to speed on the change in the will. That was his department.

I felt better having shared what I knew with Nick, and that he now knew it was my aunt's necklace in Lucy's hand. My having come clean seemed to relax our relationship. If I could call it that.

But the hidden shoe remained a secret between us.

I started driving through town, thinking I'd just go back to the hotel and spend some quality time with Noah and Maya. Maybe take them for a long walk.

Idling at a four-way stop, I checked the car to my left. We'd arrived at about the same time, and I didn't want a showdown for who would go first. I made eye contact and froze. It was the woman I'd seen with Ray two days ago. She smiled at me as I motioned for her to go ahead.

It was the same pricey BMW I'd seen before. I put on my blinker and followed her.

She led me to the bridge. My heart raced. I tried to conjure Nick's soothing voice in my head, but it wasn't working so well today. My palms started to sweat. I did my best to ignore my pending panic attack and focus on the matter before me. I knew there was a traffic light at the bottom of the bridge, and I didn't want Ray's little secret to get away from me.

I accelerated through a yellow light and tailed her several more blocks through town. When she made a sharp turn into the same motel where I'd first seen her, I couldn't react in time and had to continue down the street.

By the time I circled the block and pulled into the lot, I saw the BMW parked in a space for guests, but the driver was gone. I found a spot in the lot's corner and backed into it so I could monitor the building. I didn't know what I was looking for, but I figured I'd know when I spotted it.

It was one of those lodges that had two levels, and all the rooms exited onto a walkway with a metal railing. I could see most of the rooms from my vantage point.

I spent the next half hour playing with my phone while keeping an eye on the closed motel room doors.

A few people came and went, but no one I recognized.

About to give up, I figured I could at least get the license plate on the BMW. Maybe Nick could run the number, and we could at least find out who Ray's ladylove was.

I got out of the Subaru and walked over to the BMW as nonchalantly as I could. I tried to act cool as I snapped a photo of the car. Once done, I stuffed my phone in my back pocket and started back to my car. As I reached the Subaru, a door on the second story opened, and the bobblehead blonde stepped out.

She wore running clothes. After bouncing down the backless stairs, she checked her watch before heading down the street.

I figured I had some time.

I looked up at the closed door of room 202. A maid's cart sat several units away, but otherwise, the area was empty.

I hurried up the stairs and saw that the curtain was partway drawn on the window. Glancing through the gap in the fabric, I saw a neatly made queen-sized bed with an open suitcase on it. A round table sat in front of the window. On it were bags of chips, a bottle of whisky, and a book. Blue with pink hearts.

My heart pounded and my mouth went dry.

How many books like this that were tied to Ray could there be? This had to be what Lucy had hidden inside the green box. The one Ray had almost killed my aunt to get his hands on.

For a moment, I thought about calling Nick. But he was a good half-an-hour away, and I didn't know if we had that kind of time or if he'd even have probable cause to enter the room. And if I called the local police, they'd think I was out of my mind.

Before I could talk myself out of it, I'd backed my way against the door. Reaching back, I tried the handle. Locked.

This was getting me nowhere.

I was about to head back to my car when I saw the housekeeper pushing her cart my way.

"Hi," I said with a smile. "Wonder if you could help me?"

She came to a stop and pushed a clump of wayward hair off her brow.

"I just stepped outside to hit the vending machine, and I let the door close behind me. Unfortunately, I left the key inside."

I must have looked harmless enough, because she took out her access card and inserted it in the door.

"Thanks." I ducked inside.

I didn't have to consult a law book to know that I'd just committed a felony. I took a deep breath, but that did little to calm my nerves. The deed was done—there was no going back. I gave a quick look around the room to make sure no one was there. Satisfied I was alone, I scooped the book off the table and opened the cover.

There was a *This book belongs to:* stamp on the first page.

Below it, in loopy writing, it said: Jody Boyce.

Gulp.

I stuffed the book in the back of my waistband and looked out the window. The housekeeper and a man dressed in slacks, an oxford shirt and a tie were coming my way. She pointed toward the unit I was in.

Crap. The housekeeper had realized her mistake and must have gone to management. I eased out the door and pulled it shut behind me just as they made it to the door. I turned and walked the other way.

"Miss," the man called.

I waved a hand over my head. "Sorry, gotta go." And I hurried down the stairs, and at the bottom, I started toward my car. The blonde bobblehead rounded the corner just then, coming to a stop and taking her earphones off.

She smiled hello as we passed.

I jumped in my car as I saw the three of them meet, engaging in conversation and looking back at me and pointing.

I started the engine and drove quickly out of the spot. I didn't know if they got my license plate number and were at this very minute calling the police, but I made it to the main street and headed back to Orca Cove, my heart bouncing in my chest.

Now what was I going to do?

Chapter Forty-Two

I t was almost two-thirty by the time I made it back to Orca Cove. I was still breathing hard, and I resisted the urge to pull over and read the journal that now lay on the passenger seat.

I spent most of the drive checking my mirrors for a police car trying to stop me, but no one came for me. Still, it took a long time to calm down.

Stopping by the hotel, I rescued Noah and Maya from their shared kennel, mostly because I didn't want to be alone. Martha was on the phone, so I got out of there without talking to her. I wasn't ready to tell anyone what I'd done.

School would be out soon, and I worried about Kyleigh going home to Mary now that Ray was in jail. If she knew Kyleigh was the one who'd ratted her uncle out, there was no telling how mad Mary would be.

I parked outside the high school in a line where parents waited to pick up their kids. I took deep breaths, absently petting Noah on the seat beside me. Maya stood in the back, her head out the window, alert to our surroundings.

Once I'd calmed down, I picked up the book and laid it against the steering wheel.

The volume had been through a lot. Stains marred the cover, and dog-eared pages showed fading blue ink.

I turned to the first page and started reading the musings of a teenage girl. Unpopular, longing to fit in with the cool kids. Something I could relate to. The entries spanned about six months, each one dated. I knew Kyleigh's birthday from the birth certificate. I did the math. The last months of journaling would have been when Jody was pregnant, but she never mentioned it, which I found odd. She talked about the popular kids. One she called "the goddess" had started including her in their get-togethers. There were late-night parties at the beach and at houses when parents were out of town. The ocean spot reminded me of where Nick had taken me on his uncle's property. Jody had a crush on a boy who had gone off to college. It could have been Nick. She never named him, but the description fit.

I read bits and pieces, the beginning, the middle, and the end. Except there was no end. Not because she stopped writing, but because someone tore out several pages. Remnants of those pages, fringes of paper, still clung to the spine. I counted twelve of them. A lot could have happened during that time.

Why had someone removed them? If this journal was worth killing over, those pages had to say something that would incriminate the killer. As far as I knew, Lucy was the only one who knew what that was. And Ray, of course. But neither one was talking.

At ten to three, the school bell rang, and kids poured out of the building like ants on their way to a picnic. I stuffed the journal in my bag, got out of the car, and stood like the moms, scanning the crowd for their kids.

After the first wave of teenagers erupted, I spotted Kyleigh, alone and walking with her head down. When she was almost upon me, she stopped short, her attention on the woman closing in on us. Mary Boyce.

I braced for the confrontation. Given the information I had that Ray was cheating on his wife, I almost felt sorry for her. Almost.

"Let's go," she snapped at Kyleigh.

Kyleigh gave me a pleading look. "I have to go to work."

"You're not working for those people, not anymore." Mary grabbed Kyleigh by the arm.

"Whoa, whoa!" I held my hands out like I was trying to stop traffic. "Let's take a minute here."

"Mind your own business," Mary spat. "This doesn't concern you." She let go of Kyleigh and stepped forward, stabbing her finger in my chest. "Ever since you got here, you've put ideas in her head."

I swatted her hand away.

Before I could deliver a comeback, Maya leapt from the car and advanced on Mary, snarling and growling like she meant business.

Mary took two steps back. "Control your dog."

"Not until you control your mouth," I shot back. I looked at Kyleigh. "Would you like a ride to work?"

Kyleigh rushed over to my car and got into the passenger seat. She called for Maya, who gave Mary one last bark before she turned and got into the car.

"I suggest you concentrate on your husband's legal problems," I said. "Kyleigh's safe with us." I turned and got into the driver's seat, leaving Mary looking after us with her mouth gaping open. My hand shook as I started the car, but as I drove away, I caught Kyleigh smiling in the seat beside me.

"You're a badass," she said.

I felt invigorated.

Chapter Forty-Three

Kyleigh stayed with Martha at the hotel. After taking Maya and Noah on a quick walk, I left them with a few treats in an unoccupied room. With Jody's journal tucked in my bag, I headed back to town.

I rehearsed several explanations of how the diary ended up in my possession, but they all sounded laughable. I'd have to come up with something on the fly, like most criminals did.

A drive by the police station told me all the cruisers were gone and Nick was out and about. I had to share the journal with him. Not only could it shed some light on what Lucy had been after, but I believed Nick had a starring role in the book, and perhaps reading it would unearth some buried memory from that summer.

I pulled over and sent him a text. *You got time for a chat? I found something.*

I'm at the beach, he replied. *The one where we found Lucy.*

Be there in 5, I texted back.

His squad car sat at the trail entrance. I pulled up behind it. The sky was an ominous shade of gray, but the air was still, like the town held a collective breath. Grabbing my bag from the passenger seat, I jogged down the path, slowing as I reached the clearing where Nick sat high on a rock overlooking where we found Lucy's body. His attention was on the churning water below.

"Hey," he said, without looking my way.

I climbed up the jagged boulder and slid onto the piece of flat rock beside him. There wasn't much room, and our thighs touched before I made a conscious effort to clamp my legs together, leaving about an inch between us.

He turned to look at me but didn't say a word.

Taking the diary from my bag, I laid it on his lap.

"What's this?"

"Jody Boyce's journal."

His brow wrinkled as he picked up the book and turned it over in his hands. "And where did you find it?"

"You don't really want to know." I held my breath.

He smirked and shook his head as he thumbed through the pages. "You're like a dog who steals the remote and then brings it to you while wagging his tail."

I cringed. Pretty good analogy—I had to hand him that.

"I'm guessing you already read this," he said. "Care to give me the Cliff Notes?"

I upped the zipper on my hoodie and crossed my arms to keep warm. "After being a bit of a nerd all her life, Jody started hanging out with the cool kids. I assume that included you and Alex. She was gaga over you, by the way."

He shook his head, obviously amused.

I continued. "She wrote it during the time she would have gotten pregnant with Kyleigh, but she never mentioned it. Not about having a boyfriend or finding out she was pregnant or any symptoms that go along with it. Odd, don't you think?"

When he didn't answer, I went on. "She didn't seem to have a boyfriend. In fact, she was intensely jealous of Alex and her relationship with you. She dreamed of someone touching her the way you touched Alex." I let that settle in.

I could feel Nick tense next to me. Was it because we were discussing his love life, or did he know something? When he said nothing, I added, "Several pages at the end were torn out."

I took the book from his hands, turned to the last page, and read the last entry aloud. "I can't believe what I'm about to do. But I'm the only one who knows the truth. How can I say no?"

Nick bit his lip and took the book from my hands. "You're kidding? That's all there is?"

I nodded.

He gave a heavy sigh. "I remember Jody hanging around. Alex and I and some of the others were preparing to head off to college. Me and Alex were drifting apart. Honestly, Jody was like a stray dog who followed us around. She was as meek as a mouse, not contributing to anything that I can recall."

"I'm betting the missing pages tell us what we need to know."

He nodded. "If Lucy had the diary, did she tear them out, or did someone else?"

"Could be Ray," I said. "But she never mentioned Ray or Mary, at least not in the pages that are there. Did Ray and Mary hang out with you guys?"

"No. Ray's a few years older than me, and if I remember correctly, he dropped out of school. I don't remember much about Mary except that I would see her smoking outside before class. There has to be something in those missing pages that incriminates someone."

"Seems like Lucy came across the journal and asked Aunt Jo-Jo to hold on to it. Why? She must have thought someone might come looking for it."

"Or that something might happen to her, and she wanted the journal to be somewhere safe."

"Except Ray found out about it and cut my aunt's brake line and stole the journal. Kyleigh overheard him blackmailing whoever he was talking to?"

"I wouldn't put it past him," Nick said. "Ray is always hustling to make money."

I was about to tell him about Ray's mistress, but my cell phone dinged.

I pulled it out of my pocket. *Maya is AWOL again, can u work ur magic?* Martha.

Which way did she go?

Toward town.

I'll look for her.

"What's the matter?" Nick asked.

"Maya's missing again."

Nick looked at the sky. "Of course she is." He stood and offered me his hand, helping me down to the beach. "I'll drive."

Chapter Forty-Four

We ran up the trail to Nick's squad car. He did a U-turn, and we drove past Wiggle Butt Manor and up the hill. The chances of finding Maya dwindled the more time ticked on. I always feared a car would hit her or she would encounter wildlife even she couldn't handle. Desperation set in. I'd grown fond of the old hellion. We decided that Lucy's house was our best bet since Maya had lived there all her life. She would probably head toward the familiar.

But we were wrong. One street down, I spotted her galloping down the road. Not toward Lucy's house, but down a dirt road that looked like a dead end.

"Son of a biscuit," Nick said, making a hard left turn.

Maya upped her speed.

"You sure she's fifteen?" I said.

Nick laughed. "She's bionic, I swear."

We came to a stop in front of a chain-link fence. Someone tacked a giant "Keep Out" sign to the wire. Maya looked back over her shoulder, like she was encouraging us to follow. Then she ran along the fence and disappeared behind the building.

Nick put the car in park, and we looked at each other. It was a business. Although mostly rubbed off, I could still decipher the letters on the door. **Boyce Taxi and Collectables.** All kinds of junk and a weather-beaten yellow taxi were on the other side of the fence. Maybe it was the yellow cab that nudged my aunt into a tree. Maybe there was more than one.

We both got out of the car. I pushed the button on the gate, and a buzzer sounded. No one answered, and there was no obvious activity on the property. It looked like the business had closed years ago.

"Maya!" I called.

Nick started around the fence, and I followed. We squeezed between some overgrown bushes and the chain-link fence until we made it to the back of the building. Maya, on the other side of the fence, madly dug in the soft earth, kicking up mounds of dirt behind her.

"Gosh darn it, Maya," I called. "Come here."

She stopped mid-dig and glanced at me. But I didn't hold her attention for long, and she returned to the task at hand.

The hole was so deep, I could only see the tip of Maya's tail now.

Nick stuck his boot through the slats and hooked his fingers higher up. He climbed the fence, then jumped, landing in a crouch on the other side.

I laced my fingers through the chain link and stood on my toes.

Nick walked toward Maya. "Whatcha doing, girl?"

She stopped digging and came up with something in her mouth. She shook herself, then jumped out of the hole, walked past Nick, and trotted my way. She dropped what she'd dug up on the ground in front of me.

"What did you find, girl?" I squatted down to her level. An offering. Skeletal remains laid at my feet.

Chapter Forty-Five

Giant raindrops sputtered from the gray sky. But we just stood there, staring at Maya's find.

"Is that human?" I asked.

Nick bent down for a closer inspection. "I barely passed biology, I'm not sure. But given what's been going on, I'm not just gonna shake it off and assume it's an animal."

Maya looked at me and barked. "Good girl," I said. "How you found that, I don't know."

"She's freaky like that," Nick said. He got on his radio and called for backup.

"You should wait in the car," he said. "No use both of us getting soaked."

I'd barely noticed the rain. Maybe Ray was in even deeper trouble than I'd thought. I got back in the car and waited just as the sky opened and pelted the ground.

I watched Nick find a rope and tie Maya to a post under an awning so she wouldn't get any wetter, and she couldn't disturb the scene. Then he scaled the fence and joined me in the car.

I waited while he started the engine and blasted the heat before I spoke. "What do you know about this place?"

Nick rubbed his hands together in front of the vent. "It's been in Ray's family since I can remember. He used to operate a taxi service out of it, but he just takes calls on his cell now, and they shut down the office a few years ago. He collects junk from yard sales and picks through people's trash. He stores the stuff here and sometimes fixes it up and sells it."

"Seems like he's lost interest." Junk scattered across the property looked like it hadn't been touched in a while.

Two squad cars pulled up, and three officers got out, rain slickers over their uniforms. We got out and joined them. My hoodie was soaked through to my skin.

Two guys and a woman who identified herself as Linda joined us at the gate. The man cut the lock with bolt cutters. We walked into the yard single file. "Don't touch anything," Nick said over his shoulder.

Walking by a yellow cab, I noticed a dent in the front bumper. "Look," I said.

Nick turned back and inspected the car. "Just might be what we're looking for, but let's deal with the bones first."

At the side yard, we gathered around the hole Maya had dug. Maya's hard work eroded as the deep pit quickly filled with water.

My sweatshirt was heavy and glued to my body. A chill rattled my teeth. I pulled my hood up. Not that it did any good.

Nick walked over to the shed and came back with a shovel. He jumped in the hole. The water lapped at his ankles as he started digging, glancing up at me each time he added a shovel full of dirt to the pile. "I know Maya's not your average dog," he said, slightly out of breath. "But she had to smell something to alert her to this spot."

We soon found out what that was, as Nick unearthed a dead squirrel.

"Yuck," more than one of us said.

Nick tossed it aside. If the bone Maya dug up belonged to a squirrel, it would be in a freak show.

Maya, watching from the sidelines, tried to lunge forward like she wanted to explain herself, but the rope stopped her from getting very far.

Nick went back to digging. "Call the captain and Alex," he said to Linda. "Tell them about the bone."

While Linda got on the phone, Nick's shovel hit something hard. He looked up at us and tapped the spot some more with the spade of the shovel. He handed one cop the tool and bent down. I held my breath.

As he clawed at the earth with his bare hands, Linda rejoined the group. "What's he doing?" she asked.

"He found something," I said.

Nick stood up and took the flashlight off his belt. Clicking it on, he shone the light into the deep hole. Water pooled around it, but there was no mistaking what he'd unearthed. A skull—its empty eye sockets now staring up at us.

Chapter Forty-Six

We waited for Captain Sanders and Alex to arrive inside the taxi office, out of the rain. Nick and one of the other officers had put a tarp over the dig site after he'd uncovered the skull, wanting to preserve the scene.

"What's the next step?" I asked.

Nick put his hat on the table in front of him and shook out his dripping wet hair. He had to be uncomfortable, as drenched as he was, but he seemed to take it in stride. "First skeletal remains found in Orca Cove since I've been here."

Another cop, who had a few years on the rest of us, said, "First period."

Nick ran a hand over the stubble on his chin. "We don't have the resources to deal with this. Hopefully, Alex can confirm the remains are human. Captain will most likely call in the State Police if he hasn't already."

In the movies, local cops were usually territorial over their investigations and didn't enjoy handing over the reins to outside agencies, but real life was a little less dramatic. I liked that Nick recognized his agencies' limitations. Solving the crime was more important than his ego.

When Alex and the captain arrived, Nick and Linda stepped outside with them while the rest of us waited in the office. From the window, I could see Alex jump into the pit, and then Nick reaching down to help her out a few minutes later. She tore off disposable gloves and dropped them to the ground before they walked toward the building.

Inside, Alex lowered the hood of her jacket and looked into the expectant faces of the waiting officers. When she spotted me in the group, her pretty

213

eyes narrowed. Then she looked back to Nick. "What's she doing here?"

"She's not in the way," Nick said. "The scene is secure."

"Is the skull human?" Linda asked.

"Looks like it," Alex said. "Of course, I'll run some tests, and we need to see if there are more body parts before I can make a definitive finding."

"Calling in the state," the captain said. "Good work, crew. But we don't have the staff or the equipment to finish this. Linda and Cliff, stay here and preserve the scene until they get here. I'll give further instructions as we get direction from the detective in charge."

"I'm gonna call the judge about the search warrant on the Boyce property," Nick said. "We can at least check the trailer while the state deals with this mess. With this additional information, I'm sure she'll sign the warrant."

The captain nodded. "Ray Boyce has been a cancer on this community for a long time. I'm glad he's already in custody. We gotta play this by the book. If he buried someone on his property, no reason to think he wouldn't kill again."

Alex went wide-eyed. "You think he killed Lucy?"

The captain shrugged. "Time will tell, but who else on this island seems even remotely capable of committing such a heinous act? Now all we've got to do is prove it."

We returned to our respective vehicles as Linda and Cliff cordoned off the area with yellow crime scene tape. Luckily, the rain had stopped.

"Any idea who the deceased is?" I asked once we were underway. "Any unsolved missing persons' cases?"

Nick bit his lip. "I appreciate what you've contributed so far," he said. "I can see you have a knack for this stuff. I don't know why you didn't finish the police academy. I hope someday you'll feel comfortable enough with me to talk about it."

I patted Maya's head as she nudged me from the back seat. Today wouldn't be that day.

"However," he said, eyes on the road. "I need you to back off on policing. This isn't your case to solve."

"I know," I said, trying not to get defensive. "I'm just curious."

He pulled onto the main road and headed toward town. We drove the rest of the way in silence. "Look," he said, pulling up to my aunt's house. "I need to change into some dry clothes. I'm sure you need to do the same. The judge signed the search warrant, so we'll be heading out to the Boyces' trailer in a few."

"Oh." I couldn't mask the disappointment in my voice.

He turned to look at me. "I'm probably going to regret this, but we have a ride-along program. You'd have to sign a waiver and borrow a bulletproof vest, but you could tag along. I feel like I need to keep an eye on you before you get into trouble."

"Who, me?" But I didn't feel offended. I was beyond excited at the prospect of being included. If I hadn't been in the car, I would have jumped for joy.

"Meet me at the station in an hour."

"Sure thing." I got out of the car with Maya and went inside. After picking up Noah from the kennel, I took a long hot shower and then put on a fresh pair of jeans and layered a few shirts under my last clean hoodie. Because my sneakers were soaked, I put on my ankle boots—the only other footwear I had.

I fed the dogs and checked on Kyleigh. She was on her hands and knees deep-cleaning a kennel while a curious Schnauzer watched her every move. "How you doing?" I asked.

She looked over her shoulder at me. "I'm okay."

"You're staying the night, right?" I said.

She nodded. "If you don't mind."

"Of course, I don't. I'm heading off for a bit. If I get done in time, I'll get some takeout and meet you back here for dinner later."

"Sounds good," she said.

Chapter Forty-Seven

Linda and the other officers who had been at Ray's business met us at the station. Linda was a few inches shorter than me, but we would wear the same size vest. She offered me an extra vest, claiming it was only "slightly expired" and would still protect me from gunshot wounds, stabbings, or other undesirable things. I didn't even know what she was talking about. "It's like a 'sell by' date on eggs," she added. "You can still eat them a few days after."

It was then that it dawned on me that we could very well get into a gunfight. "Ah, Nick," I said, pulling him aside as we walked toward the conference room to discuss the plan for executing the warrant. "I forgot to tell you a minor detail."

Hands on hips, he said, "Go on."

I looked down at my feet. "I saw a gun in the trailer. After Mary left, it was gone. I assume it's hers. I thought you should know before we go barging onto the Boyces' property."

"Anything else?"

"Well…"

Nick's heavy sigh caused a slight breeze. "Spill it."

"Ray's having an affair. I saw him with another woman in town. I got the license plate of her car." I pulled up the photo on my phone and showed it to him.

He ran his hands through his hair; I imagined he'd rather use them to strangle me. "Anything else you've left out?"

My eyes met his, which were squinty with anger. Not gonna give up the shoe just yet. "Not that I can think of."

He opened his mouth to speak, pointed his finger at me, and then rolled his eyes and dropped his hand. "What's the use?" He moved past me, and I followed him into the briefing room. My heart felt heavy. Maybe it was the vest that pressed against my torso like the casing on a sausage, or maybe it was Nick sharing the info I'd just told him, and the wide-eyed stares from his peers, but suddenly I found it hard to breathe.

They came up with a plan. Everyone knew where they were going to stand, and that Nick was going to the door first. My job was to stand back and out of the way. Easy, peasy.

It was hard to keep the element of surprise on our side, given the narrow, dead-end road that led to the Boyces' trailer. So, by the time all four squad cars had pulled onto the property, Mary clearly heard us and met us in the yard.

"What's this about?" she demanded.

Nick handed her a copy of the warrant while the other officers gathered in a semi-circle around her. The German Shepherd was chained to a tree. He lunged at us, but his restraint yanked him back, and he wasn't too much of a threat. I felt sorry for him, as he had to stand back and out of the way, just like I did.

Linda patted Mary down for weapons and then asked her to take a seat on a rusty lawn chair after dumping off standing water. "Where's your gun?" she asked.

Mary gave her a hard stare and shrugged.

While Linda kept watch of Mary, the others went inside the trailer.

Mary glared at me. "You," she said. "Figures you'd have something to do with this."

Linda flashed me a questioning glance, and I swallowed my comeback about Mary's husband trying to kill my aunt. This wasn't the time.

Since the trailer was no bigger than a school bus, the search didn't take long. Nick came out holding a cell phone. He stopped in front of Mary. "This belong to Ray?"

She shrugged. He tapped the screen, and a photo of a scantily clad woman appeared behind the request for a password. I recognized the bobblehead blonde right away. "Doubt this belongs to you," Nick said.

Mary stared him down, but a look of concern flashed in her eyes.

Nick sighed. "We can have forensics bypass the password, but that could take weeks, and the judge won't be keen to release Ray from jail until we have all the details. Or you could just give me the code and move things along."

Mary crossed her arms. "I need a cigarette. I don't have any because I've been trying to quit, but I can think more clearly if I have a smoke."

Nick nodded. "We can accommodate that." He walked to his car and dug through the glove compartment, coming back with a rumpled pack of cigarettes. "Sorry," he said, offering Mary one. "They're probably stale. I keep them in the car because a lot of people used to want one last toke before they go to jail. But most seem to have given up the habit, so I haven't replenished the supply."

Mary wasn't picky. She accepted the offer and leaned in while Nick clicked the lighter and held out the flame. We all waited while she inhaled. "Code is usually 10122012, the day we tied the knot. Ray's sentimental like that."

More than one of us coughed to cover up a laugh.

"But," Mary added. "I've never seen that phone before. Where did you find it?"

"Under the mattress," Nick said.

Guess Mary never changed the sheets. Yuck.

Nick typed the numbers on the screen, and the phone opened. Apparently, Ray went to the trouble of hiding a burner phone from his wife but didn't bother to come up with a new password.

Nick walked in circles as he looked through the apps. Mary had almost finished her cigarette by the time he seemed satisfied he'd found what he was looking for. "There's some steamy text messages, and it looks like Ray made a pretty big money transfer to someone on this payment app. Ten grand. Did you know Ray had that amount of money?"

Mary sat up straighter. "That's not possible."

"Seems like he's been holding out on you," Nick said. "Maybe he's not as sentimental as you thought."

Looked like Ray was leading a double life.

Nick slid the phone into an evidence bag. "Gonna hold on to this. Anything else you want to share with us?"

Mary took one last puff on her cigarette. "Think I'll call a lawyer."

"Good idea." He tipped the bill of his hat, and we went back to our cars.

Once I was settled on the seat beside him, I asked, "Does the app show who paid and why?"

Nick put the car in gear and started down the driveway, the other cruisers on our tail. "It was some initials. Same ones of the woman who owns the BMW you followed. Says it's for Love Shack."

"Do you think Ray was planning to leave Mary?"

"Stranger things have happened," he said. "Even more puzzling, though, is where Ray got that kind of money."

Chapter Forty-Eight

W e went back to the police station. I left the vest I'd borrowed on Linda's desk, feeling twenty pounds lighter. I stood at Nick's cubicle, placing a knee on the chair next to his desk. "What's next?" I asked.

This close, I could see dark circles under his eyes. I hoped it was a consequence of the case and not that I was wearing on him. Nick pounded on the keyboard of his computer, and a mugshot filled the screen. The bobblehead blonde. She looked like she was having a bad day, not the springy jogger I'd seen at the motel. "Recognize her?" he asked.

I nodded. "Ray's girlfriend."

He scrolled past the photo to some text. "She has a record out of Seattle. Has a habit of taking care of the elderly and then swindling them out of money. Looking into Lucy's bank records, she had hired someone to help her about a month before her murder."

"You think it was her?" I leaned over his shoulder so I could read the name on the screen. "Bethany Williams?"

"I'm guessing," he said. "I was going to head over to the motel and see if she's still staying there."

I flashed a goofy smile. "Can I tag along?"

Nick laughed. "Since you led me to her, I guess that's only fair."

He started to stand, but his desk phone rang. He pushed the speakerphone button and answered. "Orca Cove Police."

"Hey, Nick, It's Linda."

"What's up?" he asked, rubbing his eyes.

"Forensics dug up a class ring. Thought you'd like to know."

Nick took the call off speakerphone. "What year?" he asked. There was a lot of nodding and "uh-hums," but I could no longer hear what Linda was saying.

Once he hung up, he stood and pulled on a slicker.

"Oh, come on," I said. "What did she say about the ring?"

Nick sighed. "It's from Orca Cove High."

"What year?"

"The year Jody would have graduated. Except she dropped out halfway through her senior year. Would she have a ring?"

I thought back to my high school years. "Most kids don't bother getting one these days. But they are available. You have to order it in advance. Maybe she didn't know she'd be leaving school when she ordered it."

He rubbed his forehead. "Maybe Jody Boyce never left town like everyone thought."

"That would mean Kyleigh's mother didn't abandon her. She's dead."

"Let's not get ahead of ourselves," Nick said. "This is all speculation. She wasn't the only person in that class to get a ring."

"But is she the only one missing?"

"I don't know," Nick said. "Easy enough to narrow that down, though. I asked Lindsey to bring her yearbook to the charity race tomorrow."

"For the dog park?"

"That's the one. Hey, you up for a ride? Linda has to work, leaving an open spot on our team. Plus, it will keep you busy and your nose out of this case."

I rolled my eyes. I was an avid exerciser. My sedentary status since arriving in Orca Cove left me feeling like a slug. I would not use my disease as a reason to sit on the sidelines. "Sure," I said, following him toward the door. "What do I have to do?"

"Meet us here at eight-thirty. I'll find you a bike and a helmet. Should be everything you need."

He held the door open, and I followed him to the car. "Let's go find Ms. Williams," he said.

Chapter Forty-Nine

"So, the thing is," Nick said as he started over the bridge. "I don't know where Ray got that ten grand. I'll need to get his bank records, and that will take time and another warrant. But he transferred it to Ms. Williams. I've got to get her to tell me why."

"Love shack," I said. "Do you think they're building a place together?"

He shrugged.

In the back of my mind, I knew we were crossing the bridge. My heart rate increased, but I tried to just focus on Nick's handsome profile and ignore my surroundings. So far, it was working.

"I still wonder about Austin," I said. "He had the best motive."

"I haven't ruled him out yet. Sometimes investigations lead you down a different path, and you discover a different crime entirely. Maybe this whole Ray mess has nothing to do with Lucy's murder."

"But if Bethany worked for Lucy..."

"If," Nick said. "We haven't established that yet."

I directed Nick to the motel I'd been at earlier. We pulled into the lot shortly after eight. It was dark out, but at least it wasn't raining. Nick called in our location on the police radio.

The BMW remained in the same spot.

"Hang back while I talk to her," he said. "If she lets me in, stay by the door."

"Got it."

The door swung open before Nick could knock. Bethany stood there pulling a suitcase on wheels with a backpack slung over one shoulder. She'd changed out of her running clothes and wore jeans and a white puffy coat.

Her shiny blond hair was straight and hung to her waist. She was beautiful in a plastic way.

She could do better than Ray.

Nick held his hands against his vest. I knew from my limited training that the position left him ready for anything, yet looked unimposing to the public. Bethany took in his uniform and stepped back. Letting go of the handle of her suitcase, she adjusted the strap of her backpack and crossed her arms. "Can I help you?"

"I'm Officer Sabato," he said. He tilted his head in my direction. "This is Ms. Calderbank. Looks like you're on your way out."

She licked her lips. "No law against that."

He chuckled, and she visibly relaxed, taken in by his charm. Boom! He had her.

"Got a couple of questions," he said. "Nothing for you to worry about, just hoping you can help me out."

She stepped back and allowed us to come inside. Like Nick said, I stayed close to the door. Nick took about five steps inside and remained standing. Bethany looked unsure of herself as she perched her tiny butt on the edge of the bed. "What kind of questions?"

"I understand you worked for Lucy Masanova for a bit."

Her eyes darted from Nick to me to the door. "Just a few weeks."

"What did she hire you to do?"

"This and that. She wanted me to help her go through the house. She was thinking of selling it."

Nick nodded. "And you found a diary."

She unzipped her jacket. "I don't know what you're talking about."

"Sure, you do," he said softly. "Blue with hearts on it."

"Maybe," she said. "There was a lot of junk in that house. You're free to look around. I don't have a journal."

"I'm aware of that," he said. "Not anymore, you don't. But did you read it?"

She played with the edge of her coat. "I don't think so."

"What about Ray?" Nick asked.

"Ray, who?"

Nick smirked. "Ray, the guy you sucked face with in the parking lot."

Bethany hung her head. "I barely know him."

"Yet he sent you ten thousand dollars."

The color drained from her face, but she recovered quickly. "So, he gave me money. Men like to give me things."

Nick let that one slide. "Love shack," he said. "Catchy song, but what does it have to do with you and Ray?"

Her face hardened. Charming or not, he was pushing her buttons. "Ray might have ideas," she said. "But he's not my type."

"So, you're leaving town. With his money."

"Money he gave me. Nothing against accepting a gift."

"Maybe not," Nick said, taking out a pack of notecards. "Not from a legal perspective, at least. You got an address?"

She stood up and put her backpack on. "I'm between places."

"A phone number?"

"I don't give that out." She walked over to her suitcase and took the handle in her hand.

The housekeeper appeared behind me. I cringed, thinking she would remember me, but she kept her head down.

"I think we're done here," Bethany said. "I've checked out, and housekeeping is here to clean the room. Sorry, I couldn't be more helpful."

Nick stepped aside, and she walked around him and out the door. We watched her struggle to get her suitcase down the stairs and into the trunk of the BMW.

The cleaning lady looked at me, and then Nick. "Hi," Nick said. "We'll get out of your way in a minute. But first, can I ask you if you've seen or heard anything between the guests in this room?"

Her eyes met mine.

"We've met," I said, hoping to derail her from telling Nick she let me in the room. "But anything between that woman who just left and a man?"

She looked over her shoulder, making sure Bethany was not in earshot. When the BMW pulled out of the lot, she seemed to relax a little. "I heard a conversation. They came into the room and didn't realize I was in the bathroom. I'd forgotten something when I was cleaning and came back in to get it."

"What did you hear?"

"The man, he asked that lady if she'd delivered the papers. She said she'd get to it later. He got real mad. He said their future depended on it. That if she wanted to continue having nice things, they needed to let the man... I can't remember his name..." She stopped and tapped the side of her head. "Sorry, it's not coming to me."

"That's okay. What else did they say?" Nick asked.

She sighed. "I'm trying to remember. Something about letting the man know that they had information that the man wouldn't want the world to know. Something about protecting his secret. They said that when... Oh, what was his name?" She shook her head. "It started with an A."

"Austin?" I asked.

She blew out a long breath. "Maybe. Something like that. Anyway, when he got the papers, he would pay big time. Something like ten thousand dollars to keep them quiet."

"That's good," Nick said. "Anything else?"

"I knew I shouldn't be listening. That if they found me.... Well, I didn't know what they'd do. But then the woman said that she would deliver the papers now, and the man said he had to pick up a fare. And they both left."

I paced the walkway while Nick took down the housekeeper's information and gave her his card. "Call me if you think of anything else," he said before joining me outside.

We walked to the car and didn't speak until we were on our way back to Orca Cove. "It has to be Austin," I said. "But I think he's broke. Where would he get the ten grand?"

"I don't know," Nick said. "Maybe that's why he's broke. He gave Bethany everything he had. I'm gonna drop you off and then have a talk with Mr. Masanova."

I gave him my best puppy dog eyes. "Can't I come?"

"No," he said. "He likes you. I'm afraid he won't be as genuine if he's trying to impress you. I've already let you be too involved. Go home and get some sleep. I'll see you at the ride in the morning."

Disappointment swelled inside of me, but he was right. I'd already seen and heard more than any civilian should.

When he came to a stop outside the pet hotel, he turned to look at me. "I'd appreciate it if you kept the information we gathered today quiet for now."

I gave him a mock salute. "Of course. See you in the morning."

I got out of the car and watched him drive away. Maybe Nick invited me to the race so he could keep an eye on me, but that worked both ways. Hanging out with a bunch of cops might keep me in the loop of the investigation.

Chapter Fifty

When I got home, Kyleigh was sitting on the front porch with Noah on her lap and Maya at her feet. Maya ran to greet me at the car and escorted me back to the house, her tail thumping all the way.

Knowing her mother many not have abandoned her, but instead had rotted away in a shallow grave with no one looking for her, it was hard not to look at Kyleigh with a newfound sadness. Police didn't have a positive ID on the body yet, but the coincidence was hard to ignore. I kept my word and didn't share the news, though.

"Sorry," I said. "I completely forgot about dinner. I got side-tracked."

"No worries," she said. "I found stuff in the fridge."

I settled on the porch beside her. My head was swimming with where the investigation into Lucy's murder had led. It was a lot to sort out. But I couldn't do that with Kyleigh beside me. So, we talked about other things. She told me she was thinking of dropping out of school, as her mother had.

"You're so close to finishing," I said. "I think that's a choice you might regret."

"It's not like I'm going to college," Kyleigh said. "What do I need a diploma for?"

"Why wouldn't you go to college?"

Her mouth dropped open. "Do you know how expensive that is?"

I thought about my student loans and the business degree I had no interest in using. "What do you want to do?"

She shrugged. "I haven't really thought about it."

"Sure, you have. If you could be anything, what would it be? Don't think about what it would take to get there. Just what would you like to do?"

"Be a rock star."

"Can you sing?"

She laughed. "Not at all."

"Me either. We could form the worst band ever."

She laughed again, and it struck me how little she smiled. "Okay, what else? You're great with dogs."

She tilted her head to the side as if thinking about that for the first time.

"One of my friends back in Jersey is a groomer. She makes decent money," I said.

"Do you have to go to school for that?"

"I think so, but it's only for a few months. We can look into it if you'd like. But everything is easier if you have a high school diploma."

She fell silent. I hoped I'd reached her on some level. I didn't want to see her become like her aunt, who seemed trapped in a miserable existence.

When she spoke again, the light that had briefly touched her faded. "Do you think Uncle Ray will go to prison?"

"He might. How would you feel if he did?"

She shrugged. "What he did was bad. Mrs. McMullen is a good lady. She took a chance on me when no one else would. I can't believe anyone would want to hurt her."

I nodded.

Kyleigh hung her head. "It's just... I don't need any more signs pointing to my family being losers."

I hadn't thought of that. "Is that why you don't want to go to school anymore? Are the kids hard on you?"

Her whole body sagged. She didn't answer. She didn't have to—her pain was obvious.

"When I was a kid, we moved around constantly because my mom always had new boyfriends. I was always the outsider. But you know what? It gets better. Life isn't always about high school. When you can move on, you meet other people. You find your people."

After rough years in high school, I found a few friends in college, but I didn't truly fit in until I entered the police academy. I felt accepted, like no other time in my life. Kyleigh didn't need to know just yet that you could be comfortable one moment and rudderless the next. That's how I felt when I got my diagnosis and had to quit the academy. But being here, with my aunt, Martha, Nick, and even Kyleigh, I was getting that settled feeling again. I tried not to dwell on the fact that I'd be leaving soon.

We turned in around ten. I didn't know how exhausted I was until my head hit the pillow. I hoped my little pep talk had given Kyleigh some hope. If I followed my own advice, my future didn't have to be bleak. I just had to find the next big thing.

As tired as I was, my adrenaline from the events of the day made it hard to sleep. I ticked through the list of what had happened that day. It started with Kyleigh's fake birth certificate. I stole the journal and lied about it to Nick. Maya found skeletal remains, which brought the state police and their forensics unit into the loop. And then there was the search warrant at the trailer. Ray and Bethany were blackmailing someone. Was it Austin? What did he have to do with the journal? Like me, he'd been to the island in his youth, although I was pretty sure we'd never crossed paths. Bethany had a history of taking advantage of the elderly. Was Lucy a victim? Did she share the journal's contents with Bethany? Were they trying to blackmail someone with the missing pages? And what did Nick learn when questioning Austin? I checked my phone. If he'd learned anything new, he wasn't sharing it with me.

I glanced at the time. Almost two in the morning. I had to ride a bike tomorrow. While I considered myself to be in pretty good shape, biking had never been my thing. I couldn't remember the last time I'd ridden.

I put my phone back on the charger and tried to settle in. Noah scooted closer, and I rolled over and put the pillow over my head. I don't know how long I lay there, but when my alarm went off, I felt like I'd had five minutes of sleep.

Chapter Fifty-One

I woke, grateful to see the sun was shining. A perfect day for the century ride.

I pulled on a pair of yoga leggings, a tee shirt, and my faithful hoodie. The thought of seeing Nick again made me half-hopeful and half-anxious. He sent mixed signals. I fell for him one minute and felt like a thorn in his side the next. I tried to take solace because he'd invited me to tag along, ignoring his statement about monitoring me like some unattended five-year-old with an agenda.

The blankets and pillow I'd given Kyleigh for another night on the sofa were neatly folded and stacked on the coffee table. Maya looked up at me from the dog bed in the corner. Strange that Kyleigh hadn't taken her to the hotel with her.

I grabbed a granola bar and a bottle of water and took the dogs for a short walk before going to the hotel to find Kyleigh. But Martha was there alone. "Any idea where Kyleigh is?" I asked.

Martha looked up from the dog food bowls she filled for the guests' morning nosh. "Haven't seen her today."

My stomach tightened. It was Saturday. She didn't have school, and I couldn't think of anywhere else she'd need to be this early. I checked my watch. I didn't have time to look for her. I needed to meet Nick and the others at the station. I reminded myself that Ray was in custody, and he couldn't cause Kyleigh any harm.

I walked down the hill and over two blocks to the police station. Around back, in the parking lot, I found Nick with a few people I didn't know and some that I recognized from the previous day. He smiled when he saw me, but he looked no more rested than he had the night before.

He had on mountain cycling shorts that showed off muscular legs but were loose enough to leave some things to the imagination. Not that I let my imagination go there. Not much, anyway. A long-sleeved T-shirt stretched across his biceps. Everyone else wore serious biking clothes. I felt like an impostor.

Nick handed me a helmet. "Alex is bringing you one of her bikes," he said. "She should be here soon."

And just thrilled to help me out, I was sure.

"What did Austin say?" I couldn't help myself.

"He's either a fantastic liar or he doesn't know anything about the journal," Nick said softly. I guessed he didn't want his coworkers to know he'd shared information about the case with me.

"He is an actor," I said, keeping my voice down, too. "What about the remains? Anything new?"

"Forensics is wrapping up. We'll have a briefing after the race, but I know they found more bones."

I cringed. It was good that they found them as I imagined it would be easier to piece together what happened, but I hated to think of someone lying there, undiscovered, all that time.

"I'm worried about Kyleigh," I said. "She was gone when I got up this morning."

Nick rubbed the back of his neck. "I hope Ray didn't get to her."

"He's in jail," I said.

"Not anymore." Nick's voice was solemn. "Mary bailed him out."

"I thought she was mad at him."

Nick cleared his throat. "You can't stand in the way of true love."

"Maybe I should skip the race and go look for Kyleigh."

Nick put his hand on my shoulder. "Not to worry, I have Karl keeping an eye on Ray."

"Karl, the same guy who slacked off on my aunt's accident investigation?"

"They talked to him about that. He'll keep watch on Ray."

This bit of news made me even more anxious about Kyleigh being gone. I'd been in the next room and surely would have heard if Ray had come for her in the early morning hours. I'd need to find her after the race and warn her that Ray was free.

Alex pulled up. She got out and greeted everyone. The guys in the crowd fell all over themselves, helping her unload two bikes from the bed of her truck. She motioned me over. With a deep breath, I came to stand beside her.

"Hi," she said.

"Hello. Thanks for loaning me a bike."

"Cycling is kind of my thing," she said. "So, I only have nice bikes. Stand here and we can adjust the saddle for your height."

I stood next to the bike, and Alex adjusted the seat for me. I swung my leg over the frame, and Alex had me put my foot on the pedal, and then she finished the adjustment. "Is that comfortable?"

"Yes, thank you."

She smiled, her contempt for me tucked away. She obviously wanted to put on a show for Nick, who had walked over to join us. "You're trusting Charlie with your Trek?" he said. "How nice of you."

"You know I'm a serious cyclist," Alex said. "I don't have relics like you ride."

Nick laughed. "Us cops don't pull the salary you do. I live modestly."

The easy banter between them continued until one of the group members let us know it was close to race time, and we needed to line up.

We pushed our bikes to the starting area. I was glad to see so many people had come out to support the agility park. I hoped my aunt was on the porch at the rehab so she could look down at the crowd.

Nick and Alex went toward the front of the group. I hung back, knowing I'd have to get my bicycle legs back as it had been some time since I rode, and I wasn't used to this bike. It would be my luck to crash and ruin Alex's precious possession. I'd have to be careful.

The starting pistol fired. The gunshot made me jump even though I expected it. Once the woman in front of me started moving, I put my foot on the pedal and pushed off, falling into pace with the cyclists around me.

We rode through the center of town. I fell into a rhythm and started to enjoy the sensation of getting my heart rate up. My foot was much better, and I thought about returning to my exercise routine once I got home.

The course led us through downtown. People lined the streets and cheered us on. For a moment, I worried we would go over the bridge, and I had a mini-panic attack, but then I saw the group ahead of me turn away from the water.

My watch buzzed, alerting me to an incoming message. I held up my wrist, and glanced down while trying to maintain my balance, which was more difficult than it should have been. No way I could stop with so many cyclists behind me.

The text was only two words long, so I had no trouble reading it.

Major pickle.

Kyleigh. My concern for her safety had been spot on. If Ray held her responsible for his legal problems, I had no doubt he'd make her pay for it. I looked for the opportunity to break away from the crowd without causing an accident. The off-ramp for the bridge was to my right, and I veered toward it, almost clipping the bike behind me. I heard the rider scream profanities at me as I struggled to stay upright. "Sorry," I yelled over my shoulder.

I sailed past the closed sign on the bridge and pumped the brakes. I heard a squeaking sound. Not comforting. As I slowed, I looked for a place to stop so I could get back to Kyleigh and ask her where she was. As I raised my watch to tap out a reply, a truck came from another entrance, ignoring the fact that the bridge was closed and barreled up the on-ramp. I recognized Ray Boyce's rust bucket right away. Karl was obviously asleep on the job. I started peddling faster, changing gears so I could make it up the steep incline before they got too far ahead of me. The passenger turned in her seat and looked back at me. Kyleigh. Where was he taking her?

If being on the bridge in a solid car scared me half to death, riding perched on a six-inch seat with nothing but open air between me and the drop off was terrifying. I had to stand to get momentum, and the bike rocked under me. The metal grating beneath my tires made traction more difficult, adding to my panic.

I kept my focus on the truck, which had stopped on the crest of the bridge. My legs burned, but I pressed on. Ray got out of the cab and walked around to the passenger side, where he yanked Kyleigh out of the truck by her hair. She stumbled backward, her hands reaching up and clamping over his as she kicked wildly. He seemed unbothered as he pulled her toward the rail.

No! No! No!

I peddled harder. Losing speed on the incline, I'd almost slowed to a stop by the time I reached the truck. I dropped the bike and ran to the railing.

We were six feet apart.

Ray had an envelope in one hand and Kyleigh's hair in the other. He was yelling, and he didn't even notice me. "Is this worth dying for?" he screamed, shoving her so she was leaning over the side, forcing her to look at what he obviously intended to be her watery grave. "We took you in when no one wanted you. You had to go nosing around!"

She screamed and managed to kick him in the shin. He cursed and looked away… and spotted me.

"Let her go!" I said.

Ray looked around as if weighing his options. The bridge was closed for the race, so there was no traffic. But now he had two of us to contend with. He didn't seem too concerned, though. He flashed a menacing smile. No one was around to intervene but me.

He shoved Kyleigh to the ground and reached into the waistband of his jeans, producing a handgun that he pointed at me. "Thanks for saving me the trouble of chasing you down."

"Run," I said.

Kyleigh rolled away from Ray, got on all fours, and then sprang up and sprinted around the truck.

"Take the bike," I called after her. She picked up the bicycle. The seat was too tall for her, and she wobbled a bit, but then seemed to gain control as she sailed down the hill.

"You just couldn't mind your own business," Ray said.

He stood outside the passenger door, between the truck and the railing. The driver's side door remained open, the engine still running.

I knew I had to keep him talking. "Kyleigh knows your secret, and she's on her way to the police with it right now."

"It's not *my* secret," he hissed.

"Okay, you and Bethany's secret."

His wild eyes went wide. "What do you know about her?"

"I know you're in it together."

His attention darted down the road and to Kyleigh as she barreled down the hill. She was going way too fast. If she didn't brake soon, she wouldn't be able to make the sharp turn at the traffic light at the bottom of the hill.

While he was captivated by his niece's reckless ride, I darted for the truck. I caught my shoulder on the door frame and swallowed the piercing pain as I slid into the seat. Ray dove for the passenger's seat just as my foot hit the gas and the truck lurched forward.

Half-in and half-out of the truck, he held on with one hand while his legs dangled in the air. The envelope was in his teeth. He squeezed off a round that whizzed by my head and out the window. The sound of the gunshot pounded on my eardrums, and I had to fight the urge to clamp my hands over my ears.

We made eye contact, and I slammed on the brakes, leaving his bonkers butt like roadkill behind me. I saw him bounce to a stop in the rearview mirror. Free of him, I pushed on the gas and started down the hill just in time to see Kyleigh go airborne as the bike left the bridge and splashed into the water.

Gunning the engine, I sped down the hill. At the bottom, I fishtailed to a stop. I spotted the envelope on the passenger floor. I'd deal with that later.

I jumped out of the truck and ran to the water's edge. Kyleigh splashed around, and I waded in to help her.

"Are you okay?" I swam to her side.

The fall seemed to have knocked the wind out of her. "I can't breathe."

Wrapping one arm around her in a lifeguard style, I struggled under her weight but managed to slowly pull her to shore while saying, "It's okay. I got you." We threw ourselves on the embankment and flopped on our backs, looking up at the crystal-clear sky and trying to catch our breath.

"Why didn't you brake?" I said, panting.

She looked at me wide-eyed. "I tried. The brakes didn't work."

Chapter Fifty-Two

I only let my eyes shut for a few seconds while I caught my breath. When I opened them, Ray stood over me. Kyleigh had scooted out of reach. He growled and then spat words out of his mouth like undercooked fish. "What did you do with the envelope?"

I sat up. It took effort to move my waterlogged body. "I sent it by courier pigeon to the White House."

He didn't get my humor. Or more likely, he wasn't in the laughing mood. He leaned over me, waving the handgun in my face. "Get up."

I got my legs under me and slowly got to my feet.

A blur of color appeared in my peripheral vision. I turned to look back at the bridge, where at least twenty cyclists rode toward us. They must have heard the gunshot. The cavalry would arrive. But I was worried that, as unhinged as he was, Ray might fire into the crowd.

I tilted my head toward the group descending upon us. As Ray turned to look, I kicked my foot at his right hand. The gun flew out of his grip, landing on the pavement ten feet away. He lunged for it, and I dove on top of him. Riding him like a bucking bronco, I held on as he crawled toward the revolver. My height advantage did nothing for me on the ground, as Ray was deceptively strong. He carried me like a mama bear carrying her cub across the road. I was an inconvenience; he would not stop. Hooking my elbow around his neck, I applied pressure and grabbed a fistful of hair.

That slowed him down.

But he persisted. He was inches from the gun when a foot appeared and kicked it out of his reach. Next thing I knew, hands pulled me off him, and

237

bodies piled on top of Ray. I scurried back, so I didn't get a cleat in the face.

My breath was ragged as I staggered to my feet and watched Nick and his buddies subdue Ray. Once he was secure, Nick sat back on his heels and looked up at me. "You okay?"

Hands on hips, I forced slow, steady breaths so I could answer him. I'd be sore tomorrow, but Ray hadn't caused any lasting damage. "I'm okay," I said.

I searched the area for Kyleigh, but she wasn't where I'd left her. I spun about and searched the group of cyclists. No Kyleigh. And Ray's truck was gone.

I ran into the crowd, questioning each person. "Did you see the girl? Long black hair? Soaking wet?"

Most of them looked at me like I'd lost my mind. But then one of them nodded. "Alex took her. She wanted to make sure Kyleigh was safe."

Alex, who had loaned me the bike without working brakes. Why didn't that make me feel better?

I pulled Nick aside. "Kyleigh's gone. Alex took her."

Nick looked distracted. His attention was still on Ray and the men who kept guard over him. "What?"

"Alex has Kyleigh," I said, more forcefully.

He nodded. "That's good. Glad she got her out of here."

"No," I said, my voice squeaky. "Something isn't right. The bike she loaned me... The brakes had been...tampered with. Just like on my aunt's car."

"Calm down," he said.

"Calm down? You calm up!"

He looked at me like I was nuts. "You've got to be kidding."

"Kyleigh was riding Alex's bike. She couldn't stop. I thought Alex seemed unbelievably happy about loaning me a bike. She meant for *me* to crash."

"Look, Jersey, I don't know where you're getting all this, but Alex is straight edge. She wouldn't hurt Kyleigh."

He scratched his head. My short time in his life would not trump his lifelong relationship with Alex. He didn't see her the way I did.

I went on. "And Ray said he wasn't protecting *his* secret. The journal had information about someone else. I think the missing pages were in an envelope he had."

"And where's that?"

"In the truck. With Alex."

He reached out and touched my arm. "Okay, that's good. She'll bring it to us."

I crossed my arms. "You gotta admit, something's off."

"We'll take Ray to the station, question him about the missing pages. Are you sure you're okay?"

I wanted to scream. Nick wasn't getting my urgency. But before I could react, a police car pulled up. Nick left me and yanked Ray to his feet, then walked him over to the cruiser and stuffed him inside. Ray stared at me through the window. His eyes narrowed, but then he flashed the creepiest grin I'd ever seen.

"Don't go anywhere," Nick said to me on his way back to the huddle of cyclists. "We're going to need a statement." He turned his back on me and conferred with his peers.

I let out a frustrated breath and shifted my weight from foot to foot. Kyleigh didn't have that kind of time. Alex's bike leaned against the rail across the road. Not the one she sabotaged, but the one she'd ridden in the race. I glanced back at Nick, who still had his back to me.

Screw it. I jogged across the street and got on the bike, leaving the chaos behind me.

But where did they go? The scene of the crime, maybe? But which one? The place where a body was buried or the place where Lucy was killed?

The junkyard was still an active crime scene, crawling with cops. She wouldn't go there. The secluded beach where we found Lucy was nearly always deserted.

It was a guess, but it was all I had.

I pulled a U-turn and started back over the bridge. The cops engrossed themselves in comparing notes about apprehending Ray, so I easily slipped past them. Going up the incline of the bridge was another story. Although Alex's bike rode smoothly, I hadn't taken the time to adjust it, and I felt like a clown riding a kid's bike. Standing on the pedals made it easier. My leg muscles were shot by then, and I almost left the bike to rely on my own two feet, but I knew the cycle would save me time on the downhill side.

During the ride, I almost talked myself out of what I was about to do. What if Nick was right and Alex wasn't up to no good? What if I'd misread her, and her only crime was that she was Nick's jealous ex-lover?

I still didn't know what those diary pages would tell us, but I knew that Alex had been one of the major players in Jody's life when she was pregnant. Someone had shared a secret with Jody. Did Jody meet her end because of it?

Chapter Fifty-Three

The only thing I knew for sure was that I couldn't rest until I knew Kyleigh was safe. And there was only one way to do that. I had to find her.

Paranoia had me testing the brakes as soon as I reached the top of the bridge. A headwind slowed me down, but as I started my descent, I gathered speed so quickly; I thought for sure I'd lose traction. I tried not to think about the fact that I was on the bridge, and I focused on the few feet in front of me.

My vision blurred as I wobbled on the bike—the open air at this dizzying height made my stomach drop into my shoes. My mind floated back to my childhood. Back to this bridge. My mom had pulled over. Gotten out of the car. She was crazed, crying about her latest boyfriend who'd cheated on her. She climbed up on to the rail until she was standing, holding on with one hand. She was going to jump.

I'd fumbled for my seatbelt. My fingers were numb, and I couldn't push the release button. Tears bubbled out of me as I groped helplessly at the contraption. Finally, a click, and I ripped the belt off me. I opened the door and jumped out.

"Please, Mommy, no!"

She glanced back at me. Determination on her hardened face faded.

I left the memory behind on the bridge where it belonged as I flew down the hill. Anger filled the space as I concentrated on the matter at hand. My mother's behavior had suffocated me my whole life. The grown-ups around Kyleigh had done nothing but let her down. I had my aunt, but she had no one. No, that wasn't true. She had me.

Thankfully, these brakes worked, and I slowed my speed at the bottom of the bridge. Taking the first right, I started up yet another hill. My legs burned.

After cutting through town, I whizzed past the hotel and found Ray's truck parked at the beginning of the trail. I opened the door and picked up the envelope off the floor mat. It had a wet shoe print on it, probably Kyleigh's. I opened it.

I didn't want to take the time to read every word, but I scanned the pages, hoping for a clue as to what I was about to walk into. Certain words jumped out at me.

Alex... She thinks the father won't want to be saddled with a baby. She vowed she'd never have children... Doesn't believe in abortion... Everyone thought she went to college....Her baby... Can I fool people into thinking the baby belongs to me?

Alex was Kyleigh's mom. I hadn't seen that one coming.

Distant voices interrupted my reading. I stuffed the pages back in the envelope, folded it in half, and stuffed it in my back pocket.

Ditching Alex's bike in the woods, I stayed off the path and pushed my way past branches, the forest floor soft beneath my feet.

At the clearing, I crouched behind an enormous tree trunk and scanned the beach. Sure enough, Alex and Kyleigh were there. Kyleigh sat on a log, crying as Alex paced before her. I moved a few feet to my right, where I found another tree to conceal me, yet I'd be close enough to hear what they were saying.

"I'm your daughter," Kyleigh cried. "You can't kill me."

I saw the snub-nose handgun in Alex's hand. "It wasn't supposed to be like this," Alex said. "If that nosy, busybody Lucy hadn't found that damn journal, none of this would be necessary."

"I can't even believe it," Kyleigh said, sobbing. "You paid Jody to raise me as her own. But why? Why couldn't you just take care of me?"

"Stop crying," Alex snapped. "I need to think."

Kyleigh wiped at her eyes with her palms. "But I don't understand. Why

242

didn't you want me?"

"Want you?" Alex threw one hand up in the air. "My own mother sacrificed everything so I could go to college. She still lets me know every day what she gave up so I could make something of myself. I had a bright future ahead of me. I would never have completed my forensics degree with a snot-nosed kid in tow. And Jody took good care of you. I kept you close so I could watch you grow up."

"Why didn't you just put me up for adoption?"

"And risk Nick knowing? He never would have agreed. He'd want to come forward and do the right thing. He wasn't ready to be a father. He had dreams, too. He wanted to be a cop."

Nick? I sucked in a deep breath at that piece of news. Terrified I'd given up my cover, I prepared for a gunshot to come my way. But they were too engrossed in their conversation to notice me.

Kyleigh kept talking. "But when my mom…I mean, Jody…disappeared, you left me with those awful people."

Alex laughed. "You really think you can handle the truth?"

Kyleigh rocked back and forth. She looked up at Alex. "You killed Lucy, didn't you? She was the only person who showed me some kindness back then. You might as well tell me the truth. You're going to kill me, anyway. Why stop now? You can't leave a stone unturned."

Alex rubbed her nose with the back of her hand and nodded. "You're right. You're a loose end."

"So, tell me. At least let me know why Jody left me. She might not have been my real mom, but I know she loved me. I remember that."

Alex stopped. Her eyes were cold, and she seemed to look right through Kyleigh. "She was going to tell. She was tired of being your mother. She'd ruin everything I'd spent the last eight years building up. I couldn't let her do that.

"If Nick would have found out that I'd kept it from him… Well. Everyone thought I went to school, but I had to put that off for a year. I couldn't stay in town because people would have known I was pregnant. But no one was surprised that Jody had an undetected pregnancy. She dressed like a bum and could have easily hidden it. She had no life anyway. I gave her a purpose."

"And you made me a fake birth certificate."

"You can't go to school without one."

"You killed Jody, didn't you?"

"I didn't mean to," Alex snapped. "I tried to convince her to just leave town. That I'd find someone else to raise you. I was already thinking about Mary and Ray. I'd pay them, contribute to your upbringing. But things got out of hand. I didn't mean to kill her..." She seemed to come out of her trance. "None of that matters now. We're running out of time. I need you to get up."

I couldn't let her hurt Kyleigh. But I was unarmed, and they were on an open beach. No way I could sneak up on them.

Kyleigh followed Alex's orders and got to her feet.

"Climb that rock," Alex said.

Kyleigh started her ascent.

Without thinking it through, I stepped out from my hiding place and cleared my throat. Alex whirled my way and leveled the gun at me. "You just keep showing up like a relentless migraine," she said.

Kyleigh gave me a pleading look from on top of the rock.

"You can't kill everyone, Alex. How many bodies will you pile up to cover your lies? The truth is out there now. It will catch up to you."

"You're wrong," she said. "Jo-Jo killed Lucy. The old bat had your aunt's necklace in her hand when she died. Then she drove into a tree because she couldn't live with the guilt. And Ray killed Jody and buried her on his property. Nothing points to me."

"Nice try," I said. "Framing Ray might have worked. But my aunt? I don't think so."

Alex bounced the gun in her hand. "Appears I still have the upper hand."

"Ray will fold on you to save himself. It's over, Alex."

"Maybe you're right," she said. "That just means I have nothing to lose by killing you. At least I'll have one thing. You'll never get your clutches on Nick."

"That may be," I said. "But neither will you. He's not even the least bit interested in you. He told me so."

"That's not true."

Out of the corner of my eye, I spotted Kyleigh inching toward the edge of the rock.

I was making Alex mad. She was so concentrated on me; she didn't notice Kyleigh getting away. The least I could do was make sure Kyleigh survived this. She'd already been beaten down, learning her whole life was a lie.

"Nick never loved you," I said. "He certainly won't love you when he knows what you've done."

"You don't know anything," she spat. "I can still beat this. You're going to kill Kyleigh and then commit suicide. I'll tell them I tried to stop you. Who do you think they'll believe? The trusted medical examiner or the newcomer who would do anything to cover for her aunt?"

Out of the corner of my eye, I caught Kyleigh coming to a stop at the edge of the rock. I took a step toward Alex to keep her attention on me. "What about Ray? He's already at the police station coughing up the truth."

She laughed. "He's a two-bit con. Jody told him about our scheme years ago. And I've been paying him to keep quiet ever since. But I never worried about him; he has no credibility. No one would have believed him if he had told. But then he got his hands on that damn journal when his trampy girlfriend told him Lucy had it. He's been blackmailing me ever since. I never should have paid him the ten grand. I should have known I couldn't trust him."

"That's a lot of people who are out to get you."

She shook her head. I could sense that she was tiring of talking. I needed to keep her engaged just a little longer. Long enough for Kyleigh to get away.

Alex might have been a lot of things, but she wasn't stupid. She narrowed her gaze, then spun about, firing a round at Kyleigh, just as she jumped from the rock.

"No!" I yelled.

I heard the splash as Kyleigh hit the water. I sprang forward, tackling Alex. Our bodies connected, and we flew several feet back, Alex landed on her back, with me on top of her. A whiff of perfume transported me back to the strange ocean smells that shouldn't have been there. The hotel. Lucy's house.

My inner Jersey exploded. I grabbed her by the hair, slammed my palm against her shoulder, and rammed my knee into her ribs.

She cried out in pain, and her eyes went wide. She still held the gun in one hand, and I latched onto it. My arthritic fingers screamed at me, but my rage was stronger than my pain. I banged Alex's hand against a rock until I heard something crack. When I realized the sound was her bones in her hand breaking, I squeezed harder.

Alex cried out in agony and released the gun, and I took control.

Staggering to my feet, I kept the revolver pointed at Alex's chest. "Don't move."

I side-shuffled toward the surf, half of my attention on Alex, who cradled her broken hand to her chest, and half on the churning sea. "Kyleigh!" I called, panic choking my voice.

I scanned the area. The sea was unforgiving, oblivious to the sacrifice it had just received.

I ran along the water's edge, my feet splashing against incoming waves. "Kyleigh!"

And then I saw her come up for air. She coughed and spat out water. But the ocean was shallow enough that she could stand. Kyleigh pointed to Alex, and I turned my attention back to her as she got to her knees.

I tightened my grip and kept Alex in my sights, knowing full well my RA didn't give me the dexterity or strength to pull the trigger. But Alex didn't know that. I kept her in my sights, listening to the beautiful sound of sirens as Kyleigh came to stand beside me.

And then Nick and several of his colleagues spilled onto the beach, still in their bike clothes.

Two of them pulled Alex to her feet and turned her around, clamping handcuffs on her wrists despite her cries of pain.

Nick came to stand by me, taking the gun from my hand. He reached for my chin and tilted it, forcing me to look at him. "I'm so sorry," he said.

I tried to answer him, but the words stuck in my throat.

CHAPTER FIFTY-THREE

"Are you okay?"

I nodded, but I didn't know if I was. "What made you come?"

Nick let out a long breath. "That housekeeper, she got back to me. She remembered the name of the person Ray was talking to. Alex, not Austin. She thought it was a guy, but once she told me, I knew your suspicions were true. Can you forgive me?"

I laid my face against his chest as his arm pulled me close. "I already have."

Chapter Fifty-Four

L ucy was laid to rest on a beautiful fall day.

My aunt had been home for three days. It was a battle getting her dressed as she couldn't lift her arm yet, but she insisted, and somehow, we got her in her favorite little black dress. She looked pretty, but only wore one ballet flat, since her other foot was still in a cast.

"I guess I can tell you now," I said sheepishly. "I found Lucy's matching shoe in the hotel shortly after finding her body. I guess Alex put it there to help frame you."

One of her eyebrows went up. "And you kept it from the police?"

"They already had your necklace. I didn't want to give Nick any more reason to suspect that you were Lucy's killer."

"Well, I hope you've figured out by now that Nick is smarter than that. He never suspected me, not really."

"I know. And I plan to tell him about it soon. He needs all the pieces of the puzzle."

I helped her in and out of the car and back into the wheelchair the way her physical therapist taught us. I was still sore from wrestling with Ray and Alex, but I kept that to myself. It was good to have Aunt Jo-Jo home where she belonged.

The church buzzed with activity. Half the town had come out for the memorial. News crews had descended on Orca Cove to cover the story of the town's medical examiner, so career-driven and wanting to please her mother, that she gave up her child and killed people to hide her misguided ambition. But today wasn't about Alex.

It was about Lucy.

The town's crotchety old woman, the librarian who scolded you for late book returns and yelled at bike-riding children, harbored a fondness for young Jody Boyce and her child. It never sat right with her that Jody ran off and left her daughter, like people said she did. She'd kept the room they'd used just how they'd left it—in case they ever came back.

Then she hired Bethany Williams to help her clean out her house. They found the journal. Bethany knew she hit a gold mine. That Alex would pay to keep its contents a secret. She met Ray in a bar, and they teamed up, and together they blackmailed Alex out of even more money. With the journal, Ray finally had proof of Alex's entire scheme, more than just his word, and he threatened to expose her. When caught in the next town over taking advantage of another senior citizen, Bethany confessed everything to police.

Ray couldn't bail out of jail this time. He was pending multiple charges. He'd be behind bars for a while.

The pieces of the puzzle were coming together.

I hadn't seen Nick since I'd given my final statement to Captain Sanders two days before. I knew his world had been turned upside down. Becoming an instant father to a sullen sixteen-year-old couldn't be easy. It was the talk of the town that he turned his home gym into a bedroom for Kyleigh, and she now called his house home. Poor girl would need a lot of care after everything she'd gone through. I imagined Nick's gentle way would help soothe her mental aches. But it would take time.

I had nightmares about that moment at the beach. When I'd held Alex at gunpoint, there was no telling how far things would have gone had I been left alone, even for a moment longer, with the woman who'd almost killed Kyleigh and had arranged to have my aunt killed. I would have pulled the trigger with my teeth if I'd had to.

Today, I spotted Nick standing awkwardly in a group of older women. Most of them were recent rehab releases, like my aunt. When Aunt Jo-Jo saw her friends, she urged me to take her to them.

I wheeled her over, and the group welcomed her with gusto. Nick looked relieved to see us. We made eye contact, and he tilted his head toward a bench a few feet away. I followed him and we sat side-by-side.

"How's Kyleigh?" I asked.

He blew out a long breath. "It's hard to tell. Maybe she doesn't hate me as much as she used to, but I wouldn't call it love."

I laughed. "It will take time. Her entire world has been turned upside down."

"I know the feeling," he said. "Never in my wildest dreams did I think I was a father, especially to a teenager."

I couldn't even imagine.

"Lucy's doctor came forward," he said. "Doctors diagnosed her with stage four cancer a few weeks before her death. We'll never know for sure, but putting it all together, it seems she hired Bethany Williams to help her go through the things in her house, knowing she didn't have long to live. That's when she came upon the journal. According to Ms. Williams, Lucy planned to confront Alex. Guessing Alex attacked her at her house, then dumped her body at the beach."

I let that settle in.

"And Bethany told Ray about the journal, and they blackmailed Alex. She didn't want me to know I was a father or the town to know she'd given up on her child." Now it would be more than Ray's word. They had proof.

"What about the body in the junkyard?" I asked. "Seems like it's Jody, but do we know for sure?"

Nick nodded. "Dental records confirmed that. And the yearbook Lindsey provided proved Jody was the only one missing from that class."

"So, Alex buried Jody on Ray's property to frame him with her murder?"

"From what we can gather."

"Ray didn't know Alex killed Jody?"

"Doesn't look like he did. He knew about the pregnancy scheme, but not the murder. He seemed genuinely shocked to learn her body was found on his property."

"How did Kyleigh take that news?"

Nick shook his head. "How does Kyleigh take anything?"

"With silence?"

CHAPTER FIFTY-FOUR

"Exactly."

I looked back at the church. Austin greeted the locals. Dressed in a suit, he looked somber. "What about Austin?" I asked.

"Guessing Lucy was going to see him to tell him about her cancer. He was her only living family member. She wanted to explain to him that while she loved him, Kyleigh needed her money more than he did."

"She left her estate to Kyleigh?"

He nodded. "Her lawyer came forward with that news. It's not much. Just the house, but I'd imagine once we fix it up, it will set Kyleigh up for a pretty good start at adulthood."

"But Lucy never made it to Georgia."

"No. I'm guessing Austin is upset about not being Lucy's heir, but he didn't kill her."

The breeze was cool, and I hugged myself. "Why did Ray cut my aunt's brake line?"

"Again, we're still putting it all together, but since Jo-Jo and Lucy were friends and Lucy gave your aunt the journal to hold on to, Alex assumed Jo-Jo knew what secrets the diary held. Ray was already blackmailing Alex. She knew he would do anything for money. She paid him to tamper with the brakes."

"And she took my aunt's necklace off her after the accident, while she was unconscious?" I took a moment to let that sink in.

Nick patted my hand. "I'm sorry. I didn't know Alex was capable of any of this. I should have listened to you."

I tried to lighten the mood. "Well, now you know to do that in the future." He laughed.

I noticed his attention shift as he looked at Kyleigh standing by the door of the church, one hand holding the other elbow. She wore girl clothes: a short, flowy skirt and tights. I wouldn't have recognized her except for the combat boots that were her trademark.

Nick rocked to his feet. "I should go. My daughter and I can stand awkwardly together."

I waved goodbye.

He took two steps forward, then turned back to me. "Kyleigh adores you. It would make my life so much easier if you'd join us later. I wanted to take her on a picnic to that place I showed you. My uncle's beach."

"I'd be happy to come."

"Two o'clock then. Do you remember how to get there?"

I nodded. He turned back to the church and took his place next to Kyleigh. It hit me then, why she always looked familiar to me. Their stance was the same. And they had the same soulful brown eyes. I watched them for a moment, knowing the road ahead of them would be rough, but envious at the same time for the father-daughter relationship I never had.

When the crowd moved inside the church, I stood and followed. It was time to bid Lucy goodbye.

Chapter Fifty-Five

Off leash, Noah trotted beside me as I kept tight control of Maya. This wasn't her neighborhood, and I didn't want to risk her running off.

My phone told me it was a beautiful sixty-four degrees with no chance of rain. A slight breeze made it feel cooler than that, and I'd upgraded my hoodie for a thick sweatshirt that hung over my jeans and touched my thighs.

The sound of crashing waves alerted me we were almost to our destination. When the trees gave way to the pebbly beach, the scent of burning wood radiated from the crackling fire in the pit. Kyleigh poked the blaze with a long stick.

When Maya spotted her, she started pulling and yipping. I let the leash go, and she darted toward Kyleigh, who caught her in a bear hug. The long-lost friends had a cuddle fest until Noah got his nose out of joint and wormed his way between them.

Nick walked up with his arms full of kindling. He dropped the twigs next to the fire and dusted his hands off on his jeans. He greeted both dogs, then turned to me. "Thanks for coming."

We unpacked drinks and the lunches Nick had brought from the bistro and ate our feast on a blanket Nick had spread on the flat rock of a low cliff.

Conversation flowed easily as Nick and Kyleigh filled me in on what island life was like in the winter when the tourists stayed away, and life slowed down even more. It sounded so peaceful; I started to imagine myself taking part in it.

Nick checked his phone, then stood. "I just got an alert from the whale watch boats. You girls are in for a treat."

We came to stand on either side of him. He looked out to sea, and we followed his line of sight. Several boats sped to the spot in front of us, about a quarter mile away, and then they idled.

Kyleigh bounced on her toes. "I know what that means!"

"Wait for it," Nick said, grinning.

The excitement between us sizzled like an electric current as we shielded our eyes from the sun, but kept our gaze on the horizon. We could see people on the boats also watching in anticipation, binoculars at the ready.

And then it started. First one, then dozens of others, as a super pod of orcas sliced through the water between land and the whale watching boats. I stood in awe as these marvelous creatures glided by us, their dorsal fins rising and falling out of the water as they passed. Even the dogs became excited, and Maya jumped up to place her paws on my chest. I stumbled and thought I would fall, but Nick caught me and pulled me to him. My face rested against his chest. I felt his heartbeat as his arm went around me.

I barely breathed as he held me steady. I had some thinking to do. And I had a secret to share. But for now, I just melted into his arms and enjoyed the view.

Kyleigh glanced our way and gave a slow grin.

It was a good day.

Acknowledgments

There are many who encouraged me and offered critiques and advice on my journey to publication. First off, I'd like to thank Mary Keliikoa, Harriette Slacker and Dawn Ius for being early readers of this book and providing valuable feedback. And to my writer's group, Laurie Cutter, Keli Esser, and Rod Langer for keeping me on task. Good friends Deneen Bertucci and Jennifer Vaughan, and my aunt, Carole Willson have also offered feedback, reading an early draft. Special thanks to my daughter, Brittany Goyette, for helping me capture Maya in all her glory. And to all the other people who have supported me on this incredible journey even if it was just listening to me talk endlessly about writing and my dream of becoming a published author. You know who you are!

To Verena Rose for believing in this series and Shawn Reilly Simmons and the people behind the scenes at Level Best Books for helping me elevate this book to its best version.

And Michael Verdun for designing a fabulous cover and capturing the "real dogs" portrayed in this series.

The support I've received for my Probation Case Files Mystery series from coworkers, friends—old and new, and book clubs has been a nice surprise. The writing community and local bookstores have also been fabulous. And my readers! Thank you for all the wonderful reviews and feedback. You are what it's all about!

And last but not least, I'd like to thank Maya and Noah who provided me with a wealth of material. Unfortunately, they are no longer with us, but they will live on in this series and writing about them keeps them close to my heart.

Without the support of my family, especially my husband Paul Hummel, daughter Brittany Goyette, son-in-law, Michael Verdun, and my mother, Beverly Schmidt, and aunt and uncle, Carole & Larry Willson, I never would have become a published author. You have always had faith in me, even when I didn't have it in myself. I love you all. Thank you for understanding why I'm always on my laptop and for riding this wild wave with me.

About the Author

Former law enforcement officer Cindy Goyette loves dogs and the Pacific Northwest. She combines these things in her first cozy mystery *Diamond In The Ruff*, A Wiggle Butt Manor Mystery. She's also published The Probation Case Files Mystery series, *Obey All Laws* and *Early Termination* and has a short story in the anthology *Lost & Loaded*, A Gun's Tale. *Obey All Laws* won an award from PSWA for best suspense. She lives in Washington State with her husband and two Cocker Spaniels.

AUTHOR WEBSITE:
   ccgoyette.com

SOCIAL MEDIA HANDLES:
   twitter @cindy_ccgoyette, @cindygoyetteauthor.bsky.social,
   https://www.instagram.com/cindy.goyette/
   https://www.facebook.com/profile.php?id=100077005287995

Also by Cindy Goyette

Obey All Laws, A Probation Case Files Mystery

Early Termination, A Probation Case Files Mystery

"The Big Mess," *Lost & Loaded, A Gun's Tale* anthology